The Night Swimmer

A Man in London and other stories

Lowell B. Komie

In 1983, nine of Lowell Komie's stories were published in a paperback edition entitled *The Judge's Chambers,* by the American Bar Association. This was the first time in its history that the American Bar Association published a collection of fiction.

In 1987, thirteen of his stories were published by Academy/Chicago both in paperback and hardcover in a collection known as *The Judge's Chambers and Other Stories.*

In 1994, a collection of seventeen stories, *The Lawyer's Chambers,* was published by Swordfish/Chicago. This collection won the 1995 Carl Sandburg Award for fiction from the Friends of the Chicago Public Library.

In 1997, *The Last Jewish Shortstop in America,* a novel, was published by Swordfish/Chicago. This novel won the 1998 Small Press Award for Fiction from *Independent Publisher Magazine.*

In 1999, *The Night Swimmer—A Man in London and Other Stories,* a collection of nineteen stories, was published by Swordfish/Chicago.

"A Woman in Prague" and a "Woman in Warsaw" were published in the *Chicago Tribune Magazine.* "Greenwald Et Cie." was published in *Chicago Magazine.* "Lederhosen Boys" in the *Milwaukee Journal Magazine,* "Skipping Stones" and "The King of Persia" were published in *The CBA Record,* the magazine of the Chicago Bar Association. "The Name, Kozonis" in *Karamu,* Eastern Illinois University, "Taormina" in *South Dakota Review,* University of South Dakota, "The Kite Flyer" in *Student Lawyer Magazine,* the magazine of the Student Division of the American Bar Association. All other stories in this collection are previously unpublished.

Published in 1999 by Swordfish/Chicago
155 North Michigan Avenue
Chicago, Illinois 60601
Copyright © 1999 Lowell B. Komie
Printed and bound in the USA

No part of this book may be reproduced in any form
without the express written permission of the publisher.

Library of Congress Catalog Card Number: 99-095130

Komie, Lowell B.

    The Night Swimmer—A Man in London and Other Stories

        1. Fiction   I. Title

ISBN: 0-9641957-2-0

This book is dedicated to the memory of my wife, Helen Komie, and to our family

With gratitude to

Mary Lou Schwall who painted the beautiful cover for this book. A talented artist and my friend.

Ann Lee who was my secretary for many of the 40 years that we have been friends and who worked on most of these stories.

Anna Leja who also worked on many of these stories and did the editing of the stories set in Poland.

Jack Hicks, Poet and Director of the Deerfield Library, Donna Hicks of the Northbrook Library, Sally Seifert of the Deerfield Library, and Anne Feeney of the Glenview Library. All friends who have always supported my work.

John Fink, in Memoriam, Novelist, Editor of *Chicago Magazine* and the *Chicago Tribune Magazine.*

Raymond R. Coffey of the *Chicago Sun-Times* who wrote a wonderful column about *The Last Jewish Shortstop in America.*

My loyal friend Lon Romanski, since our student days at the University of Michigan.

Rabbi Byron Sherwin of the Spertus Institute of Jewish Studies. He has always encouraged me.

Professor George Bornstein of the University of Michigan. He taught *The Last Jewish Shortstop in America* as part of his course on contemporary Jewish Literature.

James D. Griffith, always my supportive friend.

Miles K. Zimmerman for his suggestions and guidance.

William C. Gutmann for his photograph.

Deborah Zaccarine who did the copy editing.

And a special mention of Catherine Zaccarine who designed this book.

My appreciation to all of you and to David Komie, my partner in Swordfish/Chicago.

Contents

The Night Swimmer—A Man in London 1

Peter Freund 11

Hotel Europejski 21

Who Could Stay the Longest? 29

Skipping Stones 35

The King of Persia 43

Lederhosen Boys 51

Greenwald Et Cie. 59

The Name, Kozonis 67

Taormina 73

Conversations with a Golden Ballerina 85

The Kite Flyer 123

Queen of the Voyage 131

On the Beach—Sur le Plage 137

My Lights 145

Henry and Gitta 153

A Woman in Prague 161

A Woman in Warsaw 169

Aliyah 181

The Night Swimmer

A Man in London
and other stories

The Night Swimmer— A Man in London

WHEN HE FIRST SAW HER on that July afternoon she was seated as a docent at a desk in the Art Institute on the first floor, near the Chagall windows. A section of her face was shadowed by the blue light coming through the Chagall panels. He stopped at the desk and asked her where the Edvard Munch exhibit was located.

"Munch was a marvelous artist," she said, looking up at him. "Do you know Munch?"

"I know he was a sad man."

"Oh, he was more than sad. I'm giving a talk on Munch in ten minutes in the small gallery down the hall where they have the exhibit." She shielded her face with her hand. "Perhaps you'd like to come?"

She wore a plastic name badge, Mary Thomas, Docent. Mary Thomas, he thought, a simple name for a woman who lectured on Munch. He was a married man and he saw by her rings that she was a married woman. They'd said two or three sentences to each other and she'd issued him an invitation, and now she was blushing. It had been a long time since someone had blushed because of an invitation issued to him.

"I'll come," he said to her, and she smiled. She had a small face that brightened quickly, and short hair, graying from dark brown, with a section that fell over her face. She wore thin black-framed glasses and she seemed about forty-five, with lovely pale ivory skin. When she quickly crossed her legs, almost as a sign of her affirmation of his acceptance, the panel of her skirt opened and he noticed a black slip. Only complex women intentionally let their hair go gray and then buy expensive lingerie. He could tell by the way she shook her hair back from her eyes, and the way she immediately challenged him, that she would be a dangerous friend.

"Okay. Thank you for the invitation," he told her.

He walked away from her and went down past the Chagall panels to an exhibit of tenth and eleventh century Indian art. There was a small clay statue of the god Shiva, sculpted in a ring of fire with Shiva dancing within it, languidly flailing his four arms. One arm was used to beat a tiny hand drum. He read the description. "The god Shiva dances in a circle representing the flame of destruction, and the hand drum beats the rhythm of life."

He turned and pretended to be looking at another exhibit, and saw that she was gone from her desk. No, he didn't keep his promise to her. He didn't go back to the Munch exhibit and her lecture. Still, she was very attractive, at least he thought so. She had a certain fragrance, a Waspy intelligence and diffidence that appealed to him. He knew he'd eventually go back to look for her.

A week later he did return to the Art Institute. At first he observed her from a distance. He watched her through the glass cases, seated at her desk, briskly giving directions and answering inquiries. It was always with a smile, shaking her hair back from her eyes, and pointing with her glasses. As he watched her he thought that he could just construct a clay tableau of his own family and place it on her desk. He, Robert Gottlieb, fifty-seven, investment banker, beating the drum of his life, a small hand drum, his wife Elizabeth in her artist's smock with their two golden retrievers and their four sons. Around all of them would be a clay ring of suburban fire, and within it an old lannon stone home in Winnetka on Ash Street. The Gottlieb tableau would be set in a moveable ring of clay fire that she could twirl, and he would step up confidently to Mary Thomas's desk and ask her to just give it a spin. It would save him a lot of time. He wouldn't have to tell her about his life. He wouldn't have to lie to her.

He looked at her again through the glass display cases. She had left her desk, so this time he did go to the gallery to listen to her lecture on Munch.

She was standing in the gallery beneath a portrait of Munch and was surrounded by an audience of elderly people. It was a portrait of a sad-eyed brown-haired Munch with a pale, transparent, fragile face, a slight beard, a man in his mid-thirties. He looked exhausted and very wary.

He stood at the edge of the group and listened to her. "Edvard Munch has a museum named after him in Oslo. I hope some of you have had the chance to visit it. His famous painting, *The Scream,* which was recently stolen from the museum in Oslo and then returned, was actually modeled after the features of an embalmed Peruvian baby that Munch had seen in a museum when he was studying in Paris. For those of you that might be interested in purchasing your own version of *The Scream,* it has been widely produced as an inflatable doll and it's available in many card shops and gift stores in Chicago." She looked directly at Robert Gottlieb.

There was small polite laughter from her audience.

"But his work wasn't always bizarre or exotic. There are many beautiful portraits. Here's one of his sister Inger. Notice the full, black-patterned silk dress with a velvet collar and a gold clasp at her throat. Munch had a fear of women though, as expressed in his painting *The Vampire* against the other wall. He both loved them and feared them. In this painting, the woman is shown embracing a man, covering him with her long red hair, strands of which have fallen over his face. She's shown kissing him on the neck, like a vampire in a final kiss of death. Nineteenth century artists were fascinated by strangulation, the idée fixe of strangulatory hair—Rossetti, Baudelaire, Maeterlinck, Mallarme."

She looked at Robert Gottlieb again.

Later, she accepted his invitation to join him for a walk in Grant Park. They sat on a rim of Buckingham Fountain and he leaned over her and kissed her for the first time. Softly, on the lips. "We'll do this in London," she said. "If it's going to be done at all, it will have to be done in London."

She refused to meet him at a hotel in Chicago. It would be too dangerous for both of them. Each had too many friends who might see them together in Chicago. London would be the place, and it would have to be a hotel that no one would imagine staying at, some place out of the way. She and her husband lived in Barrington. Many of their friends traveled, but almost all of them stayed in Mayfair. It would have to be some small hotel outside of Mayfair.

So he flew to London early in August, one day ahead of her to make the arrangements. He couldn't believe he was doing it. He couldn't believe that he could be so impulsive and foolish. In twenty-five years of marriage he'd never had a love affair. He wouldn't tell her that. A few drunken gropings on the fairways of the country club after a summer dance—he remembered the paper lanterns, the sound of the band, and now even that woman and her husband were both dead. Once he'd met a woman at the Drake in mid-afternoon. She'd walked into the room dressed in a black Chanel suit, her face as waxy and pale as Munch's in the portrait. She looked once around the room, once at him, kissed him on the lips, turned, and walked out. She never returned. They occasionally danced together at the summer dances on the club terrace, but they never again met or discussed that afternoon.

He reserved a room in London at the Mornington at Lancaster Gate in Hyde Park. He'd stayed there several times before on business trips. He arrived at the hotel at midnight. She'd be there the following afternoon. It was a Swedish hotel, with the flag of Sweden flying over its mahogany and brass entrance, the blue Swedish ensign with a yellow cross. No one would look for them there. It was a small hotel and had a tiny lobby with a paneled library combined with a bar and red leather studded chairs. As a centerpiece in the library, there was a small bust of a corpulent Swedish queen slumped asleep on her throne, with her crown askew. The hotel was beautifully kept and had exactly the right texture for this love affair that he was determined to begin. He wasn't going to do it because he had suddenly turned against his wife Elizabeth. They had long ago isolated themselves from each other, and now lived in their own cubes—she, artist and mother; he, golfer and wanderer. They were still friends. He was doing this for himself, for the secret part of him that, like Mary Thomas, he had hidden away as he grew older and never discussed.

On his first morning in London he awoke refreshed and expectant. He hadn't felt that way in years. He had a breakfast of shirred eggs, a croissant, tea, and marmalade. He went to a small florist near the hotel and bought flowers for their room, a mixture of miniature pink English tea roses and a bouquet of silly paper flowers. Her plane was due at Heathrow on British Air at 3:00. She would take the airbus, she'd said. He'd wait for her at the Lancaster Gate entrance to Hyde Park.

He dressed in a navy blue jacket and lightweight gray flannel trousers. He saw himself in the full-length mirror on the closet, a tall man with thinning brown hair, a long arched nose and thin lips. He looked at his face and saw his eyebrows were growing gray, and he took a scissors from his kit and trimmed them and smoothed his hair, and put on a yellow foulard tie and went down to the bar, where he ordered a scotch. The bartender was an English woman, about forty, slim, with short auburn hair, and her hand touched his as she gave him the drink. She was the first person who'd touched him in London, and when he finished his drink, he left a one-pound coin on the ledge of the bar.

As he walked back to the lobby, a young blonde desk clerk in a black uniform with crossed keys on her lapels asked him in a Swedish accent, "You are Mr. Robert Gottlieb?"

"Yes, I am."

"Well, Mr. Gottlieb, we have a fax here for you."

She handed him the message.

Robert Gottlieb, Esq.
Hotel Mornington
Lancaster Gate
London

I am so sorry. There has been a sudden change of plans. I am unable to appear. This is not anything but cruel, I know, but it will be in the end far better this way. You would be a lovely human being if you will forgive me someday.

Inger Munch.

The desk clerk stood waiting with her receipt book. He signed the book and took the message out into the street and read it again in the sunlight. He walked with it across the boulevard into Hyde Park and sat on a bench alone in the Italian Gardens and watched the spume of the fountains. He sat still with the message in his hand, even as the wind shifted and the spray from the fountains fell lightly on his face and across his jacket and his shirt and tie. He could feel tears welled up behind his eyes. He was inordinately foolish—but she was cruel, fortuitously cruel, and he had forgotten what it was like to really be hurt. He learned one thing though, if he was going to chase after a woman halfway across the world, he should just really get a divorce.

That night he went to Covent Garden and saw Mozart's *Magic Flute*, sitting alone in the fetid balcony surrounded by British couples. After the opera, he stopped at a wine bar and then slowly made his way back to the hotel by walking down through Covent Garden to Trafalgar Square. It was humid and misty and the tables outside the restaurants were filled with couples who had been to the theaters. There was the sound of laughter and the murmur of upper-class accents as he passed their tables, the men in dark suits and the women quite elegant, their eyes flashing, lost in gossip and animated conversation. He caught a cab at Trafalgar Square back to the hotel and went into the bar and ordered an Irish Cream over ice. The same woman was behind the bar. She was busy talking to some German businessmen and then she came over to him and brought him the Irish Cream.

"Always with ice, you Americans."

"Yes, it makes it last longer."

"Oh, is that why?"

"Yes."

"So, where was it tonight?"

"Covent Garden, *The Magic Flute*."

"Mozart. I love Mozart."

He looked up at this woman, a refined, lovely woman in her early forties. Why was she working as a bartender, and why was she being so kind to him? He wasn't in the mood to reciprocate kindness. "Well, thank you," he said to her. He reached for another pound and left the coin on the bar.

"No, that's much too much. You've already left a tip this evening." She pushed the coin back to him. "Good night. Sleep well."

He took the lift upstairs. He wanted to call Chicago. He looked at his watch. It was almost 6:00 in Chicago. She'd probably be home alone, waiting for her husband to return from work. The bartender had unconsciously touched his hand again. Should he go back to the bar and tell her his story? No, that's not what he wanted. He wanted to confront the woman who'd sent him the fax. How many times had he met her in Chicago before he bought the tickets? Once at Buckingham Fountain and then only once more in a darkened lecture hall at the Art Institute. She'd invited him to a film, they sat in the back, and in the darkness she put her head on his shoulder and her hand on the inside of his leg. She had touched him in Chicago and he fell transfixed and immediately got on a plane to London. Why was he always fascinated by these upper-class Wasp women with their snub noses, their mouse-brown hair, their phony accents, their simple dresses, no cosmetics or adornment? He'd sought them out all his life—in high school, in college. He'd dated them until one by one they drifted away into the sanctuary of their families and marriage. Now even in his late fifties he'd been wounded again by one of them. He had her number in Barrington in his address book. He sipped the Irish Cream and picked up the phone and called her. After a few clickings and hollow rings her husband answered.

"Hello?" He almost asked for her. The husband said "Hello?" again. He held the phone away for a moment and then hung up. She could send him to London on a 5,000-mile fool's errand, but he wouldn't involve her husband. It was against his code. He would never involve her husband.

He tried to sleep, but the pub in the alley behind the hotel was still open, and the voices drifted up, the laughter and conversation. Finally the pub closed. He could hear people shouting good-bye to each other, and their footsteps in the alley. When the footsteps and voices all receded, he finally fell asleep.

The next morning he forced himself to go to the Tate Gallery. He took the tube. He wanted to see the Blake galleries and the paintings of Francis Bacon and Lucian Freud. He particularly wanted to see Bacon because the faces looked like the way he felt, like half his face had collapsed into molten disfigurement.

When he finally left the Tate he took the tube to Leicester Square and bought a ticket for a concert that evening at Royal Albert Hall, an all-Beethoven concert. He bought a ticket for the second balcony; he still wanted to hide, to be alone and invisible. At the concert he felt a little better. The music seemed to soothe him. He was alone again, lost in a crowd of Londoners. Some of them had the score with them and many sat in the heat of the balcony with their eyes closed, fanning themselves with their programs.

After the concert he bought a sandwich and a paper cup of tea and walked into Hyde Park with the people trailing home from the concert. He sat on a bench and ate his sandwich. The tea was cold and tasted of the paper cup. When he was done he walked from Nottingham Gate to Lancaster Gate. It took him twenty minutes to get there, and by the time he arrived the Lancaster Gate exit gate was locked. He tried it several times, but it was locked and the black ornamental iron gate and the fence were too high for him to scale. It would be impossible for him to climb out. Even if he were agile enough to get to the top, which he wasn't, the top of the fence was spiked. It was a fence maybe twenty feet high and set back, and shielded by bushes from Bayswater Road.

He started up a road looking for any opening in the fence, but there wasn't an opening anywhere that he could find, and it was very dark. He passed a small pet cemetery with headstones for dogs and cats. In the moonlight he could read some of the weathered names on the small markers. Then he passed a darkened guardhouse. There was a bridge over the Serpentine, the lake in Hyde Park, that might lead him out. He remembered seeing a bridge and a small beach with boats where families were swimming and children were playing in the sand.

He headed down the path he thought would lead to the bridge and he found the beach and the bridge, but a locked gate still prevented access to the bridge. It was also spiked and too high for him to climb. The only way out of Hyde Park would be to undress, push the bundle of his clothes through a gap in the bars of the fence, and then wade into the waters of the Serpentine. He would swim under the bridge and out to the other side of the fence. He could then slip back through the bushes to the place where he'd left his clothes, and dress. No one would see him if he was careful.

As he began to remove his clothes, he thought that this could be a kind of exorcism, a reverse baptism. He knew that the Hassidim used water to exorcise devils, so why not him? He'd been infested by a dybbuk, a tiny devil of a woman. He'd once witnessed a Hassidic exorcism at a motel in Milwaukee, three pale men in black hats and old-fashioned woolen bathing suits, immersing a man who was sobbing a woman's name.

He removed his shirt and then his shoes, trousers and navy blue jacket. He took off his socks and shorts. The night air felt cool and cleansing on his body. He should be divorced, he should ask God to give him the courage to ask for a divorce. He wouldn't have to go through this elaborate ritual of expurgation. He folded his clothes carefully and pushed them through the bars of the fence. Then, trying not to step on the rocks, he walked into the waters of the Serpentine.

The water was warm and surprisingly comforting. He twirled awkwardly three times, as he'd seen the Hassidim twirl, and cupped his hands with water and chanted her name into his cupped hands and asked God's blessing, and covered his face. Then he lowered himself into the water. He wasn't a very good Jew. He didn't know if God would answer him. As he slowly did a breast stroke in the warm water he had the sensation that a tiny engorged body was suddenly floating out of his mouth, a bloated strand of a tiny mad Ophelia in a gauzy gown with seaweed floating out of her hair, her puffed cheeks filled with stones. She floated out of him like a slimy pupa or a chrysalis inside of him, and as she left his body, the water seemed suddenly infused with the light of celebration, like fireflies in the water, hovering and dancing. It was as if he had finally disgorged her.

He slowly swam under the bridge out to the other side. The only light was from the street lights on the bridge. He climbed up the bank and walked hunched over through the bushes and found his clothes. He dried himself with his shirt, quickly patting himself dry, and then dressed in the bushes and walked out into the crowds on the street as if nothing had happened. Several laughing Indian couples passed him, two women in sandals, with diamonds on their cheeks, and yellow and orange saris, the dark-bearded men in turbans. One woman looked at him and he stared at her and she turned away.

Back in the bar of the hotel he ordered a Bushmills, drank it and ordered another.

"So, where have you been tonight?" the same woman at the bar asked him. They were alone again. She'd been reading a book.

"I went to Royal Albert Hall."

"Mozart again?"

"No, Beethoven."

"Oh, Beethoven. I'm always unhappy after Beethoven."

"Yes, Beethoven can be difficult."

"Your hair is wet. Is it raining?"

"It rained just a while. It stopped, though."

"Well, I hope you're enjoying London."

"I am, in my own way. Actually, it isn't raining. I've been swimming."

"I thought maybe you had. You're a night swimmer."

"Yes, I like to swim at night."

"I'm a night swimmer, too. There's a natatorium over on Queensway. Did you swim there? It's sort of a creaky old place."

"No, I belong to a club. I swam there."

She returned to her book.

"May I ask what you are reading?"

"I'm reading a biography of the Russian poet Anna Akhmatova. Do you know her?"

"No, not really."

"She was a marvelous poet. She had a tragic life, but when she was a young woman and already married, she was a student in Paris and met Modigliani, and they became friends. They would walk in the park at midnight and he'd shower her with white blossoms. I wish I could find a man to do that for me."

"Do you work here full time as a bartender?"

"No, I'm a stage designer. I'm saving for a trip, so I work two jobs."

"Where are you going?"

"Actually, I'm going around the world."

"Would you mind if I came along?"

She laughed and touched his hand again. "I could use a good companion. Would you be a good companion?"

"I really don't know. Probably not."

Her eyes were lovely, brown and mysterious. He would like to talk more to a woman who could teach him about Akhmatova and was leaving soon for a trip around the world.

But not tonight.

Peter Freund

HE HAD BEEN A SWIMMER in college when he married Kit Loewenstine in 1952. They were married in the garden of the Loewenstine home in Winnetka on a bright afternoon early in June and Peter and his three groomsmen had stood shyly in the receiving line, tall, lithe young men, in white linen formal jackets, standing as if they were about to momentarily freeze into a racing position and perhaps plunge into the Loewenstine pool. He had wanted his relay team there, Anderson from Butte, Grimshaw from Laramie and Armstrong from Seattle. Anderson, Grimshaw, Armstrong and Freund, Peter Freund, anchor of the University of Washington relay team, and the first Jewish Phi Delt pledge of the Seattle chapter. He had given each of his groomsmen a little sterling silver monogrammed key ring from Peacocks and his father had sent them round-trip tickets on a TWA first-class flight and reserved rooms for them at the Drake. It had been important then for Peter and the Freunds to have his teammates there. It was a matter of setting, the three rawboned Gentile swimmers in the receiving line were necessary to Peter and his family, the ultimate badge of true assimilation, three teammates flying in with seeming affection from their western towns. They were selected for their roles as groomsmen as a matter of style, a conscious understated choice much as the delicate nosegays of lily of the valley had been selected for the bridesmaids. After that June day, though, Peter Freund never again saw his three young friends.

The Freund and Loewenstine families were two old German-Jewish Chicago families. Moses Freund and August Loewenstine had each come to Chicago just before the Civil War. Moses Freund had begun with a retail clothing store and he and his sons built it into one of the largest clothing manufacturing companies in the country. August Loewenstine had started as a junk peddler traveling the southwest with a wagon full of rusting pots and when he died at the beginning of the century he owned a steel mill in Pittsburgh. Now the Loewenstine name was known throughout the world. There were mills and mines and refineries, and the Loewenstine group, Lompac, had offices in thirty-seven countries. Peter's young bride, Kathryn, was one of four Loewenstine daughters, each of them slim, fashionable young women, educated at eastern schools, and that June afternoon dressed in pink organdy and satin pumps as they stood laughing and drinking champagne in the receiving line with Peter's blond teammates.

That June afternoon in 1952 now though had diminished in Peter Freund's memory except on the occasions when he would look through the library for a book to take up to his bedroom and his hands would touch upon the padded silk binding of their volume of wedding pictures. Sometimes he would open it and flip through the pages, but now that he was in his late forties, the faces in the photographs became harder to identify and the people seemed almost artificial on the weak colorations of the fading photographs.

He was more concerned about the matter of Kit's separate bedroom. It had begun a year ago when he was named vice president in charge of Lompac's foreign division and he had begun his constant traveling. He had come in one night last winter on an Alitalia flight that was two hours late. Kit met him at O'Hare in the gray Mercedes and as they pulled out on the expressway ramp she turned coldly to him staring at him directly, her glasses up high on her chestnut hair, her hands tight on the wheel, tiny slim fingers in black Italian driving gloves.

"I've taken my own bedroom," she said, rubbing at the interior fog on the driver's window.

"Like Eleanor and Franklin," he had answered, pretending to be unconcerned.

"Not quite," she said quietly. "I just want my own place, that's all. Just my own place."

"And that's all there is to it? Nothing else?" he asked, holding his attaché case on his lap.

"Nothing else. I thought I'd try it for a while. You come over when you like. I'm not locking you out, Peter."

"Okay," he said. "If you want."

And it had begun that way, a quiet separation.

During the first six months it hadn't been particularly bothersome. In fact he rather enjoyed the privacy. He could pad around his room naked. Sometimes he would mix himself a drink late at night and sit in a chair naked and read and then get in bed by diving off from the chair onto the bed as if he were again standing at the edge of the pool waiting for the crack of the starter's gun. He would stand on the chair and tilt forward, his arms back, knees bent and push himself hard off the chair onto the bed, landing flat on his belly, his arms flailing and thrashing in swift, sure strokes as he hit the quilted silk coverlet and bounced. Also, he could do push-ups in the morning without fear of waking her. Instead of hanging clothes, he could wad his shorts in a ball and dangle socks wherever he chose, or eat a peanut butter and onion sandwich on the fresh sheets. One night he put on his Pucci robe and took his Phi Delt pin and several swimming medals and pinned them all across the velvet lapels and had fallen asleep in his chair with a dead cigar.

They still made love. They had a secret staccato knock that he used as a signal on her door. When he would rap it meant that he'd come across in fifteen minutes and she always welcomed him, although she was cross about missing her talk shows or putting aside her books.

It was only during the past few months that she had begun to turn him away. At first, she made the excuse of having headaches or being tired. Then she began to extend her menstrual periods. Her stomach began to trouble her, her back ached, she pretended responsibilities that required uninterrupted sleep. It seemed that she was sliding away from him and he from her as if they were two unsure skating figures revolving on a vast frozen arena.

He didn't want to think about it. As he traveled he sent her affectionate notes, hastily scribbled on engraved airmail tissue from the Excelsior in Rome, or in flight on Air India. He'd still arrive at O'Hare with exotic gifts, an ivory dildo from Mozambique or a Roman tear vase from the little museum they loved in Antibes. The gifts seemed to momentarily cheer her, but now more often she stayed away from the airport and Sven, the houseman, would meet him with the Mercedes and one of the gray poodles.

One evening after she had returned from a pottery course she was taking at a woman's studio in Glencoe, she came into the library where he was working on some marketing reports and said she had to speak with him immediately. As she said this she wiped her hands at the edges of her potter's smock and pushed back a wisp of hair that had fallen along her face. She closed the door.

"I've fallen in love," she said. There was something about her quiet way of making the declaration that made him believe her instantly.

"Who, may I ask?" he said to her. "May I ask who it is?"

"Joe Yalowitz. We've been together for the last two weeks."

"Kit, that crazy little New York Jew! Oh, come on now, Kit."

"Don't be superior, Peter. We're not superior people." Then she fled from the room and ran upstairs to her own bedroom. He followed her but the door was locked and he could hear her sobbing. That night, though, she came across to his room and they made love for the first time in several weeks and she was as passionate as he had ever remembered her as a young woman. By Saturday, though, he was in Addis Ababa and he sent her a filigreed ring, whorls of finely wrought Ethiopian silver, filigreed in circles as interwoven and fine, it seemed to him, as the complexities of their marriage.

When he returned to Chicago he found that Kit had gone to California, supposedly a week at La Costa. She left him a short, gay note and as a gift in her absence had enclosed in the envelope a matching ring, a slim, gold band as delicately worked as the Ethiopian filigree. He put the ring in his pocket and slid the note underneath his handkerchiefs in his dresser drawer.

He thought of moving to the Standard Club for the week. He supposed that she was in California with Joe Yalowitz but he knew he would never ask her and had he asked, she would have never told him. Yalowitz was a dermatologist in Glencoe and Peter supposed that he could call his service and find out if the doctor was in the city, but such a call was beneath his dignity. Instead, he spent the week at work and when she returned he pretended that she had never been away.

One afternoon though, when she was in California, he had left work early and had gone over to their country club for a golf lesson. Both the Freund and Loewenstine families belonged to the oldest Jewish club on the North Shore. Their courtship days had been spent in afternoons on the club tennis courts and Saturday night parties dancing on the terrace beneath paper lanterns on the bluff high above Lake Michigan. He liked to go to the club when he wanted a private moment. There would be no intrusions there. The people he would see were people he had known all his life, children of old families, secure in their wealth and following family patterns with the same dignified grace and easy sense of leisure that had always been natural to him.

That afternoon he stood at the practice tee and worked with his woods. As he watched each shot arch high over the practice fairway he thought of the one time he had seen Yalowitz. Bill and Beth Sulzberger had given a dinner party at the club an evening last summer and Peter had wandered out into the bar before the dessert course. Yalowitz was sitting at the bar with Muffy Sulzberger, who had come in from Bennington with her two college friends for her parents' party. The friends were long-haired blondes, slim and articulate, and were laughing with Yalowitz who was teaching them Yiddish phrases. Peter ordered a sherry and sat quietly at the end of the bar.

"Goyischer," Yalowitz was saying in a New York accent.

"What's that?" the Sulzberger daughter said and swished her hair at the older man. "What's Goyischer?"

"Gentile," the doctor said laughing and the college friends laughed in unison. "All of this," Yalowitz grabbed a handful of nuts and began chewing. "The goddamned burnished walls and old leather. Everything is so muted. It freaks me out. Matrons in tennis dresses, every one of them look-alikes, tan and slim and blonde. Why all the blondies? Like shiksas. A whole club of Jewish shiksas."

"Goyischer," one of the girls said again. "What's wrong with the goys?"

"Nothing," the doctor said. "It's just wrong to want to be one if you're Jewish. There's no goddamned ethnicity here. It's so Gentile it's almost vulgar."

Muffy Sulzberger jangled her arm bracelets at the doctor and pushed at a dark lock of his hair that had fallen across his forehead, pushing the hair back in place along the side of his head and patting it with her hand cluttered with Burmese rings. "Where's your wife, Doctor?" she said.

Peter had thought it all silly. The doctor had been a little drunk and the girls were putting the man on. Peter had known Muffy since she had been a tiny child standing pot bellied with a tube around her middle at pool side. Only later, when he learned that Joe Yalowitz was a widower and had seen him dancing with Kit and Kit laughing and touching her face to Yalowitz as they danced slowly and at the far edge of the crowd did Peter for a moment have a sense of being violated. Yalowitz was an intruder and it wasn't proper form, holding a man's wife the way he was dancing with Kit. It was a show of vulgarity and the doctor's dark face seemed threatening, almost alien, like a handsome Italian had stolen into the club and was suddenly doing the tarantella in front of all the members with Kit Freund.

Peter had long known that he possessed a large streak of anti-Semitism. All through his childhood he had been taught to submerge his Jewishness, to dress and act and speak as a Gentile. His parents eschewed the use of Yiddish expressions. The Freund family always had a magnificent Christmas tree, their Tannebaum, and celebrated Christmas with old German festival songs. There was no religion in the home and even the high holidays went unobserved. Peter was in school for Rosh Hashana and Yom Kippur and when the first young children of Russian Jewish families began to drift into the Winnetka school system he was ashamed of the dark strangers and embarrassed when they were absent on the holidays. The Freunds never owned a Cadillac and his mother seldom wore her full-length mink coat. Cadillacs and mink were regarded as opulent symbols of wealth. Instead Miriam Freund dressed in cloth coats from Peck and Peck, refused to have black household help and employed only Scandinavians or German couples who could whip out special pastries for the children's birthdays and family parties. He was proud of his father, a lean and aristocratic man who wore Brooks Brothers flannels and carried a battered calfskin case much like the bankers from Kenilworth and Lake Forest. Peter would wait at the station for his father with the chauffeur in the wood-paneled Oldsmobile station wagon and when the train pulled in, he would run down the platform through the veil of hissing smoke and swing into his father's arms to be driven home where his mother would be in the library with a shaker of martinis before the fire.

Kit Freund was raised in the same manner. They were both quiet, refined children, spending their summers at ranches in Montana or Wyoming while their parents traveled in Europe. In the winter the families headed for Sun Valley or celebrated Christmas in Bermuda or would take a Pullman to Miami and motor down to Homestead in the Keys where the men fished while the women and children swam and played tennis. And there was always the country club on the bluff of the lake at the core of their lives. Each Sunday morning during the summer the chain on the garage door would grind and his father would be out of the house for golf at the club with a rush of tires on the pebbled driveway. Then the children would breakfast with mother in her tennis costume and after cutting some flowers in the garden, she would be off in her car. Peter and his brothers and sisters were later driven to the club for an afternoon around the pool. At four the family would return and change for dinner and then return to the club. He could remember those long summer evenings, the little old ladies in silk print dresses on the clubhouse porch, sitting, nodding and reading in white wicker chairs. After dinner the men retired to the bar for sherry and cigars and the children would run along the verandah or just sit in the deck chairs at poolside and swing their legs and look out at the dark water and watch the stars. It was a stately conservative life and he and Kit followed the same routines in their marriage. Their friends were the children of his parents' friends. He had his permanent golf foursome at the club and Kit had hers. Their children, a boy and a girl, now both away at college, ran the same paths along the edges of the same ravines that he and Kit had followed. It was an unbroken chain that had been handed down with care and pride from each generation.

When Kit came to him for the divorce, at first he refused to believe it. They had met at the import shop on the first floor of Field's where he wanted to show her a beautiful Russian black lacquered jewelry box. She was on her way to the Friday afternoon concert at Orchestra Hall. As she approached, hurrying down the aisle at Field's, he watched her coming toward him, walking confidently in her new fall coat, pale blue wool, tailored with tiny silver buttons, a large leather purse slung over her shoulder. She was wearing a scarf around her throat and her face seemed to glow with innocence, a child's face, tanned and smooth, the eyes still wondrous, schoolgirl eyes. She looked like any young Lake Forest matron on her way to the symphony, this granddaughter of August Loewenstine, her perfume touched at him as Peter took her arm and brushed her cheek, but she turned her face away.

"Don't be silly," she said as he bent to kiss her.

"Kit, I want you to see this marvelous Russian box."

"Oh, Peter, don't buy it."

"If you'll skip the concert and come out with me now for a drink, I won't buy it."

"No, Peter, but I'll meet you after the concert. I want to talk. At the bar on top of the Hancock." She touched his shoulder and then his cheek. "Ciao, Peter," she said in a whisper and quickly left the shop. He watched her recede in the throng of shoppers until she was lost. Then he bought the black lacquered box and had it gift wrapped.

That night she asked him for the divorce. She played with a dish of peanuts as she spoke and Peter watched the patterns of the planes landing at O'Hare.

"I know I sound like a bitch."

His eyes were misted with tears. "You are a bitch."

"Okay. You finally said it."

"What should I say to you and the doctor? Mazeltov?"

"You can say bitch." She touched his hand. "I'm going now. I can't stand this." He was crying, tears glistening on his face. "I don't want to see you this way, Pete."

"What way?" he said as she left the table and ran down the stairs. "What way, Kit?" he called after her.

Two weeks after the divorce had become final he bought a black mourner's silk armband at a store on Madison Street where religious articles were sold. He was attracted by a Menorah candelabrum in the window but instead he bought the armband. A week later he also bought the Menorah and a box of small white twisted candles. It was a lovely, modern candelabrum, light blue enameled over copper with incised Hebrew letters, an Israeli design, almost a Chagall pattern. That night, he took it home and for the first time burned candles and wore the armband. He made a little altar on his night table and read in bed with the lights off, reading by the light of the candles until they burned down to stubs and at last he fell into sleep. Each night that week, after dinner, he would shower, lock his door and burn the candles in the Menorah. When he began to feel tired he would take the black Russian box where he had hidden the armband and carefully open the neatly mitered top, and then slip the black silk band on his right arm, over his robe. Kit and Yalowitz were married the day following the divorce and immediately left for Hawaii. He tried not to think of them in bed together. He knew what the scent of tropical air would be like coming up through the windows and the sounds of the sea carried by the soft winds. Still he wouldn't allow himself to cry. The armband soothed him, the tactile sense of the black silk. If he had lost his wife, he would mourn for her in his own peculiar way, privately in his room, where each night he would open his last gift to her almost as if making some votive offering to her. The box was the reliquary of the innocence that had been their youth and marriage. Six weeks after the divorce he bought a silver Citroen racing coupe and stored the Menorah in the basement in the carton where Kit had stacked the old German Christmas ornaments in layers of newspapers. He kept the Russian box though, and finally, a year later, donated it anonymously to a television charity raffle with the armband neatly folded inside it, a hidden silken black half moon.

Hotel Europejski

He was in a bookstore on Przedmiescie Krakowskie. He'd seen a book about the Warsaw Ghetto in the window, *Warszawskie Getto*. On the cover there was a photograph of a Jewish fighter just after he'd been captured. He was approaching the Germans with his hands raised and a smirk on his face. It was now mid-afternoon of the second day. The first night and day he'd spent just walking around Warsaw. At 8:00 on the second night he'd gone to the monument in Plac Grzybowski and waited for Krysia in the shadows of the trees surrounding it, but she didn't come, so after an hour he went back to the bar at the Europejski. There was no message from her. He would try again tomorrow night. When he left her in Krakow, she'd said she'd meet him in two or three days in Warsaw, either on the second or third night at the Statue of the Martyred Professors at 8:00 in the Plac Grzybowksi. If she couldn't meet him, she would call him at his hotel, the Europejski, and leave a message with other arrangements. He drank a pinch bottle of scotch at the bar and then another in his room, and with her face and the sound of her voice slowly dissolving he fell asleep on the bed in his clothes.

The clerk in the bookstore was an uncertain teenage boy who couldn't speak English, but he knew the book, *Warszawskie Getto*, and brought it down from the shelf and handed it to him. He opened the book and saw photographs of skeletal Jewish children begging on the streets, and on the next page corpses of children on the sidewalks. He closed it and bought it. The clerk wrapped it in string and brown paper.

This afternoon, before going to the bookstore, he returned to the

Plac Grzybowski. It was Saturday afternoon, the Sabbath. He'd been told that the Poles had rebuilt a synagogue there and he found it and sat at the back of the morning service. The synagogue was rebuilt of white plaster and gold. He watched the old men davening in the light that came through the new stained-glass windows. One bearded man in a prayer shawl and sunglasses sat against the eastern wall and swiveled his neck and stared at him like an angry old ostrich. It made him feel like an intruder so after a few moments he got up and left. As he walked down the front stairs, a man wearing a green sweater and binoculars muttered "Shalom" as they passed on the stairs. He answered "Shalom." The man replied loudly, "Shabbat Shalom." He'd seen the same man at the hotel and heard him speaking Hebrew, an Israeli tourist. Two boys in prayer shawls ran by him up the stairs and went into the synagogue. Two young Jewish boys in Warsaw on a Sabbath afternoon on their way to services. It all seemed so peaceful and natural.

After leaving the bookstore, he slowly walked around the brick walls surrounding the Old Town section of Warsaw. There was a statue outside the walls of a boy soldier in an ill-fitting uniform commemorating the defense of Warsaw. Some Boy Scouts came up to him as he sat across from the statue and asked him to change money. He shook his head. He sat on a park bench and plucked open the strings of the package and looked at the book. He saw a photo of an old Jewish porter pulling a cart full of bodies. Another photograph of hundreds of people sitting in the street at the Umschlagplatz waiting to be taken to the trains to Treblinka. He shut the book and tied it back into its neat parcel and walked across the square to look for the restaurant Bazyliszek. A desk clerk at the hotel had told him it was one of the better restaurants in Warsaw. There were horses and carriages in line in the Old Town square with tourists around them and stalls where people were selling merchandise. He stopped at the stall of a young woman in jeans and a denim jacket. She had a board of rings, bracelets and necklaces. She was about seventeen, with long blonde hair, blue eyes, a virginal look, almost the face of the woman rising out of the sea in the seashell in the Uffizi, Botticelli's *Birth of Venus*. A Polish Venus in a jeans jacket, with the serious face of an ancient merchant and brown teeth, one missing at the side. Always the beautiful, serious, virginal face and the rotten teeth.

He pointed to a slim gold band with a single clear green stone. "How much?"

She held all her fingers up twice. Two thousand zlotys.

He could bargain with her, the Jew bargaining with the Polish virgin. But he gave her the 2,000 zlotys and took the ring off the board. She didn't thank him, and she didn't offer him change.

He found the restaurant Bazyliszek on the other side of the square. He went up the stairs with the green ring in his pocket and ordered a glass of wine. It was a beautiful old restaurant with lots of paintings and antiques, and the waitresses were dressed in peasant costumes. Almost all the customers were foreign tourists. He was seated near a loud group of Italian men. The oldest man was the center of attention, his hands accompanying his speech like animated finger marionettes. The menu was intricate and large, entirely in Polish. There was a drawing on the cover, a horned animal that appeared to almost be half bird and half snake. He ordered a beer and mushroom soup, red cabbage salad and Bazyliszek steak. The waitress was a heavy-breasted blue-eyed fortyish blonde, in a white low-cut frilled peasant blouse and dirndl skirt.

"I do not speak English," she said emphatically.

He pointed at the items on the menu and she slowly wrote them down. When he told her he wanted Bazyliszek steak she shook her head vigorously. "Nie, nie." She turned her back and went for the maitre d' who returned with her and spoke English.

"May I help you, sir?" He was a tired looking man with spots on the faded velvet lapels of his tuxedo jacket.

"I have ordered beer."

"Yes."

"And mushroom soup."

"Yes."

"And red cabbage salad."

"Yes, sir."

"And Bazyliszek steak."

"I am sorry, sir, but you must misunderstand. There is no such thing as Bazyliszek steak. That is the name of the restaurant. Bazyliszek is half crow and half snake. It exists only in Polish legend. So we cannot serve you Bazyliszek steak. May I suggest venison or wild boar trotters?"

"You serve wild boar trotters?"

"Yes, of course."

"What are they?"

"I do not understand."

"What part of the wild boar are the trotters?"

"The trotters are the forelegs."

The waitress was staring at him.

"I will just have beer, mushroom soup and the salad. I will forget the Bazyliszek steak and I don't want wild boar trotters."

"As you wish, sir." The maitre d' gave the order to the waitress and turned and left the table. He could have turned up the volume. He could have acted like he did in the Greek restaurant in London where he did battle over their charge of 50p for bread and butter, but wild boar trotters was hardly a serious cause.

He opened his parcel again and removed the book, *Warszawskie Getto*. There was a chapter on the Jews of Lodz and a photograph of a hunchback man standing in the Jewish cemetery in Lodz, the cemetery keeper, hobbling through the broken tombstones. "The Humpback of Lodz," the eternal keeper of all the tombs of all the Jews in Poland. He drank half his beer. He would drop a green ring on each of their stones. He would bring his own version of a Bazyliszek to Poland to graze in the cemeteries, like the horned animal on the cover of the menu. He could put a green ring on the horn and then cut off the horn and use it as a green-ringed shofar to warn the Jews of Warsaw. The Humpback of Lodz standing on the Plac Grzybowski blowing his Bazyliszek horn. He closed the book and put it away and finished his beer and ordered another one and a glass of honey liqueur.

After dinner he walked back to the Europejski to put the book away in his luggage. He didn't want to carry it with him. He knew that if he had it with him he'd force her to look at the photographs and he didn't want to do that. He still had two hours. It was only 6:00, and he splashed some cold water on his face and put on some cologne.

Would Krysia show? If she did, or if she didn't, tonight would be his last night in Poland. He checked at the desk to see if he had a telephone message from her. There was no message.

He'd made arrangements to leave on British Air tomorrow afternoon. The fall semester at the law school where he taught in Philadelphia would begin next week and he'd done nothing to prepare his courses. He hadn't touched the manuscript of his book in weeks. At least he'd bring the *Warszawskie Getto* book back to Philadelphia, have it translated, and give it to some Jewish institution.

He looked at himself in the bathroom mirror. "It's time to leave this country. No matter what she says, no matter what she wants of you, just remember it's time to leave. You are not her savior or the savior of the Jews. You are not the 'Humpback of Lodz.' You are merely a fortyish, neurotic law professor chasing after a crazy Polish woman in her doomed country."

But in case she did show, he took the green ring with him.

As he walked through the Europejski lobby of faded carpet and lamps with tasseled shades and cherubs carved on stairwell balustrades, he noticed that groups of women were coming into the hotel. They were excited, gossiping and laughing. He followed some of them up the stairway to a second-floor room. The room was an ornate ballroom, and there was a string quartet playing. It was very dark and the room smelled of perfume. He saw that women were seated around the perimeter of the dance floor, the few men would slowly circle them and occasionally one would ask a woman to dance. Several of the women were dancing together. This was his kind of place, a ballroom filled with Polish women on Saturday night, all waiting for him, the Jew lover from America, his wallet stuffed with dollar bills. He would bow slightly from the waist. They'd recognize him in a minute.

There they were, behind the potted palms, all the prim blonde Polish women his heart craved, the cold, judgmental Slavic faces, the neatly pinned hair, fat ones, thin ones, young ones, middle aged, sitting with their hands folded in their laps behind the palms. All he had to do was join the circle of men. The quartet was playing a waltz. Could he waltz? Did he remember how to waltz? He used to be a graceful dancer. He remembered his dance with Krysia in the Holiday Inn in Krakow. How would he ask a woman to dance in Polish? He didn't know the words. He didn't know the verb "to dance." He walked toward a blonde with a gold cross on a chain in a white blouse and black skirt. She turned her eyes away. She looked about thirty in the dim light. He bowed to her and she stood, and suddenly he was waltzing with her, her face pressed against his; he inhaled the clean smell of her hair and her cosmetics. Her hand was light in his and she held him stiffly. He could feel the light touch of her breasts brushing against his chest. He must concentrate on dancing, and instead he was getting an erection. He turned to the side so he wouldn't touch her with it. God forbid the Humpback of Lodz should touch a Polish woman with his erection. She smiled briefly to him and he spun her out in what he thought was an intricate maneuver, and when she spun back to him he held his hand out and missed her. She shrugged and the piece ended. They hadn't said a word to each other. She nodded and went back to her chair.

He stood behind the potted palm again. Was it in a painting by Munch, the women in the white blouses, the men in black. all wraith-like dancers? He was seeing Poland now in terms of art, Botticelli, Munch. He would dance with all these women, one by one, the Zyd lover from America, one by one by one, just like the dancers in the Munch painting, around and around with the women in white blouses and gold crosses.

He waited for the music to begin again. He joined the men slowly circling the women and bowed in front of another blonde. Her eyes acknowledged him. She had a dimple in her left cheek and a tiny mole on the ridge of her right cheek. She was dressed in a checked woolen skirt and three-buttoned jacket.

"Prosze" (please), he said to her. She looked at him blankly and walked ahead to the dance floor. She smelled of expensive perfume, the heavy musk of a woman who bought western clothes at the Pewex for dollars and kept a bottle of good cologne at home on her dressing table. He still had his erection. All he had to do was press it into her and she would recognize him.

She said something to him in Polish. He couldn't reply, but he nodded. Her breath was freshly scented with peppermint. She looked at him curiously. He still said nothing. Around and around he spun her in another waltz. She turned her head professionally, biting her lips, as they circled. He was still light on his feet and he was moving gracefully, careful not to brush her with the erection, but now it was subsiding and instead he had the sensation that his shoulderblades were beginning to grow protuberances, that two small humps were forming on his back. He began to bend over as he danced.

The music ended and she smiled coldly and touched at her hair and walked away from him back to her chair.

He went behind the plants again. The sensation of his shoulderblades swelling continued and he could feel himself slowly growing misshapen, as if the wings of a dark angel had been planted like two ugly embryos in his back. Still, when the music began, he straightened and joined the men. It was a slow fox trot. He bowed in front of a woman with dark eyes and brown hair. She looked slim and attractive, except when she opened her mouth to accept his invitation, he could see her front incisors were edged in green. The perfect mistress for the Humpback of Lodz. A woman whose teeth were turning green. He would give her Krysia's green ring.

She was very light in his hands, almost a presence instead of a woman. He was fully bent over now and had great difficulty negotiating the steps. He didn't speak to her, she didn't talk to him, except that she had her hand over one of the humps and it was painful where she was pressing on it. Did she know she was causing him pain, her hand almost conical over the swelling? Jadwiga, Queen of Poland. No, I am not your lover Jagiello, first Lithuanian King of Poland. I am only another litvak Zyd. The last one, though. Be careful how you touch my hump. Do not cause me more pain. No, I will not give you my green ring. I am saving it for a friend of mine.

The woman walked away at the end of the piece and began to whisper to her friends and point to him, and they began to smirk. He could invite them all up to the room and show them a real smirk on the cover of the book, the face of the young ghetto fighter coming up from the ruins, flushed by the Germans.

He went to ask another woman to dance. He bowed in front of her. "Nie, nie," she said. He bowed in front of another blonde in a primly starched blouse, an ivory cross on a chain. "Nie, nie." He tried one more woman. "Nie, nie."

They were smirking and laughing at him. He left the dance floor and walked down the stairway to the lobby. As soon as he felt the outside air, the humps were gone and he was able to straighten his back again with no aftereffect except for a slight stinging at the two spots where the swelling had been. He went back to the lobby and looked at himself in a long gilded mirror. He was Poland's last Jew and it was time to leave.

He would go down to the river, the Vistula, and throw her green ring into the river where the rabbis used to cleanse themselves of their sins before Yom Kippur. He'd seen a painting of them in their long black caftans and fur-trimmed hats, standing at the side of the river and praying. He would throw her green ring into the river and then go back to Plac Grzybowski and if she showed, he'd explain it all to her.

Who Could Stay the Longest?

H E HAD COME TO LONDON because he knew he had AIDS and was dying and he wanted to see London one more time. Also, he had a plan. He was forty-three and had practiced law in Chicago for twenty years, at first for eight years with a large, distinguished, old-line firm of over 200 lawyers. Then, when he failed to make partner, he gradually slipped down into smaller firms, each one not quite as prominent as its predecessor, each job of less responsibility and smaller money. He never openly admitted his homosexuality at any of the firms, but it seemed that eventually he would be outed by whispering campaigns and innuendo and would be forced to resign. There was never a direct confrontation. He avoided confrontation. He always complied and left quietly. He always wore his mask of a straight conservative lawyer, immaculately dressed in his black suits or gray pinstripes, with brightly patterned silk ties and English shoes. He was a very handsome man, with clear, innocent blue eyes and English/Irish features, a snub nose, broad cheekbones with high color, and brown hair always perfectly trimmed. In a glance, Derek Haughton was a gentleman. He could have been a model in the La Salle Street windows of Brooks Brothers. His voice and manner were quiet and refined. He never argued, never raised his voice, he was always deferential, correct, politic. He'd taken his law degree at Illinois and the few straight friends he socialized with were his law classmates from those days, but gradually he walked away even from them. He lived alone and his gay life was conducted secretly, so that for the first fifteen years of his practice few people knew that he was homosexual. He was a trust lawyer and a tough probate litigator and he was very good. But he had no clients of his own. His life was too private to permit clients to intrude. He never had the desire or the ability to build networks within the bar or the banking and trust community that would bring him business. Instead, he began to spend all his spare time traveling and meeting other gay men in London, Paris or Rome, Buenos Aires or even Tokyo. He had though never in all the years really fallen in love. Not until he met Jack Norton, a young law student from John Marshall at an estate tax seminar in Chicago. Jack had been a student host at the law school seminar and Derek had asked him for assistance in finding the library for the lecture. Jack was a handsome, young blonde man in his early twenties, thin and tall and very gracious and welcoming in his blue blazer and gray flannel trousers. There had been an immediate mutual attraction.

They accidentally met again after the seminar that evening in a restaurant down the street where they both had stopped for wine and pizza. Jack was with a group of his law school friends and invited Derek to join them. That evening was the beginning of a relationship that had now lasted five years. Suddenly though, two years ago, Derek became infected with AIDS. Why, or how, he didn't really know. It wasn't from Jack. The "why" part could probably be answered, and why fool himself, the "how" part could also be answered. Even though he openly lived with Jack in Derek's apartment in Old Town, Derek early in their relationship began secretly to go to gay bars and baths and had unprotected sex. He no longer flew to cities abroad to meet discreet partners. It was as if he was lost in the frenzied rhythm of a death wish. He had no control over this secret, mysterious, animal part of him that couldn't be sated in a monogamous relationship. Intellectually he knew it was wrong, but physically he couldn't stop himself. So, on and on he went with partner after partner, still always the gray-clad, pinstriped, quiet, autocratic lawyer. But secretly, this inner rage drove him, leading him into these relationships that now would destroy him. He always protected Jack though, and had safe sex with his young lover. Derek's absent overnights were never discussed. Derek paid Jack's tuition over and above grants and loans and paid the apartment rent and all their living expenses. It was their contract. He would care for Jack and if Derek needed care someday, Jack would care for him. Ex Contractu.

Unfortunately, neither the illness nor his law firm would wait for Derek. The disease had progressed beyond cure and he stopped trying to combat it. He became thinner and weaker, his face grew gaunt. He was obviously very ill and he had lesions on his chest. His latest firm suddenly terminated him with a payment of only one month's salary. He wasn't performing, getting to the office later and later, missing days of work, failing to complete projects. His illness was never discussed. Only his work was discussed and he was judged deficient. He signed a release. They gave him a check. That was a year ago. In three months he was broke. He never had savings, not even to continue his health insurance. He was not only financially broke, his spirit was broken. He surrendered the black Porsche he'd leased because he couldn't make the lease payments. He thought of suing the firm but he didn't have the energy or money for litigation. The only asset he had was a $500,000 term life insurance policy which he desperately fought to keep in force. He'd met the last premium, but a $2,500 premium was due next week and he didn't have the money for it and had no chance of getting it. He could surrender himself to the life insurance company, tell them that he was dying, submit to physical examinations, display the lesions on his chest and then let them buy out his policy at a discount. He thought of doing that but he had too much pride to submit himself and besides it would reduce Jack's trust. He had another plan. Before he met Jack, he'd planned to leave the policy to his parents for their old age but they were dead. He'd changed the beneficiary to his estate and drawn a will leaving $400,000 to Jack in trust, one-third at thirty, one-third at thirty-five and the final third at forty. The other $100,000 he left in specific bequests to his brother and sister's children, several nieces and nephews. However, now he simply had no money to pay the premiums. He'd been living off cash advances against his credit cards for the last six months. He'd almost reached the limit on all his cards. Jack's earnings as a part-time waiter and bartender barely covered their food bills. Derek was using cash draws on one card to pay charges on the other cards and was being dunned daily by collection agents, two or three calls a day. He told them he was dying and had life insurance to pay his debts, but they wouldn't believe him. There were too many angry voices. More voices than he could understand or handle.

So, he drew one last cash advance and flew to London to get away from the angry, dunning voices and tonight was sitting in a tuxedo with a small red ribbon on his lapel, drinking chardonnay in the ornate Victorian lobby of the Hotel Russell in Russell Square in Bloomsbury. He sat on a sofa in the lobby staring up the grand balcony at a portrait of the Queen above the huge crystal chandelier. She stared back at him down the regal, marbled staircase with the icy hauteur of the young, beautiful Elizabeth. She was dressed in a blue cape trimmed in ermine. She held two scepters, one in each hand, one of Law and one of Equity. "Administer not Law so that thy should forget Equity." He smiled to himself as he remembered the rites of coronation.

"So," he said to her silently. "Your Majesty. I have a room on the seventh floor. Should I charge a bottle of Dom Perignon to my room? Take it upstairs. Drink as much of it as I can and just step off the window ledge? Would that be conscionable in Equity? My policy is paid for, I'm beyond the two-year period for suicide. If I were in Chicago, there'd just be a short notice in the paper. 'Loop Lawyer Jumps From Hotel.' Not even a murmur from the passing crowd. 'Far from the madding crowds ignoble strife.' What say thee, Lisbeth?" He held his glass up to her and drank his wine.

The lobby was crowded with office Christmas celebrants. Dozens of tall, elegant, young men, young buckos in formal dress. All hues of young men, tall, thin, broad shouldered, weak, strong, virtuous, beauteous, mean spirited, charitable, avaricious. After all it was Christmas, and they were having a marvelous time at an office Christmas party, perhaps 300 people in the hotel's grand ballroom. Young women in black dresses, elegant blondes and dusky Indian maidens with eyes shining like incandescent rupees whilst the young buckos entertained them by attempting to mount a mechanical bull in the center of the dance floor. It was a mechanical bucking bull, a machine with the huge head of a bull that cavorted and twisted as you mounted it and held onto its horns. Slowly at first, revolving and revolving, like life itself and then faster and faster with the elegant, young men and women cheering and cheering, faster and faster as the celebrant held on, tried to hold on until he was spun off, flying into the crowd. Who could stay the longest? Who could stay the longest?

He charged a bottle of Dom Perignon at the bar, had it opened and took a glass and stood in the back of the ballroom in his tuxedo with the red ribbon on his lapel. No one noticed him and he watched the mechanical bull and the wild, flailing, young men and then after finishing more of the bottle, he took it with him and quietly adjourned to the elevator and rode to his room.

He opened the old, scabbed window frame. It was hard to pull it open. The night air came rushing in, black and tasting of exhaust fumes from the traffic below, streaks of color, buses and taxis, the lights of London in invidious ribbons of color. He had written a note. He'd seen the *Merchant of Venice* last night at the Barbican Theater and he'd copied out Portia's lines about mercy. It was painful for him to even use his fingers to write but he'd laboriously copied the lines from a small leather-bound copy of the play he'd bought after the performance.

"The quality of mercy is not strain'd,
It droppeth as the gentle rain from heaven
Upon the place beneath: it is twice blest,
It blesseth him that gives, and him that takes . . ."

That would be his final note. No one in Chicago had ever shown him any mercy. Nor had he asked for any. He was outside the system. He wasn't able to join them. He could never join them. He was an outcast, never inside, always outside. "It droppeth as the gentle rain . . ." I will fall like a gentle rain, littering London's streets, a brief stain, like a condom he had seen on the sidewalk in front of the hotel, discarded in a black pool of water. He filled his glass and put the bottle down on the table beside the open window. There were electric pigeon wires to keep the pigeons off the concrete window ledge and he reached beyond the window and touched the wires with his fingers and there was a sudden arc of sparks and he burned his fingers. He winced and took a towel from the bathroom and ripped off the pigeon wires and they arced again, sending sparks down into the street, like a fussilade of a comet. He thought of Whistler's painting, trailings of color from a comet gently falling. No, he wasn't going to go home and die whimpering in Jack's arms. He would die here while he could still stand and make a conscious decision. He didn't want to die choking and bleeding to death in his lover's arms. He would be merciful unto himself. He spread his arms and slowly pulled himself through the window, twisting his body out onto the ledge. He bent his head and put his hands together in prayer and thanked God and let himself go down seven floors unto death.

Skipping Stones

SHE HAD GROWN UP ON Chicago's North Shore and gone to Boston University and Columbia Law School, and had graduated with distinction. She clerked for a year with a U.S. District Judge in Manhattan and then dropped out of the law and took a Master's in Social Work at the New School in New York City and lived in the Village for five years and worked at a hospital in Harlem. She wasn't happy in New York and eventually felt burned out, and finally returned to Chicago and resumed her career as a lawyer. She found a job with a small LaSalle Street divorce firm and, after seven more years, became a partner specializing in divorce litigation.

It wasn't easy being a woman litigator in the male club of the divorce courts, but she was a fighter and good at her work, very tough, capable of slashing, bruising argument, even when she knew the cases were clouted against her, that the judge was a political crony of her male opponent and regarded her as an enemy or political opponent, or just a bitch.

When Martha Levine began her job in Chicago, she still had the desire to help people as a lawyer. As a marital relations lawyer, she thought she would be helping people get on with their lives. She'd never been married, and now she was thirty-eight, her long dark hair showing strands of gray and lines just beginning in her face. She often wore long silk gaily colored scarves to the office and loose tops, and now in late summer, full flowered skirts with jangling bracelets and strands of Indian or Oriental jewelry as necklaces. She didn't want to harden into a man; she wanted to keep herself feminine. She didn't want to ossify into the curtness and gruffness of a man. Even though she fought with them daily, she kept her distance from her male opponents. She was polite and cordial, but not inviting, and over the years she began to intensely dislike many of her male opponents.

She had mostly women friends, but there were still a few men friends, men who she would join for dinner or go with to the symphony or Lyric Opera. No one special, just a few friends and confidants. Occasionally there would be a perfunctory kiss good night in a cab or at her building in the driveway.

Recently the man most prominent in her life had been the senior partner of her firm, Julius Frankel, who was in his early seventies, a widower and a workaholic. He had no interest other than his work and the law firm. He was constantly after Martha with his car phone before he arrived at work and then from behind his huge mahogany desk where he would leave her urgent messages: "M.L., See me immediately. J." She was tired of the messages, so tired that she'd have loved to shove one of them down his throat. His latest edict was that all associates and partners carry portable phones with them at all times—on their way to court, at lunch, wherever they were—so he or any of the other partners could contact them. Martha carried her phone, but usually shut it off, and when Frankel confronted her she told him that several judges had objected to the sound of the cellular phones going off during courtroom argument. He grumbled, but accepted her explanation. He was not only dictatorial, but in complete control of the firm, a 65 percent owner of its voting stock. Martha had a 2.5 percent interest as a partner, and she and the six other partners really had nothing to say when it came to confronting Julius Frankel. It just wasn't done, unless you expected to be shown the door.

He also craftily assigned the cases, keeping the big-money cases for himself and one or two men who were his favorites. The firm was built on Frankel's tough negotiating and trial ability. He could walk away from a divorce negotiation with a multimillion dollar settlement for his client and $100,000 in attorney's fees just on the basis of his reputation as a fierce trial lawyer. She wasn't assigned these cases. Instead, she was given second-tier cases that Julius felt "were not in the numbers." Her clients were usually women, wives of corporate executives, and the cases involved at the most one or two million dollar property settlements and $10,000 to $25,000 in fees. They were usually contested in the early motion stage, particularly on temporary maintenance for the wife. But they seldom actually went to trial and if so, were usually settled.

She had come on a long, painful journey from her social worker days. She tried to keep involved in public service cases, taking *pro bono* cases from a woman's coalition, but she found that she had very little time for *pro bono* work. She had tied herself up financially. She had a beautiful condo overlooking Lincoln Park in a slim, glass-paned Mies van der Rohe building and a white BMW convertible, a closet full of designer suits and shoes, and monthly credit card payments that wiped out her salary. At the end of the year she fought Julius and confronted him with a printout of her billing and the fees she had produced, and she received a $15,000 bonus. It was almost all gone except for $2,500. So in late July she bought herself a ticket to London. She deserved a summer sabbatical.

Why not? Ruth Bader Ginsburg was teaching in Innsbruck in Austria this summer. She had seen a photograph of her, suntanned, fit, her hair tied back with a ribbon. She looked like a young woman. Sandra Day O'Connor, where was she teaching this summer? Did she have any plans? Salzburg? No, Anthony Kennedy was teaching in Salzburg and Chief Justice Rehnquist in England, at Cambridge. If they could travel to Europe, why couldn't she? She could take two weeks in London, or maybe a week in London and a week in Paris. Her lawyer friend Julia had said to her when she told her about Justice Ginsburg's summer plans, and how young and relaxed she looked, "Martha, have you ever noticed how the facial expressions of judges change after they're appointed to the bench? Before their appointment they're just like the rest of us—harried, worried, frazzled looking, but then after they put on their robes they begin to look just like the *Mona Lisa,* with that phony beatific smile."

Of course she should take the trip. She could get away from Frankel, the firm, and the divorce courts. The stack of brown file jackets in her office were no longer people to her. They were just files, a stack of files, one after another, this one worth $5,000 in fees that one worth $10,000. They weren't people any more, and neither was she a person anymore. She had become a money machine. She needed something exotic in her life, some adventure. So in anticipation of the trip, she bought a finger ring for her thumb, Thumbelina in Europa. She knew she was losing her sympathy for her clients; she only talked to them about money. Never about their loneliness. Never asked them about their absence from sex and their loss of confidence. She just didn't do that anymore.

So two weeks later, at the end of August, she flew British Air to London for a week and then a week in Paris. She stayed in Lancaster Gate at a charming hotel that another lawyer friend, Marguerite, had recommended. She'd stayed there and raved about the service. It was a small hotel and very posh, with privacy, a quiet paneled bar, a doorman in a green swallow-tailed coat, and a lovely breakfast room. It was near Hyde Park and she would walk in the park and pretend she was Virginia Woolf or Katherine Mansfield sitting on a bench.

She even looked up an old boyfriend. She'd known Colin Rifkind when he was a pale, lonely graduate student in English literature at Boston University. He was from London and he'd been her first real college love, but he was so unsure of himself, shy and tentative, that their relationship had imploded, like one of those lovely iridescent children's soap bubbles. She knew he had gone to law school at Oxford, had married and divorced, and was now working at a London corporate firm. So she called him, and he responded warmly, and they met for a drink in a wine bar in Bloomsbury.

Instead of a tentative pale young man in love, Colin had grown into a heavy, balding, angry trial partner of a huge British firm. He'd been in Singapore for the last several years and now was involved in litigating that required constant air travel. She knew that she couldn't ever revive, or even find, the young man he'd once been, in the blowzy, mottled-faced man who roared with laughter as he told her about the managing partner in Singapore who'd been ordered back to London because "he'd been caught in bed 'rogering' the children's amah."

She was back at the hotel by midnight. So much for the revival of international love affairs. In the morning she sat with a cup of coffee at the base of the statue of Peter Pan in Hyde Park watching the children approach with squeals of delight. Had she really given Colin a chance? Why was she so closed off to men? The awful story about the amah. Perhaps James Barrie, who created Peter Pan, used to sit here. He lived in Lancaster Square. Children's laughter. It was a beautiful sound. She never listened anymore to the voices of children. There weren't any children in her life, not even nieces or nephews. Would she ever have a child? Never. She would never have a child. She sipped her coffee in the sunlight. What was the name of the little angel in Peter Pan, the angel with the wand and the fairy dust? Tinkerbell. And there she was, standing next to Peter Pan, a tiny sculpted angel with her wings folded, waiting for more children to arrive.

Two days later she was sitting in front of another statue, the statue of Alfred Dreyfus in Paris. After getting a fax from Julius Frankel with a suggested Paris itinerary, she found a book about Dreyfus with photographs of the man with dark, sad eyes, in his French officer's uniform. She'd read about the Dreyfus Affair—a Jewish officer in the French Army who in 1895 was falsely accused of being a spy. He'd been stripped of his insignia, here in the courtyard of the École Militaire, behind the Eiffel Tower. Zola had defended him in the newspapers. Eventually Dreyfus was found innocent, but only after being imprisoned on Devil's Island. Julius Frankel had sent her a fax asking her to find the statue of Alfred Dreyfus and to take a photo. It would be "a personal favor." After the photo of the statue of Dreyfus he then recommended that she go to the Holocaust Monument, the "Lawyer's Church," Ste. Chappelle, the Magistrate Courts, the old Opera House with the Chagall angels on the ceiling, "so close you can touch them," and then told her to have coffee at the Café de la Paix. Even here she was Frankel's messenger girl. She should buy herself a nose ring.

The Holocaust Monument was an underground chamber with a modern glass sculpted ceiling of daggers, a sea of glass daggers. It was in the garden immediately behind Notre Dame, and she took another photo, and then she decided to abandon Julius's itinerary and strike out on her own.

She walked to the Tuileries at dusk and rode the ferris wheel, and looked out at the magic sea of lights that was Paris, and tried to shake all the glass daggers out of her head. She was staying at a small hotel on the Left Bank, and when she returned the clerk handed her another fax from Chicago. She handed it back to him and told him to answer, "Mademoiselle est sortie."

That night she went to a boring rendition of Molière at the Comédie Francaise. She didn't know if it was a comedy; it was in ancient French and iambic verse. Most of the actors were men in pantaloons with spiked beards and plumed hats, all prancing and waving swords. She fell asleep, and after the theater walked to the bar of the Ritz. There at the bar she met a man named Jean Paul. After drinking two splits each of champagne they walked together back to the Tuileries.

She showed him the Ferris wheel and they rode up into the lights of Paris, and then at the carnival in the park below she shot clay pigeons, winning a green glass figurine of a young woman with long hair.

"I think it's Jeanne d'Arc just before she was set afire," she told Jean Paul, who was married and from Lyon. He was a lovely man, about forty-five, with graying temples and a smooth face that seemed to convey constant surprise as she told him about herself.

"Martha, she looks like you, not Jeanne d'Arc."

"But I am not a woman on fire."

"But you are a beautiful woman."

"Thank you for saying that . . . I am also made of glass. I shatter very easily. Most women do. Do you agree with that? I am a sculptor in glass. Did you know that just by looking at me? Of course not. I sculpt glass figures. My apartment in Chicago is full of them."

Just as she said that, he came to her under the street lamp and kissed her. His lips were sweet, this married corporate manager from Lyon, who had told her she was a beautiful woman. He was a beautiful man, and she told him that, and he walked her back to the hotel and gave her his card with his e-mail number, kissed her one more time, and told her he would contact her and turned and walked away into the Paris night.

She rode the elevator to her room on the fifth floor and went to her window, and walked out on her balcony to see if she could find him on the street. There was no one there. Why did he leave her so abruptly? He was staying at the Ritz. She should just telephone him and ask him to come back to her.

The red light was flashing on her phone. "Mademoiselle, you have another fax from Chicago."

"No," she said, "tell them I've left. Don't you understand?" She put down the phone. She was crying now and stepped back out on the balcony. She held the glass figure of the long-haired young woman in her hand and looked down to the street. She hadn't cried like this in a long time. She wasn't permitted to cry in America. She put her hand on the ornamental iron balcony railing, and then dropped the glass figurine over the edge and watched it fall to the street. She didn't hear the sound of it shattering. There was no sound.

TWO DAYS LATER she was back in her office, jet lagged, hollow eyed, ready for the morning court call. She could see the folded computer list of cases and room assignments waiting for her on her desk. Her eyes looked like they had been daubed with kohl. The trip had been like a dream, as if she had stepped out of her own life. But now she was back, and it was as if she had never left. The platoon of young men heading for the courts, sunglasses, hair gelled, all with briefcases, heels clicking, full of purpose and malevolence. She was full of malevolence and she lacked purpose.

One of the lawyers called out to her and stopped in her office. "Welcome home, Martha. Of course you've heard the news."

"No, what news?"

"Julius is dead. He died last week. We tried several times to fax you."

"Julius is dead?"

"Yes, D-E-A-D."

"Oh, my God!"

"He died of a massive heart attack last week in his apartment. The funeral was yesterday. There's a partners meeting tonight. I think you've got the job of probating his will."

She closed her door and sat at her desk. Julius was dead, the angry face, eyes blazing, white hair over his forehead, sitting at his desk in suspenders, shouting at clients, buzzing for secretaries, all that crazy misplaced energy and intelligence dead? Julius is dead? Gone forever? Vanished? And with it all his power over her and the lawyers in this firm, also gone, Julius is dead?

She sat at her desk and touched the list of the morning court call. If Julius was dead, she was free to leave. Why not? She could open her own office. She and her friend Marguerite. Martha Levine and Marguerite Corbett, Attorneys and Counselors. There would always be flowers in their reception room, and their offices would be done in soft pastels, her glass sculptures would be there, and Marguerite's hemp figures. Why not? Why should men be counselors to women in divorce at a woman's most vulnerable time? Why shouldn't they turn to another woman, a woman equally skilled, and tempered now by experience? It was just like the men in this office to give her Julius's will to probate. To them, probate was a woman's job. Death was a matter to be attended by women.

That night at home she read his will. After a few large bequests to nieces and nephews, he left everything to charity. Julius had no children. One of the male partners in the office was named executor. He had one strange request. He had been cremated and wanted his ashes scattered over Lake Michigan. She took care of that. She hired a pilot to fly the urn out into the center of the lake and scatter the ashes. She saved a small remnant of the ash, though, for herself in a Limoges jar, and then she put it into some special glass stones she sculpted. She called them skipping stones, and she filled them with tiny seeds of his ash and flecks of gold and miniature leaves with tiny bubbles of glass and swirls of color, swirling reds and blues that would mix with the water in which he sought immersion.

When she finished she had a small raffia basket of her sculpted skipping stones, and she went down to the beach at Oak Street near Julius's apartment. One by one, she skipped all of her stones into the water. She was alone and no one was near as a witness. Death was a matter to be attended by women. Was she being ghoulish? No, she was following his wishes: earth to earth, dust to dust, water to fire, dust to water.

The King of Persia

SHE WAS A SCRUBWOMAN in an office building in Chicago. Her name was Marya. She was a short woman, about thirty-five, with black hair and black eyes and the olive complexion of an untroubled peasant. Yet, she was a true descendant of the ancient tribes of Persia. Her face could have been cut from a bas relief in a tomb of a Persian king, a face of a handmaiden carrying a jug of water on her shoulder or a young hawk on a trident.

He was a tax accountant who worked for a large firm in the building. Richard Bernhardt was forty-two and married, with a family in a suburb. He was a lean man with the high-planed forehead of a scholar, and a dark angular face, but his eyes were blue and his family had come to this country at the beginning of this century from Cologne where his great-grandfather had been a doctor. Richard Bernhardt graduated in 1953 from the University of Chicago and became a tax specialist and now, at forty-two, a principal in his firm.

It was 1971, in the fall, when Bernhardt first noticed the scrubwoman, Marya. It was expected of the junior partners in the firm that they spend two or three evenings a week at the office. He had just been made a principal and with the change in status he was at last freed from the obligation of evening work. But after so many years, it was a habit that was hard to break. The children were young. He was used to arriving home on the 10:30 train and sharing an hour of quiet time with his wife, followed perhaps by some television, or twenty minutes or so of a novel in bed. Now that he could run for the 5:35, he disliked arriving home with the house in disarray, clothes and toys scattered over the living room, the children greeting him with shrieks of excitement and laughter. He dreaded the family dinner with his stomach still in knots from his office day. He'd rather linger at his favorite German restaurant downtown after racquetball at his club and then spend an hour or two in the quiet of his office with the door closed and the telephone off. So even after his promotion, Bernhardt spent at least two evenings a week at the office doing research, dictating memos, and reading the stacks of tax journals that he piled on his floor. Sometimes he would just sit with his feet up on the desk and pull the slats of the venetian blinds and watch the lights of the city.

He seldom paid attention to the scrubwomen. They were mostly older Polish women or perhaps Ukrainian or Slavic. He didn't speak to any of them. They didn't speak to the men. He would see them every day at 5:00 arriving in their heavy coats, trimmed with imitation fur. They'd hide in the corridor closets and change into wash dresses. Occasionally a young girl would be in the crew, a strong teenager with a fresh face, her hair in a long plaited braid. Their conversation seemed like a babble to him, guttural and undecipherable. When one of them knocked on his door and asked for his wastebasket, he was always annoyed at the interruption, the routine of emptying his ashtrays, the feather duster over the glass on his desk. He liked to shoo them in and out in a hurry before he lost his thought, the flow of his research.

When Marya first began to clean his office he wasn't aware of her. She would come in, ask for his wastebasket, touch his desk and some of his photographs with her feather duster, sometimes run the vacuum.

After a few months, he did ask her to begin watering his plants and he learned her name.

"All right, Marya, I'd appreciate it if you'd water these plants, at least once a week."

"Yes."

"Can you do that for me?" He was smoking his pipe and she took the ashtray.

"Yes, I do it."

"Thank you. By the way, your name, 'Marya,' that's a pretty name. What kind of name is that?"

"Persian."

"A Persian name. And how long have you been in this country?"

"Ten years." She spoke hesitatingly, barely looking at him.

"Okay, Marya," he fluttered his hand at her as a signal for her to leave, and she quietly shut the door.

Bernhardt bought her a plant mister and a gold watering can with a long thin spigot and Marya lovingly watered his plants. Occasionally he spoke to her. He asked about her family and learned that she lived on the northwest side and had one child, a daughter. Her husband was also a Persian immigrant. She complained that he worked too hard. After work he went to "Persian taverns." Their only child was crippled but very intelligent, a very fine student at a parochial high school. Bernhardt could sense Marya's hidden anger when she spoke of her husband. He could see it flooding in the dark eyes. She told him that she liked to dance, to go to parties. The husband seldom took her anywhere. He watched television. Marya and the daughter would go shopping alone, to church parties, picnics, always alone.

Then one evening she told Bernhardt she was saving her money. "I save my money to go to . . . . a celebration."

"A celebration?"

"Right. The King, he invite all. All Persian people to come home, to come to Teheran to a festival."

Bernhardt had read of the 2,500-year anniversary of the founding of the monarchy. Spiro Agnew was being sent as an emissary from the United States at the invitation of the Shah of Iran. There was an American entourage. "I've read about it. People are coming from all over the world."

"To Persia," she said softly.

"Yes."

"My daughter and I will be there. I have the money. Soon I buy tickets."

"And your husband."

"He will stay at home. Just my daughter and I go. We go to see the King . . . . . the Shah . . . . . we will see him."

"He is a very handsome man."

"Once I see his father. He too a handsome man. He ride a horse. A beautiful horse . . . big and white . . . the King of Persia . . . . . very handsome with medals and a hat with . . . what you call . . . long feathers." She held her duster and attempted to elongate the feathers with a gesture.

"Plumes."

"That's right . . . plumes." She smiled and the black eyes danced.

That week Bernhardt got the atlas down from the bookcase in the firm library and looked up Persia. Iran was colored green. He ran his hand over the green of Iran. It was a large country surrounded on the north by fingers of the Soviet Union and to the east by Afghanistan. Teheran was at the foot of a mountainous region with elevations of 15,000 feet and the mountains reached to the Caspian Sea. At the south there was the Persian Gulf and the Gulf of Oman and the Arabian Sea. There were provinces named Khurasan and Lahistan. Cities named Isfahan, Shiraz and Meshed. He wondered what it would be like to walk into Royal Iranian Airlines (he'd seen it advertised in the back pages of the *New Yorker*) and ask for a ticket to Shiraz. The next evening he showed the green country named Iran to his children in the family atlas and tried to pronounce some of the names. He had the children repeat the names aloud after him.... Khurasan, Isfahan and Shiraz, and they giggled but they became very serious when he told them the story of the scrubwoman, Marya, and her crippled daughter who were going to see the King.

A few weeks later Marya came into his office one evening and after she finished cleaning she picked at a few of the dead leaves from his plants and then lingered in the doorway.

"Marya," he said, "the plants are doing very well."

"Yes."

"I would like to give you something." He reached for his wallet.

"No, Mr. Bernhardt. I don't want money. It is my pleasure." She dropped the dead leaves in the pocket of her apron. "Please, if you have time... I show you something."

"Marya, I really would like to give you some money."

"No..... you good man. Very kind. I show you something ..... please? A moment." She left the room and came back with a long box. She opened the box and removed the tissue paper. Then she glanced up at him, her face shining with delight.

"It's my dress. I buy this dress for my trip."

She took the dress out of the box and held the dress over her short body. It was a long red velvet evening gown, trimmed with strips of gold framing the bodice and circling the hem.

"It's very beautiful," he said.

Marya smiled and twirled, holding the gown so the fabric swirled with her movements. Then she held the dress in front of her and dipped her body in a formal bow. "Like this.... right?" She bowed her head very seriously and slowly raised it and looked at Bernhardt.

"I like that. You do that gracefully." He clapped his hands and applauded her.

"Thank you, Mr. Bernhardt," she said, and nodded her head. She folded the dress carefully and replaced the tissue. "I have another just like it for my daughter."

Bernhardt didn't see her again for two months. He presumed that she'd flown to Teheran. He'd been in New York on a tax case for ten days in December and when he returned to Chicago just before Christmas, there was another scrubwoman cleaning his office. She was a very authoritative fat Ukrainian and Bernhardt asked about Marya, but the woman just shrugged as if she didn't understand English.

One evening during the week of Christmas he stayed downtown to buy gifts and after shopping returned to his office. With his $5,000 bonus he'd bought a stuffed koala for his youngest daughter from F.A.O. Schwarz , some Hummel porcelain figures, and a beautiful sapphire pin for his wife from Lord & Taylor. He still had $3,000 left though and he'd pop it into some nice municipals. He was thinking of the municipals when he saw Marya's shadow through the glass panels of his office.

"Hello, Marya," he said. "I haven't seen you in weeks. Did you go on your trip?" He put his packages down.

"No, Mr. Bernhardt. I no go."

"Why not? Where have you been?"

"My daughter. She have operation."

"An operation?"

"Yes. I find a doctor in hospital in Minneapolis. A famous surgeon. He fix my daughter's back with operation. He straighten her back. Now she be beautiful. She walk straight. Stand tall and straight. No longer be cripple girl. I give her operation. Cash in the tickets."

"Marya."

"No. I not sorry. I happy." He could see tears glistening in her eyes. "I happy that I could give to her. I give her new life. She be beautiful now. I will go someday to visit the King. You see. Maybe a few years. Maybe after she go to college." She brushed at her face and pushed her hair back along the side of her head.

"The dress," Bernhardt said. "What did you do with the dress?"

"I save it. I have it here in closet. To take back to the store. I take it back some night soon." Then suddenly her face brightened. "Mr. Bernhardt . . . . . you stay here for a minute? Please. Just one minute." She was out the door before he could object. He pushed the button on his digital watch and the figures glowed. . . 8:30 . . . he still had an hour before the train. He took his jacket off and hung it up and sat back at his desk and pulled the blinds up. There were long ribbons of traffic on the Outer Drive and he watched the lights of the traffic. He could see the Marshall Field's clock and the Christmas crowds of shoppers hurrying along State Street.

When Marya reappeared she was dressed in the gown. Bernhardt was shocked. She stood at the door in the gown, her hair brushed back and pinned. She had put makeup on, lipstick and green eye shadow. She stood before him transformed into an elegant courtesan. He could smell her hair spray and she seemed to him as fresh as the breeze of some perfumed sea.

"Let me see you," he said to her.

Marya slowly walked toward him. She walked behind the desk and stood beside him. Then she leaned over and gently kissed him. "You Jewish, I Persian. Don't you know what is Christmas?" she asked.

He could feel the kiss resting on his lips. He touched her face. He thought for a moment of leading her to the couch and then he got up and moved away from her. "I just want you to know . . . " he began. The words didn't come right. His voice was dry. She stood behind his desk in the shadow of his lamp, a beautiful Persian handmaiden, her face uplifted and haughty . . . she was smiling at him. He began to gather his parcels and he put on his coat. Then impetuously he handed her the tiny box from Lord & Taylor. "Here," he said gruffly. "I want you to have something. For you . . . . . I know what is Christmas." He got out of there.

Later in the cab on the way to the station he could have kicked himself. God, he was such a fool. He'd handed a $2,000 sapphire pin to a scrublady. He should be committed. Such cheap sentimentality. My God, if his wife ever knew what he'd done . . . she'd kill him. He could have given the woman the koala bear for her daughter . . . or even one of the porcelains. But the pin? For God's sake, who'd he think he was . . . some Pasha in a tent soothing his favorite dancing girl? Still he smiled as he gave the driver his customary 35¢ tip.

On the train when he settled back in his seat he began to calm down. All was in order here. The same gray heads reading their papers, bankers, lawyers, conservative men heading to the suburbs at the end of their workday. He snapped open his paper. The car was quiet, no intrusions, no mysterious eastern fragrances, just the tired faces of businessmen heading home. He began to feel more comfortable about the incident. After all, it was the one impetuous act he'd allowed himself in the last twenty years. It hadn't really hurt him. He could still buy his wife another pin and have money left for the municipals. The kids would still go to summer camp, have their orthodontia and grow to be tall bronzed young women who'd come home summers from eastern colleges and head off on European vacations with their boyfriends. He looked out the window but the window was coated with vapor. He saw the reflection of a man's face, traces of gray just coming at the temples, a scholarly looking, serious man, with glasses. He was destined to ride these trains for perhaps another thirty years... what would it be... ten thousand more rides? He snapped open the paper and began to read again.

Lederhosen Boys

WHEN I WAS A BOY, growing up as a young Jew in Milwaukee, in 1937 when I was about ten, an immigrant German family moved into a house on our block. I remember them as tall, blonde people, with two little boys named Abner and Henning, who when they first came to our block used to play dressed in lederhosen outfits in front of their house. They were ruddy-faced, blue-eyed blondes like their parents and, of course, when they first arrived, they stayed mostly to themselves, occasionally venturing as far as the parkway to poke out with sticks at stones lying in the street gutter. My mother had taught me to ask their names in German, "Was ist dein Name?" and one day I approached them and tried the phrase out. "Was ist dein Name?" I said to one of them who was crouched in his lederhosen poking stones into the sewer grating at the curb. "Abner," he said, and his brother replied, "Henning." Not understanding that they were answering me, I repeated the question again and again and each time they responded, "Abner, Henning," until finally all three of us were red faced and shouting. Then, as I remember, the little boys looked up at me disgustedly and ran back up on their porch into their house and slammed the door. My only memory of Abner and Henning other than this shouting match is later when I traded them my skeleton ring for a blue covered paper booklet, about the size and appearance of a literary quarterly. The booklet was a document of crimes allegedly committed by the Czechs against the Sudeten Land Germans. It was printed in English and contained lurid tales of rapes of Sudeten maidens by Czech constabulary, spelled out in sufficient detail to warrant a special hiding place in my closet. To this date, I still wonder about the significance of that booklet in the little German boys' background.

Were they really refugees from Hitler or was their father sent to Milwaukee for liaison with the German American Bund? I do not know.

But then, as I reached back in memory, and it is difficult because almost thirty-five years have passed, I do remember one other meeting with the little German boys. In my infancy, I was cared for by a series of nursemaids and one of them had taught me a child's phrase in German, "Der Hund Lauft die Katze nach." The dog runs after the cat. One day, it must have been during the same summer—I do remember it was after my miserable attempts with "Was ist dein Name?"—I again encountered Abner and Henning on their front sidewalk. This time, and without coaching from my mother, I tried my own phrase on them. The two lederhosen boys were bent over at the curb again at the matter of poking stones. They turned on their haunches and squinted up at me. "Good morning," I said in English, and then followed with "Der Hund lauft die Katze nach." They both immediately stood and gazed far up and down the street and then back at me again. I nodded. They nodded rather mistrustingly, I now suppose. Then I repeated my nurse's sentence, "Der Hund lauft die Katze nach." Again the two boys looked up and down the street and then at me. "Der Hund lauft die Katze nach." I said again and then again. This time they didn't bother to run into the house. They simply turned their backs to me and resumed poking their stones. After this encounter, we never again spoke, except perhaps for the matter of trading the ring for the Sudeten crimes booklet. In any event, I have no further memory of Abner and Henning.

I don't know why these memories should come back to touch upon me some thirty-five years later. I am now a lawyer in Chicago, with a family, living the suburban life, commuting to an office in the city. Yet the two little lederhosen boys suddenly arise fresh in my memory. Perhaps they come so freshly to me now because of certain photographs that I found in an old *Life* magazine the other afternoon.

About three weeks ago, on a Sunday afternoon, I drove my wife and children to Chicago to visit some friends who live in a walk-up apartment and have children who are playmates of our children. We spent the afternoon on the back porch while the children played in the courtyard, several floors below us. About mid-afternoon, the adults went shopping at a neighborhood grocery for our dinner and I was left alone on the porch with a freshened drink and some old *Life* magazines from the forties that our friends thought would be interesting. The first issue I picked up featured a photo-essay on a concentration camp that had been liberated by the American Army as it fought its way into Germany. There was a photograph of a group of Jewish prisoners dressed in striped convict uniforms, each wearing a square hat, all standing behind barbed wire. The photograph must have been taken as the GIs approached the front gate of the camp, because the prisoners appeared to be standing in an attitude of formality that I now regard as that of welcoming their liberators, although the prisoners' faces showed no expression. It was almost as if the photograph had been taken through a heavy rain and behind the rain were forms, human in shape, but coming into the lens only as shadows. There were several other photographs of the concentration camp. One was of the electric fence around the camp that was separated by a moat. Just at the edge of the moat, the Germans had screened the fence with grass and birch trees. It had the appearance of a median strip on a new highway, immaculately attended, everything orderly, the young birch saplings guyed down with wires and their fragile trunks wrapped with protective coverings. There was also a photograph of an oven and piles of human bones and skulls.

The shock of seeing these photographs in the old magazine brought memories to me of other pictures hidden deep in my consciousness. I suppose we all have these films stored within us, reminding us of tragedies, old loves, triumphs, all the categories of memory. Mine are racked up in neat files, almost, I suppose, in gray tin movie spools, stacked like they are in a projectionist's booth, with worn bits of adhesive tape on each spool identifying the subject matter. Sometimes, when I run my films, the actors, including myself, come vividly to the screen as they were in life at that time. Other times, the forms are murky, my memory having to pump and creak to keep the film going, infusing color and comment into the central events. I'm sure that I've engaged in quite a bit of re-casting and having the prerogative of both producer and director, I've altered the dialogue and events to favor myself.

But some of the films I carry within me, unedited, particularly the one of Jewish suffering, because these are films in which I had no personal participation and were merely recorded by me as an adolescent mostly from magazine pictures and newsreels. Usually these films, stripped of nostalgia and personality, were recorded by me for private reasons, probably to fulfill certain emotional needs. In the case of the film of the suffering of the Jews in World War II, the emotion it brings immediately is hatred. Not necessarily hatred of the War and all human suffering, but pure, absolute hatred of the Germans.

Now, the old photographs in the *Life* magazine immediately triggered my own films and I show them to you now, a series of photographs accumulated by me as a young American Jew and strung together in this manner.

Frame One

A blurred photo of Jewish merchants on their knees, old men dressed in formal black suits and derby hats. They are sweeping the sidewalks in front of their shops of broken glass. In the photograph a group of smiling young men in brownshirt uniforms and swastika armbands wave their clubs in mock salute to the photographer.

Frame Two

Jewish prisoners being led away under gunpoint from the Warsaw Ghetto. A column of about thirty people, marching in rows of four or five abreast, one German soldier at the front of the column. This German carries a rifle, or perhaps a machine pistol, the stock in his right armpit, the barrel pointed to the ground. He too is smiling for the photographer. In the background the ghetto buildings burn in clouds of black smoke. The Jews each carry a suitcase or a bundle of personal belongings. In the first row of the column, facing the cameraman, there appears one family, a grandmother, father and mother, and a child, a little girl of about four. They are dressed as middle-class people, the man in a tie, suit and vest, his wife in a cloth coat with a fur collar. The child with one hand holds the edge of her mother's coat and in the other carries a doll. The people all have their faces averted from the camera; only the child, in perfect innocence, stares directly at the photographer.

Frame Three

A stack of bodies piled on the back of a cart or a truck, the corpses so stiff they seem frozen, hands dangle, mouths gape with unanswered screams.

Frame Four

The station platform at Auschwitz. A photograph probably taken from a rooftop, the camera looking down through the haze of engine smoke on prisoners assembled alongside a freight train. German soldiers with whips and dogs keep the columns in order.

Frame Five

Jews somewhere in Poland being forced to dig their graves while German guards, rifles in hand, stand above them on a dirt abutment. The prisoners dig with long-handled spades, most of the men elderly and bearded and dressed in black caftans.

Frame Six

Piles of hair shorn from the bodies of gassed victims. Another pile of gold teeth heaped neatly together.

Frame Seven

A group of Jewish prisoners in tiered bunks in a concentration camp barracks. The photo seemingly taken at the moment the barracks door was forced open. There, in the light coming through the door, prisoners lie staring at the first intrusion of light. All are too weak for movement or gesture.

Frame Eight

Two children, a boy of about six, a girl of perhaps four, alone at some prisoner collection point, maybe a railroad siding. Each is dressed in a dark overcoat, the boy with a peaked cap, the little girl in a beret. They are certainly brother and sister. The boy has his arm around his sister. Each has at his side a suitcase. Each has pinned to his breast a Star of David emblem. The little girl has black curls and a baby face still softly rounded between infancy and adolescence. The boy has dark hair but his features are sharper and gaunt. No childhood gaiety lingers about them. Both gravely face the cameraman, certain of their abandonment, two lost children on their way to death, yet still together as brother and sister.

End of Film

Why did I run these films for you now? I do not know. I do know that once they have begun they must be shown through to conclusion and the process of viewing them, each time, leaves me drained. I suppose it is a form of expiation. It works to some extent, although my hatred of the Germans is by now such a basic part of me that it cannot be washed away by the showing of a few old films. Perhaps the only function the film showing serves is that it helps unreel the layers of my memory and ultimately takes me back to my childhood in Milwaukee so that the two lederhosen boys appear fresh and vivid through the grayness and agony of all the old films.

Even by running the films to clear the memory, I have difficulty remembering those days in Milwaukee. Of course, I have the other films of childhood, and these I could run to assist me, but I choose not to, because the film that I have run brings me to a certain focus that I do not want to abandon.

As a ten-year-old in Milwaukee in 1937 my vision, of course, was that of a young American schoolboy. My family was not a religious family, although both my parents had formal religious training and strong Jewish identification. But our Jewishness was more of an allegiance than a discipline. We thought of ourselves as Americans, not as Jews, except in some kind of unspoken cultural obeisance. I was busy as a bugler boy in the American Legion post marching band. My father played night softball as a graceful, dark-haired shortstop on a businessmen's team of mostly Gentile players. My parents' circle of friends was made up of Jews, a dentist, some merchants, a lawyer. But my parents were also friendly with the neighbors on the block, although we were the only Jewish family. In the evenings, occasionally my mother and father would sit with these Gentile neighbors on their porches and drink lemonade, although now I realize that none of them ever came to the house as guests and my parents never went to their homes. Still, my father would laugh and joke with these neighborhood men as I played softball catch with him in front of our house or as he stood in the evening and watered our lawn. In the neighborhood, he was the same graceful Jewish shortstop, darting here and there to touch upon and join the life of the neighborhood and then withdrawing. I suppose he was always essentially alien in their eyes, but despite being a Jew, he was viewed as a rather nice man who almost every evening threw grounders to his son on the front walk until the street lights blinked on. But as a child, I was not aware of our separateness. My friends were the Gentile boys from the block. We were schoolmates together. Although our parents observed an acquiesced separateness, we were unaware of it. Far past the streetlight hour, we played our games into the night, Red Rover, Washington Post, Hide and Seek, until one by one our fathers came out to whistle for us with that particular whistling call that I still remember and identify with those soft Milwaukee nights of my childhood.

I do not remember any overt acts of anti-Semitism among my friends or their parents. But now with the running of my film and having focused in on my life as a young Jew in Milwaukee, one afternoon in particular is evoked. Essentially the film device is selective and evocative and re-creates certain events with a clarity that justifies the pain of seeing all these old pictures. One Sunday afternoon comes into focus. My parents and I enjoyed driving to Port Washington, a little town near Milwaukee, about fifteen miles outside the city. Port Washington was really just a lake town. Like many towns that border Lake Michigan, it had some industry, but there were boats there and fishermen and a small fishing fleet. On Sundays we liked to walk out on the piers and look at the boats. Afterwards, we would stop at Smith Brothers restaurant where they served fresh fish sandwiches. But on this Sunday, I remember there was very heavy traffic on the road to Port Washington. The people seemed to be headed for an outing or picnic and the cars we passed were full of children. Then, as we came toward an iron railroad bridge, we could see that someone had painted a message in large white letters on the side of the bridge. As we approached the bridge we could see the message, spelled in whitewash, "Kill the Jews, Buy Gentile." As we came under the bridge there was a small hill and when we reached the top of the hill we could see thousands of people in the distance out in a field. The men were dressed in the brown-shirted uniform of the German American Bund and they were having a picnic and soccer games. There were literally thousands of people in that field, almost an army of men in brown shirts and military britches, the brown color of their uniforms seemed to cover the earth out to the horizon. At the edge of the highway there was a flagpole, and on the flagpole the German swastika flag was flying.

So now having run my film and having been brought back to my memories of those Milwaukee days, I somewhat understand what it would have been like for a Jewish boy growing up in Munich in the early thirties. The question is always asked, why did the Jews stay in Germany? Of course, some did get out, but most like that young

American Jew in Milwaukee whose father played shortstop on the businessmen's team, remained. The families were confident of their assimilation. They thought as Germans, not as Jews. If the Nazis were forming their divisions, it was on some distant hillside on a pleasant Sunday afternoon. Of course, this is all known, and nothing new is brought to light by these statements. But these films are my own, and I choose to run them, on occasion, in any event.

My wife and I still return with our children now and then to Milwaukee. It is only an hour from our Chicago suburb and a pleasant drive. Today, it is a huge industrial city with great factories and expressways. One evening this summer, we drove to Milwaukee and as we drove through the near west side of the city we saw a church carnival with rides and a Ferris wheel. Our children were excited so we parked the car and went to the carnival. The neighborhood people were there with their children, mostly bright-eyed little Poles and Germans, skipping around long rows of picnic tables that had been set up in a circle around a small wooden dance floor. People were drinking pitchers of beer and eating bratwurst sandwiches. An old man, full of energy, played the concertina and whistled polka shrills to the couples dancing and stomping.

It was another of those soft Milwaukee evenings and I took my daughter up on the Ferris wheel. When we came to the top, we were held there for our turn and I could look out over the lights of the city. The big, square lighted clock from the Allen-Bradley factory faced me, perhaps one of the largest clocks in the world, it stands over the city as a symbol of discipline and order. All seemed in order. I remembered a professor at the University of Michigan, Austin Warren, who had written a collection of criticism titled, *A Rage for Order*, taken from a line of Wallace Stevens' poem, "The Idea of Order at Key West." Perhaps that is it after all, the essential madness of man, A Rage for Order. As we rocked on the Ferris wheel I stared back at the huge, lighted clock. But I could feel the old films coming again, and I was glad that our turn would soon be over and we would begin our descent back to the ground before the lederhosen boys would come poking with their sticks to haunt me with more evocations. For the process of film showing is evocative and the Milwaukee night, even as you begin your descent on a Ferris wheel, already lies softly on your cheek. I have also seen Key West and there, I must report, the same soft night wind blows against those who ride Ferris wheels down.

Greenwald Et Cie.

Each morning Carter Greenwald anticipated a comfortable ride down to Chicago on the commuter train. He liked a slow train, he didn't try for an express, he always headed for the rear double seat on the second deck of the 7:51 where he could spread out and let the morning sun bathe his face through the window. The sunlight usually fell in the same arc across the rear double seat and, while most passengers avoided the glare, Greenwald liked to rustle open his fresh paper and shade the light so it fell along his left cheek and warmed the left side of his face. He always had the beginning of a migraine after the rush to the train, the left side of his head beginning to swell with the tension of fighting for a parking spot and the dash across the lot to the station with the bells of the station gates clanging. He would stand aside as the other commuters came pouring out the station door. Then he would grab around the door for his paper and twist back through the crowd and shoot up the metal staircase where, with luck, the double with its pool of soothing sunlight would still be vacant. The migraine had come with his divorce. Now that he was alone in a townhouse in Highland Park, the children away at college, and his wife Spitzy in the house on Sheridan Road in Glencoe, Greenwald began each day with a fuzzy balloon growing on one side of his head, a small tumescent balloon filled with uncertainty and fear.

Recently Spitzy had been calling at exactly 7:37, just as he was pouring juice from an oversized can of Dole pineapple/orange and fumbling with the cotton in a vitamin C bottle. Almost precisely as he would try to work one of the fat 1,000 mg slugs of vitamin C up through the throat of the plastic bottle, his princess phone would chime and he would foolishly answer, swilling the juice in his cheeks and trying to cock his head back so he wouldn't choke on the C pill.

"Carter," the voice would say, "I know you're there, Carter. I can hear breathing."

"So, I'm breathing," he would mumble and try to reach around into the sleek trays of the new yellow Hotpoint where the B-1 and lecithin bottles were stashed and poke his fingers into the bottles and pop the pills with another shot of juice. "You're breathing too, Spitz." He'd swallow the lecithin pill. Then he'd pop the little ovals of maroon B-1s down his throat with the remnant of his juice. "I can't send you another check," he'd say, glancing up at the UN calendar to see what day it was.

"Carter, you're vicious."

"I'm not vicious, I'm in a hurry and these calls are driving me up the wall. Stop calling me, Spitzy! Call your shrink. Go out to the practice tee. Go bowling."

"You're still seven-fifty short from last month, Carter. You're aborting me."

"I'm not aborting you. I just don't have it."

"Carter, why are you doing this to me? Why are you torturing me? Carter, do you think I'm really a fool? I know you. You're buying clothes. I know you're buying clothes at Brooks. And books. What about your Skira books? You think you're fooling me? Carter, I have no stomach for humor. I want that check."

He would wait a moment and then gently hang up.

Carter Greenwald was a real estate developer. His office was in a burnished copper high-rise in the Chicago financial district. He specialized in shopping center deals, and business was rotten. He had no extra money for Spitzy. Their decree called for $3,000 a month and he had been just squeaking by, but last month he had flown down to Tucson on a deal and stayed over a few extra days; now he was short $750 and Spitzy would have to be dealt with. As he climbed up the stairs on the train to the double on the second deck he thought about those nights in Tucson. He could remember the fragrance of the desert air at night and the view of the city from the hotel in the foothills. He had been alone in the bar drinking J & B twists and watching planes gliding across the mountains and landing. It had been a good time. Lonely, but a fragrant time that he could hold in his memory and refresh himself during his gray days.

The double was vacant and Greenwald spread his paper and sat down. There was no sun today so he thought about a tiny yellow cactus flower that he had seen each morning outside his door in Tucson, a bright fresh flower seamed with sunlight and hidden in the throat of the cactus. He made the flower expand in his mind, slowly opening the flower like a parasol until it replaced the missing beam of window sunlight and began to warm him and cause his migraine to subside. By the time the train got to Glencoe, his head was clear and he began to read.

He didn't like the intrusion of the Glencoe passengers. He could smell the heavy odor of their cologne as they headed for the single aisle seats and called to each other across the baggage racks. Greenwald didn't want talk on the train. The Glencoe passengers talked deals and tennis. It would be ten minutes before they'd subside into their papers. "Morry, are you feeling well? Sylvia told me you weren't feeling so well." "I'm okay, Ben. I went two sets Saturday, a little tired. How do *you* feel, Ben? Are you and Syl going away again this year?" "We already went to Paris, two weeks this summer. Rented a car and Sylvia drove, we just cocked around. Syl bought antiques. We flew over with the Klutzmans." "How's Sol Klutzman?" "Sol still comes to the office, just to make a few deals, he had a serious coronary, you know. He's all right now, knock on wood, and he was very good on the trip." "Sol's a good guy, say hello to him for me." "Oh, yeah." "Well, that's good. Sylvia, is she feeling well? . . ." Banalities, banalities. Greenwald would like to take an M-16 and spray them with their banalities, A-A-A-A-A-A-A-A-A-A right down the row of passengers. Or maybe that new little Israeli submachine gun. What was it, the Irguni? The Izaki? Empty a few clips on those fat bastards! Greenwald, a tall, bronzed, mustachioed militia man, would stand up at the end of the car, curse them in Hebrew and give them a few short bursts and quiet them down.

Greenwald stared again at the two men. They were both in their late fifties or early sixties, heavy jowled, their faces freshly shaven and talcumed. He looked at their shoes. One wore black crocodile loafers with tassels and the other gleaming black patent loafers with gold buckles. He could tell about a man by looking at his shoes. They were accountants. He wondered if their attaché cases matched their shoes. He glanced up at the baggage rack for a crocodile case but he only saw a folded houndstooth-patterned topcoat. Maybe Ben could lend Greenwald twenty thou. Maybe he should ask Ben. Lean across with the neat little Israeli snout-nose and shove it into Ben's soft tummy. Look slowly down at those fancy tasseled loafers and then up at Ben's face. He would come across with the twenty thou right there on the upper deck. Greenwald wouldn't even have to snap the safety off with a menacing click. Just shove the nose of the gun into Ben's belly and look down at his fancy shoes. Greenwald laughed to himself and snapped his paper open again.

He tried to read. The two men were silent now, quiet with their papers. The image of the brave Israeli militia man faded into window fog. Greenwald drew a finger line on the window, a slit through the vapor so he could see where he was. It looked like Evanston, the brown backs of three-flats, deserted wooden porches. He turned the line he had drawn into a triangle and then bisected it with another triangle, a rude Star of David that slowly bled into shapelessness as the moisture condensed. He closed his eyes and tried to sleep, or at least rest. He could see the towers of the city in the distance, the familiar skyline in the fog of early winter, the heavy shadow of the Hancock Building covered with mist. He stared at the city through the patch that his tracery of a Star of David had made. Then he closed his eyes again and the figure of the Israeli soldier came briefly into his mind and Greenwald began daydreaming of Haifa. He was seated in the grass on the rim of a hill overlooking Haifa. He had laid the gun down and pulled off his shoes. The same desert smell that he had sensed in Tucson came to him in the grass, but now he could feel the odor of orange blossoms, a slight scent, and the sea, definitely the fragrance of the sea in the wind. Haifa sparkled below, a white inlay of buildings, the harbor, ships, a ribbon of beach through the haze. And there was a woman with him. Who was the woman? He looked out the window and they were already rushing into the dark framework leading into the cavern of the station. Then the conductor came calling to the passengers reminding them to pick up their parcels and tickets. Greenwald fought a moment to revive the notion of the woman on the hill over Haifa, but he'd lost it and the voices of the passengers heading out of the car brought him fully awake.

Greenwald left the train and walked to a restaurant in the station. He had been breakfasting there since the divorce because he was attracted to one of the waitresses. She was a French woman in her forties, a Parisienne, gamin-faced and slim with auburn hair and warm brown eyes. She moved among her customers, mostly middle-aged businessmen, with a certain gentility, a quiet pouring of coffee refills, always a pleasant remark in a soft voice, the surprising French accent. He didn't know what she was doing in Chicago but from the beginning they seemed to enjoy a special rapport. He even began to try his rusty French on her and when he spoke to her in French she was delighted. They started a game. He would try to order his breakfast in French and she would respond with simple phrases. Soon he began to linger with his coffee until the rush was over and often she would come back to his table and stand and talk to him. He learned that she was separated from her husband, that she had one child, a daughter who was eighteen and lived in Paris. She seemed to enjoy talking to him. She told him that she didn't like American movies—too many killings, too much violence. He agreed with her. She talked occasionally about the German occupation of Paris, just a remark here and there. She had been only a girl, a teenager, but she remembered there had been a collaborator in her building. One day he disappeared; the Resistance had taken care of him. On the morning she told him that story, Greenwald went into the station drugstore and bought her a bottle of Norell. He left it next to his plate with his customary $1.00 tip and she had accepted the gift silently, not even with a look of surprise, a slight smile. Several weeks passed and he gave her another gift, some stockings from Saks. She again accepted them without emotion, sweeping the box away as she dusted crumbs from the table linen with a napkin. As time passed, there were more gifts: perfumed soap, a silk Dior scarf, some handkerchiefs. She began to unbend with him, she crabbed about her work, about how tired she was, about coming to work in a cab at 6:30 in the morning and working until 3:00; she told how in the evenings she liked to go to restaurants with her girlfriend from Paris, how she enjoyed reading but couldn't get French novels so she read in English; she liked Le Carré. He even began to joke with her, to tease her, but it was difficult because her English wasn't good enough to catch the nuances of humor, and his French was impossible. One morning he told her that his next gift was going to be something spectacular, and she laughed and stood with her arms folded and asked him to tell her what possibly could be so *"magnifique?"* He looked up at her and held his hands in front of him, his fingers together in a tent. A round-trip ticket to France. Would she go with him? How long would it take her to get ready? "*Seulement un jour, Monsieur,*" she replied with the same laconic expression she had when she accepted his other gifts.

The trip became their standard joke. She told him of a little hill town above the Riviera, Tourrettes sur Le Loup, the little tower of the wolf, a town near Vence where the two of them could stay in an old inn with swans in a pool in the rear courtyard and folding chairs under the plane trees. Each day she asked him if he had the tickets. "You are a good boy," she would say and pat his hand and hand him his English muffin with two plastic packets of jam. Then as she left him she would laugh again and turn around. "You are a good boy, but you are scared." "Scar-*ed*," she would pronounce it.

This morning, as Greenwald left the train and walked through the station into the restaurant, she was waiting for him, standing at the rear, alongside his customary table. She pretended not to notice him as he came toward her down along the aisle.

"*Bonjour, Madame,*" he said quietly as he approached her.

"*Bonjour, Monsieur.*" She wrinkled her nose at him. He crossed in front of her and sat down.

"*Que voulez-vous manger, Monsieur?*"

"*La meme chose, Charmaine.*"

"Do you want some bacon with your muffin? Crisp bacon?" She tapped her pencil on her pad.

"No, just the muffin, butter on the side."

"*Oui, sans beurre.*" She filled his cup. "Do you have the tickets?" she asked.

"Tickets, what tickets?"

"The tickets to Tourrettes."

"*D'accord,*" he said. "I will get them."

"You are not a good boy," she said and left for the muffin. As she turned away, her plastic name badge came unpinned and fell to the floor. Greenwald tried to hand her the badge but then he slipped it in his pocket and hid it in his handkerchief.

Later, when he arrived at his office, he began to think seriously about the tickets for the first time. Maybe they could stop off in Haifa and do a quick tour of Israel. He'd rent a car and they'd drive down to Eilat and lie around the pool. Then he'd fly her back to France, stop off at her hill town and shoot up to Paris and she could visit her daughter. He smiled, but then he soon lost himself in his work and dealing on the telephone, and when his working day was over he went to his club and took a fast steam bath and sauna and caught the 6:00 back to Highland Park. When he entered his townhouse the phone was ringing and he grabbed it. "Carter, you made me very angry this morning," Spitzy said. "You have a talent for wounding me."

"I don't wound you, Spitz."

"Don't start up again, Carter."

"Don't start up . . . just send money. Right?"

"Oh, Carter."

"I'm going away, Spitz. I'm going out of the country for a few weeks. I'll send the check before I leave."

"Carter, don't bullshit me. How can you afford a trip? Where are you going?"

"Spitzy, I said I'd send the money. I'll *send* it. Why should I tell you where I'm going? Just believe me. I'll call you before I go. Just leave me *alone.*" He slammed the receiver down and after they were disconnected he yanked the phone plug from the wall and made himself a scotch. Then he sat back on his couch and took his tie off and lit a cigar. His stomach was fluttering and he waited for the scotch to make it stop.

It had been a year since the divorce and she still had her teeth in his throat. If she could only meet someone with money and get married again. The alimony would end. She was driving him out of his mind! He got up and put two eggs on the stove. He stood over the pan and watched the eggs coagulate as he sipped his scotch. Maybe he should call Charmaine and tell her he had the tickets, tell her to hop in a cab and come out to Highland Park, stay with him tonight, and in the morning they'd go out to O'Hare. She was just kidding him though. She'd never go. What the hell, he was kidding himself. He knew he'd never go. He knew he'd never get out of Chicago. He was a bullshitter. Spitzy was right. And he was too tired, he knew he was too tired. Old now and alone and tired. He did his dishes and poured himself another scotch and lay down on his couch and covered his eyes with the newspaper and fell asleep.

When he awakened it was midnight and his back hurt. He went up the cantilevered stairs to his bedroom. He brushed his teeth and took his clothes off. He wondered if he'd be able to sleep again. He opened the drapes and looked down at the street. Nothing. A few kids wheeling their cars. All the chic little stores shuttered up tightly, suburban darkness. He should have moved downtown after the divorce. No, it would be lonelier downtown, staring at the city from a highrise. Resignedly, almost automatically, he went to his closet and took out a large cardboard carton.

He put the carton on his bed and then he went over to his desk and opened a drawer and removed a small leather lockbox with a combination lock. He spun the tumblers and took out a woman's wig and makeup kit. He wondered if he had become a transvestite. No, he wasn't a transvestite. He wasn't queer. Not Greenwald the Israeli militia man. He laughed. He was young. Young again and his face was bronzed and he was standing in the desert in the warm wind, the scent of Tucson came to him again, the yellow flower, hidden deep in the cactus, slowly opening in the warm morning sun. He was so lonely.

Then he remembered the handkerchief. He went to his laundry hamper. A black wicker hamper that he had bought at the custom bath shop in Glencoe. The shop where Spitz had blown $500 on gold faucets. He looked for his crumpled handkerchief and found Charmaine's plastic name badge. Then he went back to his bed and opened the large cardboard box. He removed a long crumpled rubber pattern, a pneumatique, like a child's blow-up water monster. It had a needle valve, and Greenwald began to blow on the valve. He was crying now, blowing on the valve and crying. The pattern of a woman began to inflate. Slowly, slowly, the air from his lungs bringing her to life, first distorted, her legs beginning to swell and then her breasts and her face. He paused a moment and he was shaking. He had to remember to buy a pump. It was too exhausting to blow her up every night. But he was so damned tired. He just couldn't remember things. He took a gulp of air and blew on the valve and her face popped into shape. He found the makeup kit and applied gloss to her lips. He sprayed her ears and her breasts with Norell mist. He arranged the wig on the doll and combed her auburn hair. He removed a black uniform from the carton and dressed the doll. He tied her red apron to her waist. Then he pinned Charmaine's name badge on her right breast. He carried her over to the window and stood her up and held her, her hair touching lightly on his cheek. Greenwald stood with her and looked out at the street and far across the rooftops he saw a plane blinking away from O'Hare. They stood together and watched it.

The Name, Kozonis

"The Name, Kozonis" is my first published short story and I wanted to include it in this collection. It was published in the fall of 1973 by Karamu, *the literary magazine of Eastern Illinois University, Allen Neff, Editor. I will always remember Allen with gratitude. He was a literary man and a gentleman who lived too short a life. I was so excited when the story was published, I drove down to Charleston and took Allen and his staff members out for a lunch of hamburgers and beers at a local tavern. My son Jim went with me and went fishing in the river there and caught a nice fish. Also, I will always remember coming home from the office on the train and finding my entire family at the station waving the acceptance letter from* Karamu. *They were as excited as I was. Shortly after "The Name, Kozonis" was published, in the spring of 1974,* The South Dakota Review, *John Milton, Editor, the literary magazine of the University of South Dakota, published "Taormina," which I have also included in this collection.*

THEY WERE A YOUNG GREEK COUPLE. The wife was a short, pleasant woman, about twenty-seven, grown a little plump, and as she sat in our living room she tugged at her skirt in nervous, prim gestures. They had come for cocktails. My wife and I had met them in the neighborhood about two years ago and now the young husband was being transferred to Arizona. We asked them over for a good-bye drink and to wish them luck.

A few months ago they had retained me as their lawyer to obtain a change of name decree. Their family name had been Kozonis and they had it changed to Chase. So the cocktails also celebrated the new name as well as the new job.

I liked both of them. They weren't pretentious people. The wife had worked as a teacher in Chicago for many years while the husband went to De Paul business school at night. This was his first real promotion. He was being transferred from Chicago to Phoenix as division sales manager for a hardware manufacturer. They were very excited over the prospect of the new job and a move to the Southwest. So we talked quietly with each other and watched the snow falling outside the window and sat in front of the fire to drink a special bottle of retsina that the husband brought to us as a gift.

I thought of the day they had first come to my office to discuss the change of name proceeding. They had brought their little girl with them. Her name was Tina, a very delicate child, with huge black eyes. The parents were quite anxious about the role Tina would play in court. I told them it wouldn't be necessary to bring her along, but they regarded the hearing as an event requiring the participation of the entire family; the change of name was to be their secular baptism. They had deep feelings of regret for the severance of the old name and yet the new name, Chase, promised assimilation and acceptance in their new life, far removed from the sanctuary of Chicago's Greek community.

On the day of the hearing they had arrived in my office with Tina, all naturally quite excited. I remember the wife had a small new fur cape and the husband wore a dark suit, the little girl in a lacy dress with puffed short sleeves and a tiny cross on a thin gold chain on her chest. The hearing took only a few minutes. The judge asked them if they had ever been in bankruptcy or convicted of a crime. When the wife shyly shook her head, the judge stamped the decree and wished them luck. "Good luck to you, Mr. and Mrs. Chase," he said. The husband and wife smiled and Tina showed the judge how she had learned to curtsy. I remember the wife whispering to the child, "Tina, make your bow for His Honor." The child looked up at the judge with her dark eyes and then taking her lacy dress at its corners, stepped back with a tiny foot and gravely bowed.

The logs in the fireplace were very dry and quickly flamed up, filling the living room with sudden light. My wife turned the lamps off and we sat and watched the fire. The young couple sat on the floor, the husband propping up two pillows against a chair and the wife, carefully spreading her skirt, sat next to him. The fire played its shadows against their faces. My wife went into the kitchen for some cookies that she had baked and I joined the husband in another drink of retsina, both of us beginning to feel the warmth of the wine, the husband's face flushed with the wine and the heat of the fire as he filled my glass.

We talked about the neighborhood and about their regret at leaving Chicago and their friends. Then my wife came back with the cookies and little paper napkins to keep the crumbs from falling on the carpet.

I asked the husband about his parents. I remembered once being introduced to his father. I had been walking the children to Lincoln Park and across the street I had seen Tina and the husband and wife. We all went over to say hello and walked together to the park where the husband's father was waiting. He was sitting on a park bench, his hat pushed down over his eyes, dozing in the sunlight. I was introduced as the lawyer who had procured the change of name for the family and the father reacted to me coolly, barely acknowledging the introduction. Tina climbed on the old man's lap and he stroked her fine hair with his rough hand and squinted at me in the sunlight. "So, you the fella," he said. The old face was hidden from me by the child's face, the child's face was mute and accusatory, and her dark angelic eyes seemed to project her grandfather's anger. He bounced the little girl on his knee and held her serious face up to me, pinching her cheeks up above the ridges of her cheekbones so that she looked like a furious little owl. "The name, Kozonis, good enough for me," he said. That was the end of the conversation. Then the old man took the child and hand in hand they walked down the sidewalk toward the park zoo. Tina skipped to keep up with her grandfather and then she ran out ahead of him, looking back at him shyly, until she hovered at the rim of a covey of walking pigeons. When the old man caught up with her the pigeons burst in frenzy all around them and the grandfather lifted Tina upon his shoulders, the little girl reaching for the birds, her arms joyously thrown up to the sky.

I reminded the husband of the time I had met his father in the park and I remarked that the old man had seemed quite angry with me. The husband looked up at me and then reached in his pocket for his pipe. He said his father was indeed very angry and had not really forgiven them.

Then the husband told us a story of a trip that he had made with his father to Crete as a young boy.

It seemed that when the husband was about ten his father had taken the boy with him on a journey to Crete. The boy was his only male child and the father yearned to return to the father's native village with his only son. The mother and the little sister were to be left at home. So during the summer of the boy's tenth birthday, the father and son flew to Athens and then went by ship to Crete where they were met by one of the father's friends from the village.

The young husband leaned back and put his arm around his wife as he continued with his story. They drove by car from Khaniá along the coast to Rethimnon and then inland to Spili. He pronounced the names of the Cretan towns carefully and exactly, lingering over the syllables that required the slight lisping sound of the Greek language. Then they proceeded by donkeyback to climb the high mountain range that led from Spili to Idhi and he told of the tinkling sound the bells on the donkey's halters made in the wind that came down the mountain trails. He remembered the excitement of his father, how the old man would kick the donkeys and pull and heave the beasts through the narrow gorges and mountain passes.

When they arrived at his father's village they were told that they had come in the middle of bandit warfare. That there were bandits up in the hills around the village who had been terrorizing the villagers for months and that some militia from Khaniá had come in just before them with orders to kill the bandits.

The husband refilled his glass and tapped his pipe into an ashtray. He was quite serious with the storytelling, his eyes growing darker, resembling the dark fierce eyes of his child and his father.

Then he told of how he had been awakened one morning by his father. The old man was wild and laughing. He took the boy to the village square where the men of the village had assembled in a small crowd in front of the coffeehouse. He pushed the boy through the crowd. Some militia men were standing there and they had the severed head of the bandit chieftain on a stick. They passed the stick proudly from man to man, then to the father and then to the son, and then around the full circle of men back to a soldier who drove the stick into the ground and took his red militia man's throat scarf and wrapped it around the bandit's bleeding throat. Then they left the head on the stick in the village square for a week to burn in the Cretan sun. There was no more trouble thereafter with bandits. The rest of the trip, the young husband said, had dimmed in his memory, except that he remembered that he had slept in a hut on earthen floor and drank goat's milk. He also mentioned the beauty of the cypress trees.

He had finished his story. He looked at me to see what understanding I had reached of his father's anger over the change of name and the young couple's decision to move away from the family. I nodded my head. The young husband was pleased. Then gracefully he stood up and gestured to his wife. He reached into his pocket and pulled out a clean white handkerchief. Then seriously, snapping their fingers with great dignity, looking into each other's eyes, Mr. and Mrs. Chase began to dance a traditional Grecian dance, in front of the fire, as the snow fell on the Chicago streets and in the wind outside the windows came the little tinkling of donkey bells as a proper farewell to the name, Kozonis.

Taormina

A MAN OF WAR BIRD was alone in the sky. It was gently gliding on uneven puffs of wind, climbing with the drafts and ebbing and sailing downwind in a long even trajectory, its wings spread in a black V-curve against the sunlight.

There were two men below in a little fishing skiff that was rigged with two passenger swivel seats and a large outboard motor. The boat was moving out under the viaduct and crossing under U.S. Highway Number 1 that separated the Florida Bay from the Atlantic. The guide stood in the rear, steering with an extension rod that connected to the steering shaft and throttle. He was bent over and looking out across the water for the channel markers that marked the green deep water from the brown patches of weeds and mud banks. He had been a guide in the Florida Keys for twenty years and was deeply respected by the local people for his ability.

"You see that Man of War, Al?" the passenger asked. He was a short, heavy man, about thirty-five, wearing a straw hat and windbreaker.

"He's looking for food," Al said. "You watch him now. There he goes." The bird fell dropping into the water heavily with a splash and then came up again, laboring with his catch, his wings shedding water from the fall as he moved away into the sunlight.

"They're rascals, all right," Al said, laughing. "Usually wait for another bird to make a catch and then they come on in to steal it."

"I saw a roost of them once, in the backwaters out of Key Largo," the passenger said.

"They roost with the pelicans, you know," Al said. "There're lots of them up where you were but down here some days you'll see the sky just black with them."

"It's a good day for fishing, isn't it, Al," the passenger said. He sat back on the seat and surreptitiously unhitched his belt a notch.

"You bet it's a good day, Mr. Spiegel," Al answered. He was still standing, looking for the channel markers and following the long green swirls of water. He was excited to be working in off season. "It's about an hour's ride into the backcountry, but there's trout out there on the reefs. We'll have a good crack at them. Don't worry, we'll catch fish."

They were heading out into the Florida Bay now, the thin strip of Upper Matecumbe Key and the bridges across the highway grew less visible. This was famous fishing water, green in sections and blended with hues of dark purple, alive with fish and birds overhead. The ride was getting rougher and the boat thudded and bumped its way along the water, rising and crashing down hard on the chop. Spiegel felt it in his lower back and sat straight and with his back away from the seat to take the impact of the fall of the boat with his feet like a rider posting his horse.

"See that muddy water, Mr. Spiegel? That's mullet."

The water was muddied in a large section where the mullet had been bottom feeding. The mud rose in a hazy section of water for almost 500 yards ahead of the boat and then the water became green again.

"There must be a lot of fish in there," Spiegel said.

"There's millions of them," Al said. "They're vegetarians, you know. Bottom feeders. That's old mullet, all right. They won't take to a hook." He pulled a cigar from the pocket of his wool shirt. "Smoke a cigar?" he asked.

"No thanks," Spiegel said. He thought for a minute about smoking and then he remembered his office ashtray, always filled with butts, a round orange ceramic ashtray that his sister-in-law had given him. He decided not to smoke and he looked away into the sun, letting it warm his face.

Al slowed the boat down and shifted into reverse for a few seconds. "Get the weeds off my propeller."

"How far out we going?"

"See that little island away out there? Just beyond that. Now you tell me if it gets too rough."

"It's okay."

"Well, I had a man and his wife out here the other day, they wanted to do some fly casting and it was choppy, just about like today. I gave them an awful bouncing. 'We're tough old Yankees,' they said. 'You just keep going.' So I did."

Spiegel could feel the fat bouncing on his chest. He swiveled his chair around forward and put on his sunglasses. The salt spray hit him and there was a salty taste he could feel with his tongue at the corners of his mouth. It was about two in the afternoon. The sun was beginning to get hot against his face and the salt burned on the ridges of his cheeks. He thought about sucking on one of the oranges he had brought along and then he reached down below his feet into the cooler and passed up the oranges for a bottle of chocolate drink. The cooler was nothing more than a compartment filled with a large chunk of ice. Al had made a fuss buying the ice and bait back at the dock, kidding with the owner about the price. When they shoved off, as he pushed them away form the pier out into the channel, he turned and yelled, "Two dollars worth of shrimp, Earl. Mark it down, you hear? Be sure and tell Bud." Spiegel had been sufficiently impressed.

They were passing a chain of lobster traps that bobbed on white floats. Spiegel could see a fishing yawl marked with rust anchored in one of the coves between two keys off to the right. He saw a man working with the traps in a dinghy just beyond the yawl. They drew near the ship and passed around it. The man had disappeared beyond the ship and they were both close enough to it to see piles of blue and red nets on the deck drying in the sunlight.

"Commercial fisherman," Al said. "Lives on the boat. His boys bought him that boat."

The man came into view again behind them. Spiegel watched him pull at his oars with an uneven jerking motion, first one oar, then pausing, then a jerk with the second oar, almost a stab at the water. He was very graceful with his rowing, no body, just all shoulders and sudden little movements with his shoulders and wrists.

"That fellow be fishing trout soon as he's cleaned out those traps," Al said. "He'll come in with fifty, maybe a hundred trout using shrimp and regular old bamboo pole."

"Well, let's get out there before he beats us to the fish," Spiegel said.

Al laughed and leaned over to open the bait hatch. He moved his fingers quickly through the water in the hatch several times and then shut the wooden cover. "Got to keep our shrimp alive," he said. "Don't worry none about him, Mr. Spiegel. He's in no hurry."

They had come a good distance now and soon the commercial fisherman was out of sight and they were past the few little coral keys into open water. They passed the channel markers of the inland waterway and then headed out about two miles for the reef. The water quickly lost its milky appearance and now it became a very pale green with the brown of the reef clearly visible directly in front of them. Their boat left a long path of foam across the open water. A group of porpoises, about three or four, passed to their left. They arched steadily in and out of the water with their curved backs glistening in the sunlight as they dove and came up again on top of the waves. Spiegel sat quietly. He had always in fishing and hunting found great pleasure in the last few minutes of the approach. It had been a long time, almost a year, since he had fished. He wanted to fish well and he could feel the anticipation in his legs.

It took them about fifteen minutes to reach the reef. Al cut the motor as soon as they hit the outer edge of the weeds. They glided into the brown shallow water smoothly and Al waited until they had the full effect of their glide and poled to the edge of the first large patch of green water they saw and secured the boat right at the lip where the weeds fell away into the clear water. He drove his pole into the weed bank, hard into the mud, and then lashed the pole back to the boat so the boat would be steady against the current and would face directly into the clear water. "Let's go fishing," he said. He was very serious now and worked very quickly.

The guide reached into the bait box for a shrimp and found a fat one, then holding the bait in his fist with his left hand so that just the shrimp's big eyes and feelers were exposed, he worked the hook into the slit at its tail with his free hand and then slid the hook down around the backbone. The shrimp curved along the length of the hook and covered it completely. The hook had two barbs, one little barb on the shank and one on the curve.

"Now when a trout takes to this bait, Mr. Spiegel, you let him have it for a minute, then whip it into him good." Al quickly threw some shrimp out into the water directly ahead of them for chum and tied his own line with a small white bucktail and threw it out with a straight cast.

"You cast right out into that green water," the guide said. Already some needlefish were working on the chum. They came skipping on top of the water after the shrimp.

Spiegel pointed his rod and tried to cast out past the needlefish, but one of them grabbed his bait immediately as it hit the water.

"Shake him off," Al said. "Shake him. Bring your bait in fast."

Spiegel brought the shrimp in quickly but its head had been cleanly torn off.

"Those little bastards," Al said. "Get out of here," he shouted.

Al baited the line again and tossed it back into the water. Spiegel waited a moment for the needlefish to move with the current and then threw out toward the far edge of the clear water where the brown sea grass formed the outer rim of the reef. His cast was long and he pulled back just as the bait was about to drop in the grass. The shrimp hit the water right at the edge of the weed bank.

"Too much arm," Al said. "Use your wrist, like this." He threw his bucktail off the other side of the boat with an easy motion. "It's all in the wrist," he said, demonstrating.

"Now bring it back slowly," Al said. "That's too fast, slower."

Spiegel slowed down the return and brought the shrimp through the water back to the boat.

"There should be fish here," Al said. "Those trout will be working across this reef with the tide. Throw out to the left."

Spiegel worked the line out with his wrist in a high cast toward where the guide was pointing. He wound the bait back slowly and then the rod suddenly went down in a sharp curve as a fish hit the shrimp. He waited until he could feel the full weight of the fish and then brought the rod up sharply with both hands and set the hook with all the power of his forearms in a sharp upward snap of the rod.

"That's too much fish for trout," Al said, quickly moving forward.

"You stand back and let me bring him in," Spiegel said. "Just be ready with your net."

"You get him," Al said. "But bring him up nice and close so I can reach him."

Spiegel stood up and held the butt of the rod hard into his stomach. The fish was running against the drag and then stopped and turned in toward the boat. He felt the release of tension from the line as the fish came toward him and he bent down and reeled in his slack quickly. The line came hard again and he now began to work the fish. He held his rod high, then came down for slack reeling fast, now up again feeling the fish, then down fast, taking all the slack the fish would give him. The weight of the fish pushed the butt of the rod into him as he used his stomach to anchor and lever the rod, first up, dragging the fish through the water, then down, reeling hard for slack. After about three minutes of working with the fish he brought it alongside the boat and swept it in toward the guide and his net.

Al picked it up carefully with his net and looked the fish over, holding it just under the gills.

"Jack crevalle," he said. "That's a nice jack."

"He was heavy enough," Spiegel said.

"That's a big, fat jack," the guide said. "About seven pounds. You want to keep him for a mount?"

"Where will we put him, in the baby's room? The kid wakes up crying every morning as it is." Spiegel thought the fish looked something like his kid though, big and fat and blowing hard.

"Okay, back you go," Al said. He held the Jack in the water and let him go.

"Well, thank God for the first one," Spiegel said. He could still feel the strain in his wrists and the burn from the rod just above his belt, but he was happy with the first one gone.

Al was standing in the back of the boat and he began urinating over the side. "That was a damn nice jack," he said. "They give you a good fight, don't they, those buggers." He zipped his fly and sat down and offered Spiegel some coffee from a thermos.

"Watch that little breather hole on the cup, turn it away from you," he said.

The coffee was black and strong, bitter and metallic tasting. "You fish better than you cook," Spiegel said with a smile to the guide. There was a string of cormorants, little black sea ducks flying off to the right, and Spiegel drank the coffee and watched them fly up into the sun.

By now, it was almost mid-afternoon. The sun was high in the sky, directly over them, and he took his fisherman's cap off and sat with the coffee and his eyes closed to the sun.

"You get enough of that sun and you'll catch yourself cancer," the guide said. "I've had six cancers cut off my cheek in the last ten years."

He pointed for emphasis to a round, smooth scar under his right eye. "Skin surgeon in Homestead cuts them out for $250."

"I've got a surgeon on the Diner's Club who has your man beat," Spiegel said. He was feeling very jaunty now with the first fish gone. There was no one out here to bug him, no law partners, no wife, just sky and birds overhead. He could feel the sun boiling into his bald spot and he wondered what it would be like to someday be set free only to learn in a dermatologist's office in Rio or maybe Portofino that one had developed cancer of the bald spot.

"Maybe they could sew in a little Plexiglas flap," he said to Al. With his eyes closed though, he knew there were no dermatologists in Portofino.

"Where, on my cheek?" the guide said.

"On my head," Spiegel said. "Maybe your man in Homestead could do it."

"You pay him cash money and he'd remodel your ass," Al said. Then he stood up and threw his bucktail out toward the weed bank again in a straight, hard cast.

They began to fish again, steadily and intently, in the way of men who, having felt each other out, were satisfied that each would do for the other, at least for this one afternoon. It was a good enough comradeship to allow them to be quiet with each other.

Al was cute with his bucktail. He threw it out in a looping cast and then, imitating the motion of a fish, would dance it and jiggle it on top of the water. Spiegel watched him retrieve the lure with a slow drag followed by a whipping motion, a short snap of the rod and then a long, slow drag again, the lure first alive and then almost still in the water.

Al would be a good man to have around in Portofino, Spiegel was thinking. If one was suddenly to grab the first jet out, Al would be a good man to go free with, a good steady companion. Al was all right. A little bowlegged, perhaps, for the beach at Taormina, but nice, even teeth under the carcinoma scar. The sun was getting very warm and Spiegel could feel the sweat trickling down his nose onto his chin. He wiped the sweat away with the back of his hand and began thinking of a cold can of beer. He watched Al working for a fish. We should have brought some beer along, he thought. He could really go for an ice-cold beer. Maybe Al will catch us one, good old even teeth will cast out and catch a six-pack, properly chilled. Or maybe he'll find us a beautiful young mermaid. Spiegel sniffed at the sweat hanging from his nostrils. He closed his eyes and saw a young, slim girl rising from the sea, amulets of green seaweed around her neck.

"They aren't moving through here yet," Al said. "You sit there in that sun with your cap off, Mr. Spiegel, and you won't be fit for fishing." Al brought his bucktail in and unlashed the boat from his pole where it was holding in the mud. He pulled the pole out and began to push them to the edge of another green hole along the fringe of the sea grass.

Spiegel put his cap back on. "You ever been to Europe?" he asked the guide.

"Hell, no." Al was grunting with the effort of poling. "I got all I can handle right here." They had moved about thirty yards and Al looked around and then drove his pole into the mud again and lashed the boat to it. "Let's get busy," he said, pointing with his rod.

The guide was in the water first with his bait and something took it immediately. He brought it in alongside the boat with a long, sweeping motion. "Catfish," he said. "Good-for-nothing fish." He held his rod between his knees and put on a pair of leather gloves. Then he took his clippers from his bait box and clipped off all the barbed whiskers around the mouth and threw the catfish back.

"They can really cut you, those ugly bastards, worse than sharks."

"You gave him a good haircut," Spiegel said.

Spiegel began casting again and brought back a little barracuda that Al handled with bare hands, holding the fish well back of its jaws.

"You ought to get me to take you fishing in Italy," Spiegel said.

"I'm lucky if I get to go up in the backcountry turkey shooting with my boy."

"We would be a big hit over there," Spiegel said. He was still thinking of Taormina. "Your boy would love it." If the weather was bad they would fly over to Tangier and while Al and the boy hunted in the mountains, Spiegel could sleep late and take his coffee and almond cakes on the terrace in his bathrobe. In the afternoon, they could meet and together walk in the hills and watch the women harvesting blossoms from the orchards to make perfume, beating the tree trunks with sticks to bring the blossoms down.

There were some pelicans coming in off to their right and they landed on the edge of the reef and began to look over the operation. Spiegel threw right in front of them and a fish hit his bait on the first cast. "Lucky pelicans," Spiegel said.

"That's trout," Al said excitedly. "You stand up. Don't lift him out of the water to me, you hear? Just bring him in slowly and keep him down. They got weak mouths. You can pull the hook right out of his mouth."

Spiegel brought the fish in easily and Al leaned over with the net. He picked the trout out of the water and pulled the hook with its half-eaten shrimp and tossed the fish into the storage compartment at the rear of the boat.

"That's a keeper," Spiegel said. He heard the fish violently flopping inside the storage chamber. It had been a big, silver fish, heavily lidded and slime covered, brought up from beneath the dark cover of the sea-weed, flailing its smooth, silver tail and bleeding at the mouth. Now it was frenzied and beating itself to death underneath the wooden hatch. Al kept a foot on the hatch while he baited Spiegel's hook again. He wiped the fish slime from his hands along his trousers.

"How do you know that wasn't a mermaid, pal?" Spiegel said. "Take a look."

Al winked and opened the hatch for a second. "I'll double-check," he said. "No, that's old trout."

"Are you sure?"

"No, that's just plain old trout."

"You double-checked."

"That's just a mighty tasty trout."

"You aren't giving me some of that conch double-talk?"

Al laughed and threw back at the pelicans with his bucktail and another trout came almost lunging out of the water at the lure. He brought the trout in, dropped it into the compartment and went back high and far into the water all in one movement. He was holding the tip of his tongue at a corner of his mouth as he jerked his lure lightly along the edge of the sea grass.

"Get to fishing now," he said seriously. "They're out here all right. I can see them. All we can use and then some."

Another fish came twisting out white from the water after the guide's feather.

"Catfish, get away, get away!"

Al pulled his line out and away and then just as quickly his rod went down and he was back home with trout and out again in a long cast to the same spot.

The pelicans began to move in now, grunting and coming cautiously with their wings half raised as they swam into the trout.

Spiegel stood up and threw right in front of the leader. The bird stopped momentarily and then Al tossed some heavy chum to the left and away from the trout and the birds slowly moved in the direction of the shrimp and began to feed.

"They're like my partners," Spiegel said. "They want their share."

"They'll have it, too, if you don't get busy." Al put his rod down and pulled the boat around the pole so the boat stood directly between the birds and the channel where the men had found the trout. He turned and threw more chum past the birds.

Spiegel began to work again and brought three trout in with three casts, taking the fish easily, all with the same shrimp.

"Three for three, coach," he said, laughing. "When do we bunt?"

"Bunt, hell, you get back in there before those birds come back."

Spiegel could see them gulping and shaking the shrimp down, with their back feathers high, riding the current about a hundred feet away.

"They're still safe in the bull pen. Should I phone them?"

"Give them some more chum. Throw them some more."

Spiegel reached into the bait box then threw the chum high and a little short.

"Knuckleball," he said. "I should have spit on it."

Al was busy moving trout. He would sweep a fish through the water, pull it up into the boat, hold it under his foot and rip his lure out. He had stopped bothering with the storage chamber. The rear of the boat where he was standing was soon filled with fish, bleeding and flopping and beating about and slipping against each other.

The two men, working hard and quietly, took about forty trout in ten minutes. Then Al touched off the motor and they got out of there.

They rode just off the edge of the reef where Al slowed down and then while drifting he put on his gloves and grabbed the trout, slapping them on the ice one by one, as he laid them in the compartment.

He picked the biggest one up by its tail. "This will go six pounds. It's a big fish."

"I can't see my wife cleaning it between gin hands."

"Oh, no, I'll fix it up nice for you. Filet all the bones out. How many do you want for dinner tonight?"

"How many do you need for two people?"

"I'd say four or five."

"Well, then, you keep the rest, or if you don't want them, I'll take them back to the motel and give them away."

"I'll take them. But you keep all you want. Make sure now." Al reached back and throttled the engine again.

"I don't clean for everyone, but I'll have time for four or five." He was satisfied with the way the division was going. His boy would clean the other fish tonight after supper and tomorrow morning before work Al would take them down to Marathon and sell them for at least twenty bucks.

Spiegel slept most of the way in except for a moment when Al woke him up to watch some bonefish tailing off one of the little keys near the dock.

After they had tied up, Al washed the trout off with a hose at the edge of the dock. Then he cut their heads off and cleaned the fish. He wrapped them in waxed paper and gave them to Spiegel. Al's share went into a big soda water cooler in the back of his station wagon.

Spiegel wrote out two twenty-dollar traveler's checks and added a five dollar bill and handed them to the guide.

"Thanks much, Mr. Spiegel. Maybe you'd like to go after bonefish tomorrow? There's nothing like them in these waters."

"Sorry, pal, but we're leaving on a 4:00 flight out of Miami."

"Well, maybe you'll come down in June for tarpon."

"Is that when they run?"

"Oh, yes sir, tarpon fishing's really good down here in the summer. But write before you come. I might be booked heavy if they run well."

"Listen, Al, you did a nice job for me. Someday we'll go fishing again."

"You come back, now. You'll really like it, you hear?"

The two men shook hands and Spiegel watched Al climb into his car and drive off. When he passed, Al gave Spiegel a little wave and shouted, "You all come back . . . okay?"

Spiegel got his gear together and walked down the dock and then up the road where his wife was waiting in the Chevy station wagon.

The windows were rolled down and he could smell the odor of her hair spray. She had the spray can propped up on the open glove compartment door and she was using the rearview mirror to comb her hair out.

"So, Fisherman," she said. She was combing and holding her hair pins between her teeth.

"So, move over, Margo . . . phew!"

"A minute," she said with the pins. She gave her hair a squirt and began carefully putting the pins in place.

"Sol Gorsky called you three times on the ship to shore." She gave her hair another squirt. "He's flying to New York tomorrow and he wants you to meet him."

"Sol Gorsky is a momzer."

"All right, so he's a momzer."

"Just get your ass in gear, Margo. I'm tired. I want a shower."

"Forty seconds, darling. You want Momma to be beautiful don't you . . . you want pretty Margo."

Spiegel stood outside the car waiting for her to finish. There were some prisoners down by the bridge painting beams underneath the span and an old guard sitting on his haunches in the afternoon sun with a rifle across his lap. The men were from the state prison, mostly blacks, dressed in gray trousers with white stripes along the trouser sides, like a men's softball team. They painted with languid strokes, slowly in the heat, but they had an expectant mood about them whenever they gathered together, as if their team was about to suddenly break from the bench and move out to the field in long, even, graceful strides. Spiegel watched the men for awhile and then he put his tackle box on the roof of the car and looked out at the ocean again. By squinting, he thought he could still see one bonefish tailing, but the late afternoon sun made the water dark and with a little wind blowing it was hard to see the fish in the motion of the wind on the water.

Conversations with a Golden Ballerina

This is a section of a new novel. It's included to add a little humor to the collection. Arthur Fabricant originally appeared as the central character in "The Kisses of Fabricant," published in Chicago Magazine. *The story has now been expanded and, like David Epstein in my novel,* The Last Jewish Shortstop in America, *Arthur Fabricant, fifty, is a sort of anti-hero juggling multiple relationships with women. One of these women is the Golden Ballerina from the Chagall statue on the plaza in front of First Chicago Bank who has stepped out of her "deep freeze" hiding place to converse with Fabricant. She's every bit as mysterious and dangerous as "deep throat," Nixon's nemesis in the Watergate scandal. Who is this Golden Ballerina? Who is she really? The action opens with Arthur trying to get up nerve to break a date he foolishly made with a twenty-four-year-old art teacher to go see a film, Fellini's* City of Women *and also to break off the relationship. He then visits the mysterious and beautiful Golden Ballerina who confronts him and suggests he try to put some order into his life, although she's hardly qualified to become his romantic advisor.*

THE NEXT MORNING ON THE WAY TO HIS OFFICE, he promised himself that he would call the young art teacher and break the date. He was much too old for her. He had no interest in seeing Fellini's *City of Women.* She was beautiful though she did look like a treacherous young Egyptian princess when she played the Irish flute for him. He had enough treacherous Egyptian princesses in his life. He should look for a mature woman, his own age. Sydney, his therapist, was right. He should find a woman his own age and climb out of the jardin noire of the young. It was full of asps.

He liked to visit the Chagall monument on the way to work. It was in the plaza of First Chicago Bank, a long rectangular mosaic of tiny tiles of Jewish peasants dancing, people right out of Sholem Aleichem. Jewesses with canted eyes and kerchiefs on their heads, whirling and dancing, men sowing seeds, other men playing clarinets and dancing, chickens and angels falling from the sky, lovers strolling and kissing.

At one side of the monument there was a glistening mosaic of a ballerina in a golden dirndl with flowers in her hair and a bouquet in her hands. The monument was a magical Chagall elegiac to Chicago, the buildings of the city and the lake etched in a colorful backdrop to the peasants dancing. The Golden Ballerina was his favorite, especially on days when there was a touch of sunlight. The tile pieces of her costume would reflect the sunlight and he liked to stop in front of her and stare at her and occasionally talk to her and tell her his troubles. She never answered him.

Until this morning.

"Arthur." He heard a woman's voice in the wind softly calling to him.

He stared at her. She seemed to be beckoning to him with her arms outstretched.

"Are you speaking to me?"

"Do you like to dance, Arthur?"

"No, I don't dance."

"Can you do the hora?"

"I've never tried it."

"Come, Arthur, and dance with me. You'll be my partner."

She had a lovely voice and a soft accent.

"I think I'm having an out-of-body experience. You'll have to excuse me."

"No, I'm really talking to you, Arthur. I've seen you come here at least twice this week. You look so lonely and so unhappy. You should learn to dance. I'll teach you how to find happiness. Hold out your hands to me and we'll dance."

"I don't like to dance. I seldom dance."

"If you won't dance, I don't know if I can help you. I'm a ballerina. I can help you only if you'll dance with me. If you won't even try to dance, the only thing I can suggest is to put an ad in the paper. Put a personal in the Jewish papers, even the Polish papers. There are some good Polish women who come to the shtetl and dance with us and hire our klezmer players for their weddings. Find a good peasant woman who can cook and keep house. If you won't dance with me, at least bring her to me and I'll look her over for you. Stop already with all these young women. They only bring you unhappiness and misery. I know all about that. Believe me, I've brought men misery, particularly one man. And now I'm a prisoner here, trapped in this frieze. I'm a prisoner of love and politics and I'm in deep frieze. I could write volumes about love and misery."

"What's your name?"

"My name? Don't you recognize me? We don't give names. They won't allow me to give my name." Her golden bodice flashed at him in the sunlight and suddenly she became silent. Only her canted eyes stared at him, challenging him. The sounds he heard were the sounds of city traffic. Her voice was gone.

Had she really spoken to him? He'd been having wild dreams lately, daytime dreams of all his old loves stretching back to high school. Their faces were so fresh and now the ballerina had joined the chain of faces and just as quickly had left him and disappeared.

IN HIS OFFICE ON THE FIFTY-SECOND FLOOR of the Bank building, he thought about what she'd told him and he began writing an ad. He wrote in the neat block printing of an architect with an elegant black and gold Waterman pen he'd bought in Paris on his honeymoon.

> Jewish man, in his early fifties, rather playful, interesting, often supportive, likes music, art, occasionally watches the Bulls and the Bears. Will travel to Europe, London, Paris, a Francophile, literary. Financially secure and recently divorced. Looking for Jewish or perhaps a Polish woman, lusty, with an intellectual bent. All serious inquiries will be answered. No game players.

Maybe he should eliminate "no game players." No, he kept it and finished the ad with a bold signature and a special flourish, a design that he always used to sign his architectural drawings; the symbol was the coda of his firm, an Arthur Fabricant fleur-de-lys.

Then he phoned the two Jewish papers and one Polish daily and faxed each of them a copy and left his phone and fax numbers.

Next he called and broke the date for the Fellini film. He was in an action mode, a direct action mode. His persona was on "enter." All he had to do was extend his finger and touch his "delete" button, and erase the young art teacher from his life. She was right. He didn't want to make an emotional investment in her. He didn't want to make an emotional investment in anyone but himself. Call that selfishness, he called it common sense.

"Arthur, are you really breaking our date for the movie on El Salvador?"

"Yes, I am. I'm sorry, I forgot, I thought it was Fellini's *City of Women,* but in any event, I can't make it."

"Why? I thought we could be friends. I told you we could be friends."

"I'm really looking for a woman who's more lustful."

"And you don't think I'm lustful?"

"No, you play the flute beautifully but I don't think you're lustful."

"You mean I won't go to bed with you. That's what you really mean."

"No, I didn't say that."

"Arthur, don't ever call me again."

"I won't. I promise I won't."

"Please don't. And stop sending me postcards."

He'd forgotten about the postcards. He'd sent her cards of a series of Bauhaus-designed furniture, tables and chairs. Okay. So he would just erase her from his life. What about the others? The woman who thought she was turning orange. The woman who criticized the way he ate his lobster Gae Kow. The brain was much faster and more magical than any computer. He could just push his own "delete" button and erase them all from his mind.

T**HAT AFTERNOON HE WENT TO HIS THERAPIST'S OFFICE** and told him about the experience with the Golden Ballerina.

"Do you think she really talked to me?"

"What do you think?"

"I think I was talking to myself, Sydney. Talking to my inner androgynous self. "

"Go on."

"I was talking to my feminine side. She wasn't talking to me. I was doing the talking. I'm tired of all these neurotic, young women. I've erased them from my mind. I broke the date with the twenty-four year old."

"Good. You've got how many, almost thirty years on her?"

"She was annoyed with me."

"She'll get over it."

"And I've put an ad in the Jewish papers and the Polish paper. A personal ad. I should meet a lusty Jewish or Polish woman according to what the Ballerina told me."

"She was right, Arthur. Find someone who can cook for you. A Jewish woman, not a Polish woman. Someone your own age and background. I would rather have a plate of golden latkes waiting for me when I get home than a Golden Ballerina."

"That's you, Sydney. You love food. I like food, but I can go without it. I want someone who'll go to bed with me. She doesn't have to be a cook."

THE FIRST ANSWER CAME the following morning. There was a fax waiting for him at his office.

"I don't know about a Francophile. What good have the French ever done the Jews? What about Alfred Dreyfus? What about the concentration camp at Drancy? What about the Jewish children the French loaded on the trains—the trainloads of children? How can you be a Francophile? But the rest is okay. Financially secure is okay. A 'literary man,' I don't know about that. I too am financially secure. A widowed Orthodox Jewish woman, forty-nine, with a grown daughter out of the house. Thanks be to God. I am a gourmet cook and I play the keyboard. But I am very, very religious and I'm considering leaving the U.S. for eretz Israel. I cannot find an honest, decent, Jewish man in Chicago. I'm definitely not a game player. Occasionally mahjongg. I am only really interested in the game of life and am looking for a serious man who is able to make a commitment. I do not want a schlemiel like Golda Meir's Morris. If you want to call me, go ahead and do it. I like men of action."

She left her phone number.

She sounded interesting. A tough, shrewd woman, but interesting.

He called her and made a date to see her that evening, Friday. "Get here before the sun goes down," she told him. "I don't go out on dates on Shabbos."

He drove up to her house in Skokie. She lived on the top floor of a yellow brick two flat. He drove his 1986 Alfa Romeo red racing coupe. It was his prize possession and he kept it constantly garaged under a woolen blanket, but he felt good about this evening and he took the Alfa out and even wore his Borsolino Alpine hat with the speckled feather of an Italian pheasant and his mesh driving gloves he'd bought in Rome. He loved the smell of the leather seats of the powerful car and to touch its highly varnished dashboard and its gleaming burled wooden gearshift. He easily overtook the traffic on the Outer Drive in short bursts of the powerful engine and he was confident in his driving.

When he arrived at her house, the stairway was dark and she greeted him standing in shadow at the top of the stairs.

"What kind of hat is that?" she said with her arms folded.

"It's Italian. It's the kind of hat an Italian gentleman would wear walking in the mountains. My name is Arthur Fabricant."

"My stairs aren't that steep."

"Why are they dark? I can hardly see."

"They're dark because Shabbos is about to begin and I can't touch anything. I can't even turn off the lights. So I have an automatic timer switch that turns them off an hour before sunset."

She invited him in and he sat in front of her television with his hat in his hands. She was an attractive blonde woman, a little plump, with an expressive face that broke into happiness and disdain with equal ease. She sat suspiciously, with her ankles crossed, staring at him. She had trim ankles and nice legs and she was short. In his cloudy memory she looked like an aging Jewish Betty Grable who had stopped dancing years ago, but still kept the inner rhythms that had tantalized men like Caesar Romero and her husband, Harry James.

"I'll get right to the point," she said looking at her watch and offering him some grapes in one gesture. "We only have maybe fifteen minutes before sundown and then you have to leave. I'm a very religious woman. My name is Trudy Altschul. Your name is Arthur Fabricant. You said it already. Pleased to meet you. I'm looking for an observant man. Already, I don't like the hat and the Italian mountain talk. Are you a Jewish man? Your ad said you were a Jewish man."

"I'm a Jewish man."

"Where do you live?"

"On the North Side in a high-rise."

"No, before, where did you grow up?"

"On the North Shore."

"So you're one of those assimilated Jews."

"I'm not Orthodox. I'm not Conservative. If anything, I'm a Reform Jew. Also what do you mean by assimilated?"

"Do you belong to a synagogue?"

She crossed her legs and he heard the swish of silk and he saw that she was wearing a purple slip trimmed with lavender lace.

"I belong, but I only go for the high holidays."

"I don't think we'd get along." She looked at him. "Here, have another grape, have a peach. Do you like peaches? Take one home with you."

He found himself taking the peach and fondling it as if it were one of her breasts.

"You seem to be a gentleman though, Arthur. Why the divorce? What happened? Why did your wife leave you?"

"Why did your husband leave you?"

"He left me because he died."

"Oh, I'm sorry. Very sorry. I thought you were divorced."

"No. He was a good man. An angel of a man. He left me very well off. I have more than enough. I'm very comfortable. I don't need a man to support me." Her lips were pursed. "But I miss having a man in my life."

"So do I qualify?"

"How would I know? What happened to your wife?"

"She left me."

"Why?"

"For another man. A professor from the University of Chicago. She ran off with him to Israel. I don't know why. I still haven't really answered that to myself. I think maybe because I was too involved in my work. Also, I was too self-involved. I was always running around the world doing projects and not paying enough attention to her. She found a lover and dumped me."

"Any children?"

"Two, two girls."

"They're not with you?"

"No. They're both in college. One's at Stanford. One's at Michigan. They blame me for the divorce, so I have very little contact with them. I just pay the bills."

"That's a shame, a man should be close to his daughters. That's a real shanda. Also your wife ran off to Israel? That's where I want to go. To Israel. I want to live in Israel. In a condo in Haifa. I've even got a place in mind."

"I don't want to live in Israel. I like it here in America."

She shook her head. "Have you ever been there?"

"No."

"I don't think we're for each other. I think you're overassimilated, Arthur."

"Would you like to go to the movies with me, Trudy?" He heard himself asking her in an almost disembodied voice as if he were his own ventriloquist.

"The movies? I don't go to movies. By the way, what's your occupation?"

"I'm an architect."

She stood up and offered him some coffee candy wrapped in gold foil. "Here, put these in your pocket and watch the stairs carefully as you go down. I don't want any lawsuits if you fall. You have my number. I have your number. Maybe one of us will call. Maybe not. Only God knows what two people will do."

She stuck out her hand and shook his and led him to the door. Her hand was soft and warm. "Shalom, Arthur," she said quietly and gave his hand a little squeeze and closed the door. "Good night, Arthur Fabricant," she said. "We may meet again. Maybe. Maybe not."

He was alone on the dark stairway and carefully picked his way down.

H<small>E HEARD FROM</small> T<small>RUDY</small> A<small>LTSCHUL</small> the following evening.

"Hello," he answered the phone. He'd just finished shaking a chicken breast in a plastic bag of bread crumbs and his hands were covered with bread crumbs.

"Is this Arthur Fabricant the architect?"

"It is."

"This is Trudy Altschul from yesterday."

"Good Shabbos."

"Shabbos is over, Arthur. Now, I want to talk business with you."

"Sure." He gave the bread crumb mix bag another little shake.

"You're an architect, Arthur. What firm are you with?"

"I'm with my own firm."

"Where's your office?"

"A. Fabricant and Associates in the First National Bank building."

"Are you a good architect?"

"Of course, I'm a good architect. I've won prizes, international prizes."

"Can you build an Eruv for a group of synagogues?"

"What's an Eruv?"

"Can you design a fence to be strung around the city? An Eruv is a sacred place. A fenced territory where Jews can walk on Sabbath without violating the laws of the Sabbath. Where they can run errands, pick up their children. Do necessities. As long as they stay within the enclosure, it's okay. They can come and go on Sabbath as they please as long as it's within the Eruv."

"You want to build an Eruv around the whole city? You want to string wires around the whole city?"

"Why not? Why should Jews have to stay in an enclosure only around their synagogue? Haven't we been in enough enclosures? Can you design it?"

"Of course, I can. But don't you have to get permission from the city council?"

"We'll get the permission. You just design it. How much will you charge us? I represent a group of poor synagogues. Ordinary people, not fancy North Shore people. We don't have much money. Not like your North Shore temples."

"I'll have to think about it."

"It would be better, Arthur, if you can make it invisible."

"An invisible Eruv? String invisible wires?"

"Sure," she said. "So the goyim can't see them. God forbid, they might think we're trying to pen them in. What's so hard? Just make the wires invisible. Use your imagination. An architect is supposed to have an imagination; call me tomorrow night and give me a figure."

"I'll think about it."

"Arthur, don't think too much. Just do it." He heard the phone click.

She was an interesting lady. Very direct. He liked that. He was much too obtuse; it took him forever to make up his mind about anything. Sure, he could string wires around her neighborhood and create her Eruv. Just use the existing telephone poles and get permission from the phone company and the city council. But he could see the headlines. "Jews Try to String Secret Wire around the North West Side. Architect Claims It Will Be Invisible." Maybe, if he got it high enough and the wires were translucent, it would be invisible in the sunlight. The light would pass right through it. Chicago didn't have enough sunlight though; what about winter? What about low-flying planes or kids climbing the poles with wire cutters? But around the whole city? What a furor that would create. "Jews Try to Pen in Gentiles. Invisible Wires Secretly Strung around City." Still, the Eruv was an interesting concept. He knew that the Jews in London, in Highgate, had tried to create an Eruv in a fashionable London residential section. There'd been an immediate court action. Had they tried to enclose Highgate Cemetery? He didn't know, but there'd been a big fuss in the London papers.

H E DECIDED TO CALL THE WOMAN he'd made a date with to hear a reading of Anna Akhmatova. He also wanted to break that date. What did he know about Anna Akhmatova? Not much. He barely knew how to spell her name. Akhmatova had been a beautiful, young Russian woman poet, lithesome, a long oval ivory face framed by wisps of hair, regal looking. She'd been married to a brutish man and took her revenge with her lovers and her fragile and elegant love poems. Late in life, she was an old woman, standing in line to visit her son at one of the Moscow prisons. He would rather listen alone to Akhmatova's poems than spend time with his friend listening to her talk about her problems. He dialed the number.

"Hello, Gail?"

"Yes," cautiously.

"This is Arthur Fabricant."

"Oh hello, Arthur."

"You know Gail, about our having planned to listen to the lecture on Anna Akhmatova."

"Yes."

"I won't be able to make it."

"Oh Arthur, you know, I was just about to call you. I can't make it either."

"You can't?"

"No."

"Well, I'm sorry."

"Don't be sorry Arthur. We'll try to get together some other time. I liked the reading of Gerard Manley Hopkins by the nun, didn't you?"

"By the nun with the lisp?"

"Did she lisp? I didn't notice."

"I thought she was cloying."

"I thought she was very good. How can you call a nun cloying?"

"Gail, may I ask you what you meant that night when you said you wouldn't come back to my apartment with me because it would be much too lonely?"

"I meant the two of us would be alone together there."

"And that would be too lonely?"

"Yes."

"I see."

"Do you really Arthur?"

"Yes, I think so."

"I mean people together can be so alone that they're not really together. They're just together alone."

"That's what I mean by cloying."

"You just don't understand me, Arthur."

"No. I think I do. I really do understand you. I need someone less uncertain of herself, someone who can at least entertain the idea of being lustful in a relationship."

"Lustful? You don't think I could be lustful?"

"I don't think you even think about lust."

"You mean I'm not interested in a sexual relationship with you."

"No, you're not interested in intimacy."

"No, I'm not, Arthur. I'll go to poetry readings with you. I'll go out for Chinese food with you. But I'm not interested in a sexual relationship with you."

He sighed and held the phone away and he could hear her voice still echoing through the plastic.

He pushed the "off" button and the voice disappeared.

I N THE MORNING, on the way to the office, he thought of stopping to see the Golden Ballerina to talk all this over but it was too windy in the plaza, so he went directly to his office building. He crossed the plaza, and the only sound was of huge corporate flags whipping in the wind. On each sleek office building named after a corporation, there was always a huge corporate flag. The AT&T flag, the USG flag, the Bank One flag. Why did they need these mammoth corporate flags?

He liked to stop at the Quotron machine each morning. It was on the second floor of the bank in the private banking section. He wanted to look over the morning stock prices and check the Dow. He had a little trick that he used to pick stocks. He'd follow some conservative, well-dressed corporate man to the machine and wait behind him. Then, when the man had finished, the machine would show what stocks he was looking at. Usually it was Bank One since most of the customers worked for the bank, but occasionally he'd find an opportunity. Today the man ahead of him left GYMBOREE on the screen. Why GYMBOREE? He'd seen GYMBOREE at a shopping center in his neighborhood. Kids bouncing on space-age trampolines. Anxious mothers waiting with their arms folded as their kids morphed into bouncing martians inside huge plastic bubble enclosures. Did some banker know something he didn't know? He called his broker and bought a thousand shares.

"Hello, Alfred? Alfred, I want a thousand GYMBOREE at 8¼."

"All right, Arthur. But why GYMBOREE?"

"Why not GYMBOREE, Alfred?"

"Okay. You've got it."

"Thanks, Alfred."

That afternoon at lunch he headed for a Chinese restaurant he liked and as he crossed Wabash Avenue at Lake Street he saw a young Oriental woman with a rucksack studying a map. She was short and moonfaced with round, wire-rimmed spectacles and short black hair, but very fresh looking, like a moonflower.

"Can I help you?" he said to her.

"Yes. Can you tell me where is The Museum of Contemporary Art?" She smiled at him and her face came alive with curiosity and energy.

"Yes. I can help you. The museum is about ten blocks north of here. You can walk or you can go over to Michigan Avenue and wait for a bus. The 151 will take you up there."

"Oh, thank you, sir." She smiled at him and the sunlight flashed on her glasses. She bowed her head and as she began to turn away he asked her if she would like to join him for lunch at the Chinese restaurant.

She looked at him inquisitively.

"Why don't you join me for a cup of tea or if you haven't eaten, have lunch as my guest."

"Oh, sir, that would be most pleasant," she replied graciously. "I've had nothing since breakfast."

He held the door open for her and when they entered together, the hostess and his regular waitress looked at him suspiciously.

The young woman told him she was a psychiatric nurse from Hong Kong and she worked in a mental hospital there. "It is a very exhausting job. The patients can be most trying and demanding."

"So you came to America to find some relief?"

"Yes." She poured him some tea ceremoniously in a Chinese manner.

His regular waitress looked like an elegant Chinese movie star. She was beautiful, perfectly made up, glossy lips, thin, arched eyebrows, perfect cheekbones, a high silk mandarin collar. The nurse seemed plain beside her. His waitress obviously couldn't understand what he was doing with this moonfaced young woman from Hong Kong, but she was patient and courteous while they ordered. She even said a few words to the young woman in Mandarin and then left to get their orders.

"My name is Arthur. What is your name?"

"In English, Elaine. In Chinese, Miu Ling."

"And where do you live in Hong Kong? Do you have an apartment of your own?"

"Oh no. I stay with my parents. Also my brothers and sisters. I am the eldest."

He guessed that she was in her early thirties.

"I know you should never ask a woman her age."

"Why don't you guess the range," she answered adroitly.

"I'd say in a range of thirty to thirty-four."

"That's close. How old are you, sir?"

"The range? Why don't you guess my range."

"I'd say very youthful." She smiled warmly at him and offered him a lychee nut.

"Do you care for a lychee?" she said, holding up the lychee nut in a spoon.

"I'll have one."

"Very sweet."

"Am I younger than your father?"

"Oh yes, sir. Considerably younger, Mr. Arthur."

"Does your father work?"

"No. He is retired."

"What does he do with his time?"

"In the mornings, he does tai chi exercises with his friends in the park. In the afternoons he plays mah-jongg and drinks tea."

"And your mother?"

"She is what you call a 'stay at home.' She cooks, she sews, she is not a modern woman. They were very poor people. They came to Hong Kong from a small village, from a small farm."

At the end of the lunch, he exchanged calling cards with her. She wrote her name, an ornate, complicated vertical series of letters that she explained was her name in Chinese. He drew the Arthur Fabricant fleur-de-lys. He asked her for her phone number in Hong Kong and she wrote it on her card. He wrote his home phone on his card. "If you need a friend in Chicago, or some help, call me," he told her.

They shook hands and she headed up the street and he stood watching her until her blue rucksack disappeared in the crowd and it became just a dot of color. That's how people always disappeared out of his life, they just merged into nothingness. Sydney would say to him, "That's how you let people disappear out of your life. You just watch them go." It was nice though to have a Chinese psychiatric nurse as a friend. She also gave him her number at the YWCA in Chicago. He could call her there. She would be here only two days. It was hardly any solace though to have her phone number in Hong Kong. What good would a phone number in Hong Kong do him on a lonely night? He would have probably been better off if he had just pointed the way to the museum and hadn't invited her for lunch. He didn't need to add another young woman to his sad collection.

That night, he worked late on the Eruv project and when he took the elevator down from his office, it was past ten. He'd had some sandwiches delivered to the office and a small bottle of Montrachet. The night man in the lobby called out to him, "Good night, Mr. Fabricant." He decided as he crossed the square in front of the bank that before finding a cab he would visit the Golden Ballerina.

He walked down the stairs to the plaza. Just before he left, he'd called "Voice Broker," the automated service of his broker. It gave him the numbers on the Dow and his stocks. He liked to listen to the robot voice of "Voice Broker." He would give the name of the stock and "Voice Broker" would talk back to him and give him the close. It was all done in the dull voice of computerese, repeating exactly what he'd asked for in computer tones, no inflections, no shadings, no inklings of triumph, no sighs of despair, just pure computerese. "The Dow Jones Industrial Average," he would intone. "The Dow Jones Industrial Average," the computer would repeat. The Dow was up 24. GYMBOREE closed up ¼. Maybe he'd buy another thousand shares tomorrow. Children bouncing. He'd invest in children bouncing. It wasn't a very stable investment, but then life itself wasn't a very stable investment. If he could bounce from Elaine to GYMBOREE and now to the Golden Ballerina, all in a few steps, children bouncing on trampolines that looked like satellites of Mars might not be such a bad investment. He was foolish, though, for having stayed in his office late to work on the idea of the Eruv. It would probably never be built.

When he walked down the stairs to see the Ballerina, she was standing outside the monument dressed in a gray traveling suit, a double-breasted stylish jacket with large red buttons and a long, black, slit skirt. She looked like Chekhov's love, his actress love from Moscow, Olga, only she wasn't holding a fur muff. Olga who? He couldn't remember the name of the actress from the Moscow Theater Chekhov married when he finally broke away from his sister and his mother. Her name was Olga Knipper. He smiled to himself as the name came to him. Olga Knipper.

"Where are you going?" he asked the Ballerina as he approached her.

"We're all leaving tomorrow. We're going back to Israel to a kibbutz near the Sea of Galilee. But Arthur, please come closer. I want to tell you something. They're taking me to Israel against my will. I'm drugged. I think they're giving me Prozac or something they slipped into my bowl of kasha. I don't want to go. I've become their prisoner. You don't understand. You don't recognize me, do you? You think I'm made of stone and chips, a mosaic lady. I'm not, I'm a real person. Don't you recognize me? I've been drugged and put in here. Drugged by Kenneth Starr and his agents. Oh, Arthur, please help me. Ask me to dance, I'll tell you the whole story. They believe in dancing. If you ask me to dance, they'll say it's okay. But see that little guy in the frieze balancing an enormous carp on his head. That's Shloime. He's my personal bodyguard. He watches over me constantly. So first ask his permission. Tell him we just want to dance for a moment and I told you to ask his permission."

There was an orchestra assembled behind her. Not really an orchestra, but a quartet of elderly black musicians, and all the Jewish peasants were standing outside the frieze and were watching them. The quartet began playing "Sophisticated Lady." Even, Shloime, her personal bodyguard, the young man with the enormous fish on his head, began listening and he consented to their dance with a curt nod of his head.

She moved toward Arthur Fabricant and he could sense the fragrance of her hair. "Who are you?" he asked her. "Tell me, really, who are you?"

"Dance with me, Arthur." She held her hand out to him. "Before I leave, just one last dance and I'll tell you all about myself." She kissed him on the lips and he was filled with longing for her. With one kiss she captured him. Nothing like this had happened with any of the other women. She was like Salome and she had an aura of lust, almost a golden aureole of lust shining around her head. She gathered him in her arms and with her lips on his ear, they began to slow dance.

She whispered. "Don't let them take me to Israel, Arthur. If they do, come and rescue me. You've got to help me. I've been abandoned by everyone, Arthur." She had the aroma of a fresh spray of white lilacs and her black hair was silken on his cheeks.

"They say they have cottages at the kibbutz, even an Olympic-sized swimming pool, Arthur."

"How would I ever reach you in Israel?"

"They have a telephone and a fax. I just slipped a note into your pocket with the numbers."

The quartet now switched into "Missed the Saturday Dance" and he spun her around and around toward the plaza while all the Jewish peasants, animals and characters from the monument watched them dance. The klezmer players stood alongside the angels, the donkeys with garlands of flowers twisted in their manes watched, the beautiful young peasant girls in kerchiefs and dirndls whose canted Levantine eyes were shining with tears sat on the donkeys and watched. Even Shloime with the enormous carp balanced on his head watched them dance.

At the end of the song, everyone applauded and he kissed her on the cheek. "My name isn't really Ruth. It's Monica," she said softly, her eyes shining, and then she kissed him again tenderly on the lips. "Ruth is the name they've given me. They won't tell me my real last name. They've been giving me Prozac, so much Prozac. I think I'm really Monica Lewinsky, not Ruth, an Israeli dancer. I think Kenneth Starr and his people kidnapped me and stuck me in this deep frieze and now they're shipping me to Israel to put me into some kind of nunnery for wayward Jewish girls. It's like a Jewish convent."

"If you're the real Monica Lewinsky, Ruth, then who's that woman who went before the grand jury in Washington?"

"That woman is a female impersonator. She's a spy. An Arab transvestite. A nightclub singer from Jehrico. Her real name is Wedad, which in Arabic means "Love." She's a Hamas spy and Hamas has taken over Starr and the whole inquiry by supplying them with this woman. She is simply lying and lying. Starr doesn't think she's Clinton's concubine. He knows she's a female impersonator supplied by Hamas. She never had an affair with the president. She blew a poisoned dart into his ear and drugged him and then hypnotized him and he confessed to all these things. None of which happened. Hamas programmed her to bring the government down so the right-wing Republicans can take over the country and Hamas can take over Israel. It's a deal between the two of them. Hamas gets Israel and Starr and his bible salesmen get Washington. All because Clinton has this meshuganeh dart in his ear. If you could only get me out of here and fly me to him, I'd pull it out with one kiss in his ear. Clinton would be freed from this horrible curse and the country would be saved. Here, let me show you, Arthur." She leaned toward him. Her lips were so very soft and she had a definite scent, the smell of the flowers in the hills of Galilee, a distant lavender scent. "There, Arthur. Did you feel that? I also kissed you on your ear and put a pomegranate seed in your ear with my tongue. A tiny heart-shaped pomegranate seed. It will make you come to Galilee and save me. We could be lovers forever."

Just then, Shloime the young man with the enormous carp on his head, walked down from the frieze and tapped Arthur on the shoulder.

"Listen, dude, you've been dancing long enough with Ruthie, she's gotta go now."

"Who are you? Where are you taking this lady?"

"Who am I? Never mind who I am or where we're taking her. The lady don't want to dance no more, fella." He began tugging her arm.

"Why do you have that enormous fish on your head?" he asked Shloime.

"Fish? What fish? I don't have a fish on my head."

"You have a huge carp balanced on your head."

"There's no fish on my head, dude. You keep saying that and I'll put a fish on your head. Besides, the lady is out of here. She ain't Monica Lewinsky no matter what she says." He began pulling her toward the frieze.

"Arthur, please help me. Please. Don't let them get away with this. Don't believe him. I am Monica."

"The dress. What about the blue dress and the stains?" he called out to her as Shloime tugged her back toward the frieze.

"Stop it, Shloime. Let me talk to this man." She pulled at the carp's tail and the fish began to flutter and knocked him off balance away from her.

"If you're Monica, explain the dress and the stains. Why did you turn the dress over to Starr? He wouldn't have had a case but for that dress."

"The stains were just ice cream stains, Arthur. The president and I snuck out one night and went to a Dairy Queen and took a walk around the neighborhood. He wore a black toupee and a gray beard. He looked like Castro. No one spotted him and we just held hands and walked to the Washington Monument in the moonlight. He wanted to show it to me. He bought me an ice cream cone and I just spilled my cone on my dress."

"But the FBI lab . . ."

"The DNA test was rigged. Starr's men got to the FBI and schmiered them to rig the test results. Those stains weren't even ice cream, they were yogurt. Not even vanilla, vanilla with strawberry swirls."

Shloime staggered back and pulled at her arm again. "All right, Ruthie, that's enough."

"Listen, Shloime, if you let me out of here, we'll fly together to Beverly Hills. I'll take you to a friend of my father's who's a big plastic surgeon there and he'll cut that fish off the top of your head and you'll be a free man."

"There's no fish on my head." Shloime patted the top of his head and the fish twitched its tail and burped. "And you're not Monica Lewinsky, Ruthie."

"Did you see that, Shloime?" she said.

"See what?"

"Shloime, your fish just twitched its tail. Every time you lie, it twitches it tail."

"Okay, so I have a little bit of a fish on my head. So what. It's not like what Monica did with the president, Ruthie. There's no comparison between a carp and fellatio. Anyway, say so long to the dude here. We're outta here. You'll see your pal here in eretz Israel."

He motioned Arthur aside. "Ruthie, get back into the frieze. I want to talk privately to your friend."

Shloime waited for Ruthie to leave and then spoke to Arthur.

"Let me warn you, fella. Don't come to Israel. Don't even think of it. This lady is a head case. A real head case. She thinks I have a fish on my head. There's no fish on my head. Her name is Ruthie. She's not Monica Lewinsky. She's Ruthie Margolis from Haifa. She works in a bookstore there. You know, like some Jewish girls think they're Anne Frank. She thinks she's Monica Lewinsky. So you want my advice? Stay away from her. Don't get mixed up with her. Sure, she's a beauty, but so what. She's not Monica Lewinsky. She's Ruth Margolis from the Steinmatsky Bookstore on Karnovitzky Boulevard in Haifa. We only brought her along because she's a beauty and she can dance like Salome. But she's a real meshuganeh. My advice, dude, stay far away from her. I knew a woman just like her once. A real meshuganeh lady. So if I have a fish on my head, she put it on me. It's the curse of Jean Feigenbaum. You get involved with Ruth Margolis, she'll put a fish on your head, the Curse of Ruth Margolis. I'm warning you."

Shloime left Arthur, shook his finger at him, ran up the steps and grabbed Ruthie's hand. "Don't say I didn't warn you." He touched the tail of the carp and the huge fish began to swim both of them right back into the center of the frieze and they were gone.

Suddenly, everyone disappeared, the Golden Ballerina, Shloime the Fish Boy, all the Jewish peasants and donkeys and angels. It was silent on the plaza and Chagall's mosaic figures had completely disappeared. The huge monument went blank like a giant outdoor blank movie screen in the Chicago gloom.

Arthur Fabricant slowly walked back out to the street alone and hailed a cab back to his apartment.

THAT EVENING, AFTER DINNER, he called the number of the Chinese psychiatric nurse at the YWCA.

"Hello?"

"This is Elaine."

"Elaine, this is Arthur Fabricant. Do you remember me from lunch?"

"Oh, of course, Mr. Arthur. How nice of you to call me."

He could picture her glasses perched on her nose and her round face wreathed in a smile as she sat on the edge of her bed with her rucksack over her shoulders.

"Elaine, you're still in Chicago."

"Yes, yes, Mr. Arthur. I fly to New York tomorrow."

"I want to ask you a question, Elaine. As a psychiatric nurse have you ever come across delusional personalities? Someone who thinks they're someone else? I've met a woman who seems to have this problem."

"Oh, of course. Our hospital in Hong Kong is loaded with delusionals. We have one man who thinks he is Jiang, another Mao, another Chou En-lai, another Chiang Kai-shek. Another man thinks he's Madame Chiang and he talks in her voice, another Confucius and talks in his voice, another Sun Yat-sen and so on and so forth. All very weird and very sad. The noise in the unit is like a cacophony. Is that an appropriate English word? An amalgam of voices, all in discord, none in harmony."

"A woman who believes she's Monica Lewinsky, how would you treat her?"

"Monica Lewinsky, 'The Great Enchantress'? We would treat her with re-education. We would send her to a camp in the countryside."

"You wouldn't give her Prozac?"

"Oh no, in China we don't give Prozac. We may use certain herbs. Sometimes we place acupuncture."

"And this destroys the delusion?"

"It may. It may also help the person live peacefully within the periphery of their own consciousness. For instance, if the woman you speak of truly believes she's Monica Lewinsky, 'The Great Enchantress,' acupuncture could reduce her desire for enchantment."

"But not return her to herself."

"No. That would take a long period of re-education in the countryside. That's why we have camps. Two or three years in a camp and she will lose all interest in her adopted personality and return to her real self. Then we release her. She returns to society as a whole person."

"Well thank you, Elaine. That's a nice analysis. Have a great time in New York. If you need my help, please call me anytime."

"Oh yes, Mr. Arthur. Thank you. I do indeed have in you a gracious friend in the States. I hope this woman with the delusion does not affect your tranquility. But if she does, feel free to call me in Hong Kong for advice. Women who are not tranquil within themselves can cause turbulence in the lives of all who come in contact with them. In our re-education camps we teach them how to make wonton soup and to slice wafer-thin pork and other useful activities so that when they return to society they will be productive and find husbands who appreciate good soup and quiet evenings at home with lychee nuts and tea and mah-jongg tiles clicking and the grandfather clock ticking. I love those sounds. Those are the sounds of my own house, the great clock pendulum ticking, the mah-jongg tiles clicking, the sweet smell of wonton soup with pork wafers and tops of green onions and bamboo shoots. Oh . . . I'm getting homesick and carried away."

"No, I understand. You miss your family. I understand. Thank you, Elaine. I'll be in touch."

LATER THAT NIGHT he drove his Alfa out to Trudy Altschul's house to meet her and the president of the synagogue board. Trudy and a little old man who looked like a Jewish monk in a business suit were seated at her dining-room table.

"This is Mandel Elegant, the chairman of our board."

"How do you do, Mr. Elegant."

The old man extended his hand, as limp as wet parchment. He was tiny, with no hair and a wizened face, and only one good eye. The other eye, dulled with rheum, was like the dead eye of the carp on Shloime's head.

"Mandel doesn't hear so good so speak up and talk loud to him," Trudy said, raising her voice and picking at imaginary bits of lint on her bosom. She wore a tight black dress and a white woolen knitted shawl of loops and a pink wax flower at her throat.

"Mandel Elegant," the old man said, his face distorted with a grimace. He was very suspicious and looked at Arthur as if he were a Yeshiva bocher. "You're the architect?"

"Yes sir."

"Trudy here says you're a good architect, not a gonif." The old man coughed in a tissue and inspected his phlegm and extended a bony finger. "You can build our Eruv around the city of Chicago?"

"Why around the entire city of Chicago, Mr. Elegant? Why not just around the neighborhood of each synagogue, around a few blocks in each neighborhood?"

"No, no. What good does it do to have an Eruv around a few blocks? What if there's an emergency somewhere? What if we have to go somewhere outside of the neighboorhood? Suppose I have to be somewhere on the South side or the West side? Not that I would ever go to the South side or the West side because, God forbid, I might get my throat cut. But I should have the right to go there. This is America, right? Jews should be able to walk anywhere. Even on Shabbos, particularly on Shabbos. I don't want an Eruv that would just wind around a few neighborhoods like a prison wall. I want it around the whole city. The board can't afford it, but if you can do it, I'll pay you personally."

His face broke out into a half smile that was really a leer, a paroxysm of a smile. "If it costs me a million, so what. Two million, I don't care. At my age, what do I care? The government will take everything anyway. But not the Mandel Elegant Eruv. That they cannot take. You name the Eruv for me. Jews will be able to take a walk along the lakefront on Shabbos and look at fish if they want to. Or like in Warsaw, we could walk to the river and cast our sins away. We could walk to the Vistula and throw away our sins. Why not toss our sins into the Chicago River? The Catholics can go to confession and swallow those little wafers like tiny matzos and melt away their sins. Why can't the Jews walk to a river on Shabbos and toss away their sins?" His eyes were glittering with pleasure. "Would it be so bad to be able to go anywhere in the city on Shabbos? That's freedom. That's real freedom, the American way. With the Eruv you go anytime, anywhere, anyplace. Jews in Chicago will really be free. So you build it. The Mandel Elegant Eruv around the entire city. Make it invisible though. No Gentiles can see it, no one can know it's there. No one will know it exists. God forbid, if the Gentiles see it, they'll think we're trying to put them in a prison."

"I told Mandel you told me you could make it invisible," Trudy Altschul said patting Arthur's hand.

"I never said I could make it invisible."

"Just hang it from the sky." The old man pointed up. "Hang it up in the sky. Make it come down invisible from the sky. No one will see it."

Arthur closed his eyes and envisioned a huge strand of gossamer spider's web encircling the entire city. "All right," he said. "I'll try. But I won't promise. I'll make a model."

"One or two other things," Mandel said. "A statue in the park. My statue. I want a statue to be there. A statue of me in Lincoln Park with my arms out like this." He spread his arms with difficulty and winced. "Like where they have Shakespeare in the park. I want a little plaque, like Shakespeare's plaque. It should tell how I came to America from Poland and made my fortune and left most of it to Uncle Sam and then built the Mandel Elegant Eruv. But it can't say what it is or where it is, God forbid. Just that I built it and left it to the Jewish community."

As Arthur was about to leave, Trudy walked him down the stairway and pressed two caramel candies wrapped in gold foil in his hand.

"Arthur, I also want you to build for me a Succoth Hut in my backyard. I already have a Succoth Hut but it's a pre-fab and the rabbi won't bless it because he says its machine made and I need a Succoth Hut made of natural materials. So I want to consult with you. The rabbi will bless the sides of my hut but not the roof. The roof must be open to the heavens, he says, like a tree. It must be made of boughs and leaves. The rabbi says my roof has staples in it. I should remove the staples and replace the slats of wood with tree branches. So I did that, but now, he says, he discovered staples in my side walls. If I remove those, the walls will come tumbling down. But he won't bless a Succoth Hut with staples in the roof or the walls. I have to consult you as an architect." She squeezed his hand and moved closer to him. He could sense her peppermint-scented breath. Just then, the lights went out in the hallway.

"Is it Shabbos again, Trudy?"

"No, no. It's just my Shabbos light regulator. It's also my stairway light regulator. It only leaves the light on long enough to get down the stairs."

They stood together in the darkness and he had the feeling that she was waiting for him to kiss her, but he knew that Orthodox women were not allowed to kiss men other than their husbands. The worst sin she'd commited so far was to press candies into his hand.

"Good night, Arthur Fabricant," she whispered to him in her peppermint-scented voice. "If you build me a new Succoth Hut, I'll serve you dinner in it under the harvest moon. I'll make a beautiful dinner for you."

"Thank you, Trudy. Have you thought of leather thongs instead of staples? You could hold the sides together with leather thongs. That's a natural material. The rabbi would bless leather thongs."

She moved away from him and went up the stairs and turned the lights on and fluttered her hand good night.

"If I want leather thongs, I won't need an architect. I could hire a Boy Scout for leather thongs."

She closed the upstairs door and the last thing he saw was the swirl of her dress and the flash of her ankle.

W̲HEN HE RETURNED TO HIS APARTMENT there were two women waiting in the lobby. One was an attractive young Indian woman with golden open-toed sandals. She was dressed in silken pantaloons and she had a red spot in the middle of her forehead, a bracelet of tiny silver bells, and her black hair was tied in a long pigtail. She was really quite beautiful with black, flashing eyes. George the doorman told him she'd been waiting for almost half an hour. She was reading a paperback covered in a plain wrapper and she lowered her eyes when he looked at her.

"I think she's from India," George said to him. "Something about answering your ad. The other lady is a Polish lady. She's been here almost an hour. She's also come for the ad."

"Who came first?" he asked George, who had the seamed, wrinkled face of a Chinese foo guard dog. He wore the uniform of a full admiral of the Doormen's Corps, blue with gold braid on his visor, gold epaulets, a golden-corded right shoulder and a gold lanyard holding a silver whistle. His uniform was appropriate for the decor of the lobby, which was mostly silken damask and golden-patterned wallpaper.

"The Polish lady was first. She beat the Indian lady by thirty minutes."

George was a consummate consumer of tips. He handed George a five dollar bill which the doorman took with a little salute.

"I'll see the Polish lady first, George. Buzz her into the lobby."

He sat down at a table in the lobby and removed his Italian mountain borsalino hat and his driving gloves and received the Polish woman at a small antique wooden desk in the paneled lobby. The desk was set beneath two portraits of eighteenth century English gentry, a lord and his lady with lace collars and jewels at their throats.

The Polish woman approached and he stood and helped her with her chair.

Her face immediately reminded him of Picasso's drawing, *The Acrobat's Wife.* Her hair was coiled on her head and she had slanting, high cheekbones and thin eyebrows, an almost ivory face, without cosmetics and thin lips, a very pale face, yet quite beautiful, a very sad face. It was too sad to be the face of a young woman. She was in her mid-thirties, very short and thin and her clothes were obviously European. She wore a full woolen skirt, a tweed jacket and a silk blouse with a high, lace collar closed at her throat by a pin, a square enameled portrait of a cowled woman.

She handed him a small bouquet of withered flowers, six miniature pink roses wrapped in green tissue paper. She held the bouquet upside down like an inverted cornucopia.

"These are for you, sir." He heard the slight European accent.

"Thank you. Thank you very much." He took the flowers and she blushed.

"You've come in response to the ad?"

"Yes, the ad in the Polish newspaper."

"And you're Polish?"

"Yes."

"Where in Poland are you from?"

"From Czestochowa."

"I know Czestochowa. That's the city of the monastery of *The Black Madonna*. The famous painting that's the holy icon of Poland."

"Yes, Mr. Fabricant. I wear her portrait." She pointed at the enameled pin at her throat. "It is unusual that you should know that."

"No, I've been to Poland. I'm an architect, I had a commission there. Do they still have the procession every year, people on their knees going up the hill to the monastery to see the painting? I forget the name of the monastery."

"Jasna Gora."

"Yes, Jasna Gora."

"Yes, they will always have such a procession." She touched her throat again and color came to her cheeks. "She is our lady of Czestochowa, our holiest lady."

"They call her 'The Black Madonna.'"

"That is right. You know so much about Poland, Mr. Fabricant. She is 'The Black Madonna' because it is believed her face was seared by gunpowder and smoke in a battle fought against the Swedish hordes. The Polish defenders held up her portrait and she repelled the Swedes. Her face was blackened with the smoke of the battle and pierced by arrows. That was tragic. Yet, Poland was saved by her intervention. This we believe."

He could see that as she told him the story, her eyes were glistening. Also, he noticed that she had lovely hands; long, tapered, graceful fingers.

"So, you bring flowers to me in her honor, to honor her memory."

"Yes, that is part of the reason," she said speaking so softly he could hardly hear her. "And also to honor you and perhaps the beginning of a new friendship. In Poland we bring flowers to our friends."

"You hold the bouquet upside down?"

"It brings good luck holding the bouquet upside down. We also place flowers on statues of holy figures and on holy icons. We believe in the healing power of flowers."

"May I ask your name?"

"My name is Stephanie."

"Stephanie, do you cook?"

"Cook? No, unlike most Polish women, I am not a cook. I take most of my meals out in inexpensive cafeterias or restaurants."

"Are you interested in food?"

"Not particularly."

"When you eat, what do you have?"

"Very little. Mostly tea. Herbata. Tea and bread. Chleb. Tea and bread and perhaps, marmalade. For the evening meal, perhaps a soup, a hearty soup."

"You're very slim. What do you like to do, Stephanie? What are your interests?"

"I go to church. I visit with my Polish friends. I love to read. I am very interested in literature. I like flowers and gardens. I visit museums, art galleries, occasionally the theater. I mostly go to church on the weekends. I like liturgical music. Flute and organ music. Also Chopin. I love Chopin, on the harpsichord particularly."

"And you think we could be friends?"

"I must first know more about you, Mr. Fabricant. I have read your advertisement, but may I ask, what are your special interests, Mr. Fabricant? Do they coincide with mine?"

"I must be honest with you, Stephanie. I'm going through a kind of metamorphosis. I'm sort of in a chrysalis. Do you know that word? I don't know if that's the right word. I'm trying to come out of my cocoon. I'm a divorced man and the divorce was very painful. My wife left me for another man. I try not to think about it and perhaps that's why I keep going out with women who are much too young for me. I'm trying to prove that I'm still attractive. But I know better and I'm beginning to dislike myself for it. I see myself as being weak and foolish. I know I'm not exactly a treasure."

She looked directly at him with her clear, innocent pale blue eyes. It was the first time she looked up directly at him.

"I am also a divorced woman, Mr. Fabricant. I have commited the sin of becoming divorced but I could not stand my husband any longer. We were not suited for each other. I made a mistake. He was French. I was Polish. It was like Chopin and George Sand. In the end, they were not suited for each other."

"You don't like the French?"

"Not any more. I've learned my lesson. I am not a Francophile as you advertised you are."

"Do you have any children?"

"I have no children. Do you have children?"

"Yes, I have two daughters, both in universities. I'm not in touch with them very often."

She put her beautifully tapered long fingers together and said something softly in Polish.

"What kind of work do you do, Stephanie?"

"In Poland I taught English literature at the Jagellonian University in Krakow. Here I teach English and Polish literature at the University of Illinois in Chicago."

"So you understand with your literary background what I meant by chrysalis."

"Just as in *The Metamorphosis* by Kafka, Gregor Samsa was in a chrysalis. I understand. Did you know that at the end of his life, Kafka wanted to go to Israel, to Tel Aviv to open a small restaurant? He was in love with a woman named Dora. She was a Zionist and they planned to go together to open the cafe. She would be the cook and he would wait on tables. That was their plan."

"And you think we could be friends like Kafka and Dora? We could open Kafka's cafe here in Chicago?"

She smiled for the first time. "Perhaps. I think I would be willing to make the experiment."

She reached across the desk and touched the top of his hand with her beautiful fingers and he was immediately attracted to her as if he'd been touched by the whirring wings of an ivory-throated hummingbird.

"Stephanie, could we have dinner together? Meet somewhere in the evening for a simple dinner? Perhaps next Thursday in the evening?"

"Yes, it would be agreeable."

"Could you leave me a card with your phone number?" He reached for his wallet.

"No. I have already written it out in anticipation of our meeting again." She handed him an old-fashioned, large-sized calling card with her name neatly printed out in ink, "Stephanie Agnieszka Kroleska," with her address and phone number.

"I'll call you later in the week, Stephanie," he said to her and shook her hand.

"I will look forward to our meeting, Mr. Fabricant," she said quietly.

George buzzed her out. She looked back through the glass once and then walked out through the front entrance.

"Send the lady from India in, George," he said putting Stephanie's bouquet of miniature roses down under the elevator table so that the bouquet would be out of sight.

THE INDIAN LADY APPROACHED HIM in a swirl of golden veils and as she sat down there was the essence of some strong scent, perhaps patouli. She moved gracefully with the sound of tiny bells tinkling from silver bracelets on her wrists and ankles. She wore an orange sari and ropes of red, blue and black beads around her neck. Her head was covered with a white, silver-trimmed, silk scarf and her trousers were silken and threaded with silver which offset her golden sandals. Her face was very intense, beautifully featured, a long, thin nose and dark eyes and two half-moon crescents of painted silver dots arching down each cheekbone, and a red dot in the center of her forehead like a red opal.

"You are Arthur Fabricant, sir?" she asked pulling her patouli-scented scarf over her head so that she looked like an errant Indian princess who had just wandered out of the ashram at the palace to secretly meet with him.

"Yes, I am Arthur Fabricant, and you are?"

"I am Sudha Tanjoree Markowitz."

"Markowitz, are you Jewish?"

"Yes, of course, I am a Jewish woman from India." Her eyes locked in on his. "Are you surprised to meet a Jewish woman from India?"

"Yes, particularly in Chicago. Where are you from Sudha?"

"Not Sudha. I hate that name. Call me Tanji, that's what my friends call me. I'm from Delhi."

"And what are you doing in Chicago?"

"I work for the Bank of India. I'm a loan officer. They have a branch here."

"How did you learn of me?"

"Your ad on the Internet. You're on the International Dating Network. I saw your personal and called. I was curious, so I came up. Just like the Polish woman. Although I haven't brought any flowers. Why are you hiding her bouquet under the table, Mr. Fabricant?"

"I don't know. You're quite observant, Tanji. But I suppose as a lending officer you would have to be."

"Well, it's quite obvious that she brought you a bouquet of roses."

"Yes, she did."

"You can be direct with me, Arthur. I am used to analyzing information rather quickly."

"All right, Tanji. I will be direct with you. I have always had the dream of visiting India. In my dream, I would rent a houseboat in the Vale of Kashmir and meet a woman there."

"You would not want to go there now. There is a war there in the Himalayas. It's not a place to meet a woman."

"Yes, but in my dream, the woman comes to my houseboat. She's dressed in a beautiful sari just like you are, but she's veiled."

"Like a harem woman?"

"Yes, and she has silver finger cymbals and she begins to dance and I am completely entranced and seduced by her. The boat slowly drifts out into the perfumed water and we lie on silken pillows and make love under the swaying paper lanterns."

"So are you asking me what that dream means? To interpret your dream?"

"No, I'm not finished. I fall asleep. She gets up and leaves and just before going ashore, she drops a match and sets the houseboat afire and shoves it with her foot back out into the current where the wind takes it with me asleep. It becomes my floating pyre. I drift aflame, the boat disintegrates and I am incinerated."

"I'd say you're very mistrustful of women."

"You're probably right."

"Have you ever been married?"

"Yes, but it ended in divorce."

"It's a very sad dream, Arthur. What should have been beautiful and lovely turns into a disaster."

She held her hands in the vertical Indian prayer position and pointed them at him as if she were blessing him.

"If you were a loan applicant at my desk at the bank, I would turn you down. I wouldn't even send you to the committee for review. That's my analysis. I hope you find peace, Arthur. But I don't think I'm the woman who can bring it to you. You seem like a very complicated man."

"I don't know, Tanji. I don't mean to frighten you. But I really don't see all women as pyromaniacs. Also, I'm learning that what I want is a nurturing love and an uncomplicated, intimate relationship that nevertheless has passion."

"That's what we all want, uncomplicated passion arising from intimacy. And instead we all wind up incinerated on our own floating pyres."

"That's rather cynical. I can see you're also complicated."

"I'm not so complicated and I'm not afraid of men." She shook the bells on her silver bracelet to accentuate her statement and he heard the faint tinkling of the bells and he reached out and touched her patouli-scented hand. Then she leaned toward him, "You don't really think I'm a pyromaniacal harem dancer, do you Arthur? Even though I'd reject your loan application, that doesn't mean you can't trust me and that I'm incapable of an intimate friendship. I just don't mix the bank's business with friendship."

"Tanji, do you know a good restaurant around here that does good tandoori chicken? Perhaps we could go there together? Maybe next Friday evening? Someplace where we could listen to the sitar and talk and get to know each other. If you could leave me your name and phone number, I'll call you and confirm, but I'm quite certain I could make it if you could."

She took a small notebook from her purse and tore off a piece of paper and wrote her phone number and gave it to him. She then stood and touched his face gently with her hand. "Friday night, Arthur. There's an Indian restaurant two blocks away on Oak Street. I'll just meet you here at six and we'll walk over there." She removed one of the beaded necklaces from her neck and dropped the necklace over his head. She didn't look back as she left through the glass lobby doors, pulling her sari around her, disappearing as quickly as Stephanie whose bouquet of tiny withered roses he now retrieved from under the elevator table.

So what had he accomplished? Really nothing. He'd broken two dates and now he had two more. He was right back where he'd started even though he'd been given a bouquet of roses and some beads. And even worse, now he was on the Internet.

He quickly called the Jewish and Polish newspapers and left voice mail messages to cancel his ad and asked them to immediately take his personal off the Internet. He slept fitfully that evening trying to avoid the floating Kashmir pyre dream and to prepare himself for the morning. He knew it would be a difficult morning. He had an appointment with Trudy Altschul and Mandel Elegant to inspect the model he'd made of the Eruv.

The model he'd built could be seen only by taking a boat out into Lake Michigan where he'd constructed a working model of the Eruv just inside the breakwater. Trudy and Mandel Elegant both objected to having to go out into Lake Michigan, which was often treacherous, but Arthur insisted and hired a yacht and a captain and crew for the excursion. Fortunately, it was a beautiful, sunlit morning and Arthur, dressed in a white yachting outfit and captain's hat, met them at the Monroe Street Yacht Club where he'd rented a sleek cabin cruiser with a Jewish captain and an all-Jewish crew. The crew members were dressed in white bellbottoms and red and white striped jerseys and white sailor caps. The captain was a former gun runner for the fledgling Israeli Navy and had been sworn to secrecy about the Eruv project.

Mandel Elegant was dressed in a yachting costume, a yachtsman's jacket and captain's hat. He wore a navy blue double-breasted flannel jacket with gold anchor buttons and a silk cravat with a design of tiny golden anchors and white rubber-soled yachting shoes and white trousers. Trudy wore a red, white and blue sailor's blouse with blue stars on the white sailor's collar. She had a red straw bowler hat tied with white streamers and a full white pleated skirt almost to her ankles.

As soon as they left the harbor, they were seated by the captain beneath a large green canopy at the rear of the ship and served a catered lunch. Arthur ordered the lunch delivered in silver chafing dishes from his favorite Russian restaurant. There was matzo ball soup served in tiny lovely china cups, miniature matzo balls with chopped vegetables, Russian style. The soup was followed by blinis with salmon caviar, then cheese and meat pierogis served with applesauce and sour cream in honor of Mandel Elegant's Polish background.

They were each given patches by the captain to wear behind their ears for seasickness. For dessert they had Russian tea and apricot strudel. No alcoholic beverages were served. Before they visited the Eruv site, the captain had been instructed to slowly cruise along the lakefront. The topic under discussion was not the Eruv but the impeachment hearings before the Senate.

"They're picking on the Jews again," Mandel Elegant said squinting with his one good eye at the Chicago skyline in the bright sunlight.

"How so?" Arthur asked.

"Who do they call as witnesses these small town, shaygus house managers? Two Jews and a Black. Monica Lewinsky, Sidney Blumenthal and Vernon Jordan. Do you think they done that accidentally? No, they done that on purpose. What does goyischer America care about subpoenaing two Jews and a Black? Nothing. Bupkes." He spit into the wind and just missed Arthur's face. "This way they can blame everything on the Jews and the Blacks."

"Mandel is right," Trudy said re-tying the streamers that held her hat on against the wind. She folded her arms. "Those goyischer congressmen, the managers, Mr. Asa Hutchinson of Arkansas. What does he care? There're no Jews in Arkansas. And that choir boy Mr. Lindsey Graham of South Carolina. Another assassin from a district with no Jews."

"I haven't thought of it that way," Arthur answered.

"Sure," Mandel Elegant said." So who do they subpoena from the whole country? Two Jews and a black. The prosecutors would love to crucify them. And Henry Hyde, the crybaby with the white minister's hairdo. He's mad because he never had a Monica as his intern, only some guy's wife did he steal and break up the marriage. He's got the conscience of a herring, Henry Hyde. By the way, Arthur, who pays for all this, the fancy boat, the captain and crew, the fancy lunch?"

"I'm paying for it. You and Trudy are my guests."

Trudy looked at Mandel and the old man was suspended in disbelief, his one good eye glittering suspiciously at Arthur. Mandel took off his captain's hat and daubed his forehead with a starched napkin and then pulled the brim of the captain's hat down almost to his eyes.

"So why do we have to go out on the water to see the Eruv?" he asked Arthur. "Tell me. Enough yachting already. If we keep cruising back and forth like this, Congress might investigate us. Three Jews on a boat on a Sunday afternoon."

"Maybe that Bob Boyd of Georgia, that little fat-faced womanizer will come after us," Trudy said. "Or maybe Sensenbrenner the millionaire hatchet man from Wisconsin."

"All right," Arthur said signaling the captain to turn around and head out to the breakwater where he'd built his model. "I've incorporated all your ideas into the model. Something that will encircle the city and hang from the sky, yet be unobtrusive and invisible. Believe me, it wasn't easy. But then I got an idea from the Bible, from the biblical parable of Jonah and the whale."

"The whale swallowed Jonah and tried to eat him like gefilte fish," Mandel Elegant said. "I don't like it already. I don't even like gefilte fish unless I put sugar on it."

"Please don't think of Jonah, Mandel. Think only of the whale."

"What's a whale got to do with this?" Trudy asked.

"It's not the whale. It's the concept of the whale."

Trudy put her hand over her mouth. "I think I'm getting a little seasick. The boat keeps rolling. Can't you tell the captain to stop it from rolling?"

"Don't think about the boat. Think about the whale. How the whale spouts water up into the air."

"All right already. Enough of the whale," Mandel said. "I don't want the Mandel Elegant Eruv to be named after a whale. Look at *Moby Dick*. I read that when I first came to America. Was it named after a whale? I guess it was. I don't remember who wrote it, but I don't want my Eruv named after a whale."

"Your Eruv won't be named after a whale, I promise you. It will be the Mandel Elegant Eruv."

They began to approach a tower that had been built into the lake, a tower of black, latticed scaffolds that looked like a small Cape Canaveral launch pad and they slowly began to circle it.

Arthur handed them each a pair of sunglasses.

"Now put the glasses on and watch. Close your eyes and count to seven. Then say the password, 'Sholem Aleichem,' and you'll see your Eruv."

The old man pointed a bony finger at the tower and in his squeaky, high-pitched voice called out the password, "Sholem Aleichem" and as he pointed, just to be sure, he said it again backwards, "Aleichem Sholem."

Suddenly, with an electronic signal from Arthur's hand, a missile erupted from the tower and whooshed up into the sky in a perfect liftoff trailing blue and white vapor trails, one - two - three - four - up - up - five - six - higher - higher - seven - and then the missile exploded and disappeared leaving a tracing in the sky of a perfect blue and white fence made of vapor contrails that slowly began to drift over and encircle the entire lakefront. It was a vapor fence, drifting higher and higher up to about 15,000 feet where it stopped and hung over the city like *The Hanging Gardens of Babylon*. The blue and white colors of Zion, the Mandel Elegant Eruv, invisible, hung from the sky, already minutely dissolving, twenty-four hours later it would disappear entirely as if it had never existed.

The old man tilted his ostrich neck and watched through the sunglasses. Trudy put her arm around Mandel and whispered something into his ear and he nodded agreement. She pursed her lips and glared at Arthur.

Then Mandel Elegant turned to Arthur and said, "A Boy Scout could have built that. Just vapor trails, pretty pictures in the sky. For vapor trails I don't need an architect."

"But Mandel, it has everything you asked for, the concept of confinement, encirclement, invisibility, it lasts only twenty-four hours. We could shoot it up once a week on Friday night at sundown until Saturday at starlight. We'd need maybe six or seven towers to do the whole city."

"Who pays for the torpedos?" the old man answered. "For torpedos we don't need an architect."

"Arthur, I told you wires," Trudy said to him. "Wires is what Mandel wants."

"Wires?"

"Arthur, wires," she said again. "Invisible wires. Why should that be so hard? This is too fancy, too complicated, too high maintenance. So we come out here in a boat once a week to fire this off? How do we get out here in the wintertime on the frozen lake? With sled dogs?"

"No, we load the towers once or twice a year and store the missiles. The whole thing works electronically. We push a button on the shore. You could do it from your living room."

"It's no good, Arthur," Trudy said to him dropping two golden, foil-wrapped coffee candies into his breast pocket. "Go back to the drawing board and tell the captain to take us back to shore. Mandel is beginning to turn a little green and I don't feel so good. Let's have some tea and then you go back to your office and tear up your drawings and give us wires."

So HE GAVE THEM WIRES. If it was wires that they wanted, he would give them wires. All he had to do was design connections to the existing telephone wires. The telephone company had already strung an Eruv around the entire city. He'd just hook it up. He'd design connections that could be strung in the gaps of the existing system. If the telephone wires ran for 195 blocks north and south in parallel grids, he'd just hook up both ends of the existing system. He'd have a perfect rectangle completely encircled by wires approximately five miles wide and twenty-five miles long. The connecting wires he'd install would be fiber-optic wires that'd be translucent. No one would see them. The 195-block Eruv wouldn't be too beautiful. It wouldn't run along the lakefront. Shabbat strollers wouldn't be able to look at fish or toss their sins away into the Chicago River, but it would be a complete Eruv, a contained space, 195 blocks long and 50 blocks wide, cutting through the heart of the city. Also, it wouldn't cost very much to build. He envisioned five miles of spools of fiber-optic wire at each end and a truck of technicians, maybe two people, to string the wires at night. The truck could be disguised as a cable-television truck and the wire stringers would be dressed in black. They'd have to be very tough, like Jewish ninjas, but armed. Two Jewish ninja wire setters, armed with every conceivable weapon, automatic pistols, machine pistols, knives, stun guns, electric prods, Mace, pepper-spray canisters, an entire arsenal at their fingertips as they make their way secretly at night through the Chicago alleyways to string wire. They'd be passing through some of the toughest, most violent neighborhoods of the city. Two well-armed Jewish ninjas could do it. That's all it would take.

He contacted Jewish Vocational Service the next evening, and they sent over a man and a woman who arrived on a motorcycle, a black Harley "Fat Boy." Arthur met them in the alley behind his building and talked to them while they sat with the motorcycle running. The man was huge, dressed entirely in black, with bulging, tatooed forearms and arm muscles, his head was shaved and he had a neck as thick as a pro football lineman. He was a first cousin of the champion pro wrestler Bill Goldberg. He was a duplicate of Goldberg, powerful, mean and nasty, with a huge head and bull neck and tiny angry eyes. David Goldberg, cousin of the champion, sat on his Harley "Fat Boy" and revved the chortling engine as he listened intently to Arthur's instructions. David Goldberg was named after the Warrior King of the Jews and he'd named his Harley, "Lil David," with scroll lettering on its gas tank. It had Star of David red blinking taillights and side running lights. David Goldberg, cousin of the national wrestling champion, a mammoth Jewish ninja, supplied with only one phone call to JVS.

His coworker on the jump seat was a very pretty seventeen year old named Judith Trumpeter, who held onto David's waist and his sparkling, studded motorcycle belt. She looked like a tough, teen-aged, Jewish waif with a duck-feather haircut. Judith Trumpeter was also a Jewish ninja named after a great Jewish heroine. Judith had a round face with a jewel embedded on her chin and on each eyelid. Her eyes were black and unclouded with fear. He cheeks were so full of passion and daring that they glowed orange with intensity. She was very silent and that was a wonderful attribute for a Jewish ninja, silent but deadly. Her skill was wire stringing and climbing. A perfect pick by JVS. She could climb telephone poles faster than a black squirrel. She could climb with a spool of wire slung around her neck and and attach a wire to the top of the pole in five seconds. Then she'd dive down off the top of the pole into David Goldberg's massive arms. They'd jump back on the Harley and roar down the alley to the next pole. They could easily string two miles a night. David said they could do the whole job in a week.

"We'll show you how we do it," he said in a deep-voiced Oklahoma accent. He pulled a black throwing knife from a pocket inside his leather jacket. "Pick a telephone pole, sir, any pole. Just point to one, sir."

Arthur pointed to one.

The black knife hurtled through the air and stuck quivering at the bottom of the pole. A perfect throw.

Judith Trumpeter was off the cycle in a flash, used the knife as her first foothold, and scampered up the pole in three or four seconds. She called out, "David" . . . and like a dark nightingale, spread her arms and floated down into his waiting arms and dropped to the ground and bowed as if she'd just floated down from a high wire (which actually she had).

"Judy used to be with the circus. She just got tired of all the travel."

"That was magnificent," Arthur told them. "I couldn't believe you could do that."

"We can do twenty, maybe thirty poles a night," David said. "But we'd have to be paid in advance. One thousand a night and you supply all the ammo, Mace and pepper gas and two bulletproof vests. There'll be junkies in those alleys, plenty of gang bangers, whores, pimps, thieves, winos, all kinds of good people. They won't like us coming through their turf. I've done this midnight alley work before, pulling cars. It's dangerous work."

"No, I think a thousand a night, in advance, is very reasonable. But we don't want anyone killed. That's why we have to rely on your speed and surprise. I see you can get in and out in a few seconds. That's just what JVS told me."

"No one will even see us, sir," David answered. Judith nodded her head. She remained absolutely silent but her eyes were sparkling. She jumped back on the rear seat and hugged David's studded belt. "If they do see us, I know how to buy them off. Just offer them free cable. Judy can hook them up for free cable while she's up there. We'll just give them a free cable hookup and they won't pay any attention to the Eruv wire."

"Okay, it's a deal, but I have to have you meet my clients, the members of the synagogue board. I'm sure they'll approve it. Come tomorrow night. Right here, same time, and give them a demonstration." David Goldberg nodded approval and Judith said nothing. He revved the fringed handlebars of the Harley and smiled at Arthur.

The Harley then bucked and roared down the alley, its Star of David taillights blinking away into the darkness.

The Kite Flyer

THE FIRST KITE HE FLEW out of his window had a golden dragon on its face, a triangular pale blue kite, and the dragon glittered in the weak Chicago winter sunlight as the kite rose above the office buildings on Michigan Avenue. It had a yellow plastic tail and the kite would rise, swoop down, and rise again as he fought to pull it up so it would fly free above the buildings. When he succeeded, he anchored it by tying the string to one of the handles of his windows. He flew it for maybe fifteen minutes, then reeled it back in and closed the window.

Frederick Marcus had been a lawyer for over forty years in Chicago. He was a solo practitioner with an office in a rather undistinguished older brick building, hidden in a crevice between two slick modern high-rises sheathed in aluminum and steel. He had slightly cut the index finger on his right hand pulling the kite back into his office. He sucked his finger and wrapped it in tissue. Why was he flying a kite? He didn't really know why he was doing it. The Tibetans flew kites out the windows of their lamaseries to try to communicate with the spirit of God. Why couldn't a Chicago lawyer do the same thing? He could even tie bells to the tail.

A man on the train this morning was reading a memo in Pakistani. He leaned into Marcus as he bent to give the conductor his ticket. A young woman clerk at McDonald's in the station where he stopped for a cup of tea, very pretty, petite, Spanish accent. "Where are you from?" Marcus asked her. "Quito, Ecuador." "I met a man once from Guayaquil, on a ship on the way to Europe," he told her. He was always too garrulous. "Enrique. He had a gold cigarette case and he raised horses in the mountains and brought them down to the sea to exercise them in the warm salt water." The young clerk stared at Marcus and then she smiled. "Buena suerte en los Estados Unidos," he said to her as he left with his paper cup of tea. He passed a beggar on the bridge. The man had no teeth and desperate eyes. He was Marcus's age, about sixty-five. "How are you today, sir?" he said to Marcus and shook his cup. "I'm okay, how are you?" "Got cirrhosis of the liver, got it bad." "Here's a dollar." "Thank you, sir, God bless you, sir."

Lately his clients had been paying him in cash. A widow for whom he'd drawn a living trust and a pour-over will and health care and property powers of attorney, after the will signing, turned to him and said, "I owe you a thousand dollars, Mr. Marcus, right?" Then she reached under her skirt and unpinned a tiny cotton purse from her stocking, opened it, and counted out ten $100 bills and put them on his desk. "You can't trust anyone in the city, so when I carry big money, I carry it there." She straightened her skirt. She was about eighty, a petite white woman, bright blue eyes, still very pretty. "When I was a kid I was a hatcheck girl in New York, and I learned how to hide money. I worked at a place owned by the Mafia. There was always lots of cash around. I quit that job though, because one night after work the owner raped me in his office. He was an awful man, and I got pregnant from him and had an abortion. I've had a lot of bad things happen to me. I've been married three times. The last man though was a kind man and I loved him. He left me enough so that I could live decently. I'm all alone now, and when I go I want my daughter to have what I have. So it's worth a thousand dollars to me. Besides, my memory's slipping. I want to provide for my daughter while I can still use my mind."

Another man came in, a black man in his early seventies, dignified, with easy laughter. He wanted a premarital agreement. He'd been living with a younger woman, about fifty-five, but she'd torn up two prior drafts of the agreement. The understanding was that if she stayed with him and cared for him, he'd leave her his house, which was fully paid for and worth about $100,000. Marcus had charged them $450, which the man paid in installments, the final installment in cash. He'd taken down his trousers and removed a small wallet from under his long underwear. "I always carry a hundred dollar bill here because my neighborhood is so full of gang bangers I have to hide it here." He handed Marcus the $100 bill and laughed and pulled his trousers back up. "If she don't sign this one, I think we can forget about it."

> *On the way to work today there was a young fresh-faced lawyer wheeling a skeleton down the street on the way to court at the Daley Center. The skeleton was hung on a rolling platform. "Is that real?" Marcus asked the young lawyer. "I don't know." "Poor man," Marcus said, as the young lawyer stood with the dangling skeleton waiting for traffic to clear. At the Daley Center people were being searched and patted down before they are admitted to the courtroom floors, their bags and packages run through X-ray machines. Slim guards in black uniforms with electric batons guarding the gates of justice. In the Daily Law Bulletin at the newsstand counter, on the first page, a lawyer won a $9.7 million malpractice verdict against a doctor who failed to treat a pregnant woman for severe diabetes. The child was born retarded. If the young lawyer with the skeleton brought that kind of verdict home today, he'd have over $3 million and he wouldn't have to wheel the skeleton down Washington Street.*

As Marcus came up the escalator at the bank, there was a blinking red sign:

SARA LEE
INTERNATIONAL TAX CONFERENCE

> *He punched out his stocks on a computer at the bank. The last man had punched Fedders Corp. Maybe he should buy Fedders on a hunch. He punched K for Coke. Except K was Kellogg. He suddenly couldn't remember the Coke symbol and he didn't know how to look it up. He'd bought Coke at 28 and sold it for 35. Now it was 74. So much for his acumen at picking stocks. He'd have to rely on clients reaching into their underwear for cash. It was a strange way for a juris doctor to make a living, but it was better than having to attend the Sara Lee International Tax Conference.*

The next time he flew the kite was for no particular reason. It was a sunny winter day. People on Michigan Avenue were bundled up against the wind, but they felt the sun on their faces. There was a group of Peruvian pipers standing in the slush playing their fifes and hand drums on the square of the adjacent office building. Squat little men with bronze, ancient Indian faces of Incas, wearing heavy blue and white frayed woolen capes. The sound of their pipes fluttered above the people on the street. He should go down there and stand with them and fly his kite. He could wear the shawl of an ancient Jew and blend in perfectly, perhaps blow his shofar horn in syncopation with their hand drums. Everyone should have a personal hand drum to beat out the rhythms of his life, the inner rhythms. He opened the window and let the kite go, and it quickly filled with wind and the golden dragon unfolded and opened up into the currents. He tried to guide it over and above the Indian fifers, but it swept higher and soon was out of sight and had run to the end of the spool. He would have to get a new spool, a professional kite flyer's reel. He had trouble reeling the kite back, but this time he didn't cut himself and he let the dragon glide for a few moments on a short halter before he closed his window. He had six messages on his voice mail. The eye was flashing six times.

The next morning he deposited the $100 the man had taken out of his underwear. As Marcus crossed the Daley Plaza he met a lawyer friend who told him his partner had forgotten his keys to the office this morning and had bloodied his hand pounding on the door to get someone to let him in. "He's in a foul mood." "Tell him to calm down," Marcus said.

In front of the State's Attorney's office there was a man on the sidewalk holding a sign:

> THE MEMBERS OF LAW ENFORCEMENT
> IN THIS CITY ARE ALL CRIMINALS
>
> THE STATES ATTORNEY IS A CRIMINAL
>
> GRAVE INJUSTICES HAVE BEEN COMMITTED
> AGAINST MY FAMILY AND I
>
> THE STATES ATTORNEY AND HIS OFFICERS
> SHOULD BE INDICTED

Suddenly the man with the sign was gone. Marcus looked up and down the Daley Plaza, but the man was gone. In the newsstand box, a Spanish language newspaper with the headline, ¿BUSCA LA JUSTICIA? (Is this justice?) It was a story about a man now on his third trial accused of murdering a young girl. Twice his convictions and death sentence have been reversed. Do they have the right man? Marcus stared at the headline, the strange inverted question mark preceding it, and a single line: ¿BUSCA LA JUSTICIA?

This morning he has three calls on his voice mail and eighteen saved calls. He's too tired to erase the saved calls, he doesn't want to listen to them. Then he has a sudden burst of energy and erases all his saved calls, all eighteen. "Hello, Mr. Marcus, this is . . . . [erase] "Mr. Marcus, it's . . . . [erase] "Fred, I'm calling about . . . . [erase] He delights in doing this, erasing the calls with a burst of blipping, he erases all of them with his index finger, like a demonic one-note pianist, until his entire backlog is wiped clean and he's ready to face the day. Voice mail costs him $10 a month. He has to make some money today. He can't fool around. He's only taken in about $575 this week in checks. It's the third week of the month and his billing is just trickling in. Last week he had the clients who magically pulled cash out of their clothing, so he'd been taking it easy, listing to the Inca pipers and fooling around with the kite.

Today would have to be a serious money day. He only has $300 left in his checking account. He has a rule in running the office: he always pays his bills immediately, and never uses his savings to run the office. So today he needed to stop flying the kite and listening to the hand drums and pluck a $2,500 retainer from the four black women coming to see him about problems with their aunt's will. He felt anxious about the appointment. He felt the fine bones of his face. He suddenly saw himself as having the tiny facial bones of an anxious ferret. There was a manic beggar on Michigan Avenue who always kept a pet ferret in his cap and stroked it as he called for coins. If Marcus had become a trial lawyer, he would have made millions. Again today in the *Law Bulletin* another lawyer brought home two multi-million judgments in one day, one in a contractual dispute, a bench trial, the other in a legal malpractice case, both in one day. Two million in a day, and he, Marcus, was figuring how to hit on these poor black women for $2,500.

When he met them in the waiting room he could see two of the women were crippled; one had a walker and one had a cane. They greeted him with animation and laughter. Could he take money from these poor women? He should see them *pro bono*. Were they laughing at him? Maybe if he wore a black hat, a caftan and a hidden beeper on his waist like an elderly Hassid waiting for the coming of the Messiah, they wouldn't laugh at him. If he wore a beeper, he could be called back to Jerusalem through a tunnel under the oceans by Rebbe Schneerson, the ancient sage of the Hassidim. He would be introduced to God as a lawyer in his fortieth year of practice who finally did something *pro bono*. He hadn't taken a *pro bono* case since he was a kid lawyer volunteering in his neighborhood at a legal clinic.

The granddaughter, about twenty, was sweet-faced and bright. Her two aunties were both crippled, in their forties, one with a walker the other with a black cane. Her grandmother was a tired-faced woman exhausted by life and the strain of living in the city. They were all urban poor from the heart of the city, and the blonde receptionist in her stylish Irish tweed skirt and pink cashmere sweater looked disdainfully away from them as they walked down the corridor to Marcus's office. The woman with the walker was in pain and she could barely walk the short distance down the hall. The others went ahead.

When they were seated, she became the angriest, demanding that the three-flat left her and her sister by their aunt, their mother's older sister, be sold, that they couldn't afford to pay the expenses and taxes. She and her sister would each realize more than $20,000, but their mother who was living on the third floor would be out on the street at seventy-five with no place to live.

"That's wrong, Auntie," the young granddaughter said. "Absolutely wrong. Can't you both see that's wrong? Grandma's lived there for twenty years. You tell her, Mister Lawyer."

"First of all," Marcus said, "I'm not going to charge you for this conference. I want you to know that. I just want you to relax." He unconsciously felt a throbbing at his waist, as if his invisible beeper had just sounded.

They all looked at him without any change of expression. They would never trust a white man wearing a suit.

"I think your granddaughter is right. Why sell the building? It was left to you two daughters free and clear. All you have to do is fix it up. You'll each have an income for the rest of your life."

"The tenants aren't paying rent. This man in the back owes over twelve hundred dollars."

"Put a five-day notice on his door."

"We can't even get Mama to move downstairs." The daughter who could barely move her legs was still very angry. "We could rent her upstairs flat for six hundred dollars."

"Why should Grandma move? She's lived up there for twenty years," the granddaughter said again and pointed her finger at her two aunts.

"Can't you get someone else in the lower flat?" Marcus asked. "Someone your mother's own age who she could be friendly with. They could watch out for each other."

The crippled daughter was beginning to calm down. "I suppose we could put it on the board at church, get a church lady."

He realized that all they wanted was a mediator. They looked at him as if he were a judge. He could resolve this dispute and set this family straight for several generations.

Marcus stood up, like a judge.

The women looked at him and the room was quiet. No one spoke.

"Your mother stays in her flat." He folded his arms. "You don't have to go into probate. Probate would cost you twenty-five hundred dollars. You'd have to pay a lawyer to do that. You don't need a lawyer. With the money you're not going to spend, you could fix the flat. Just file your aunt's will. The filing costs nothing. She left you some insurance policies. She has no bills other than her funeral. She even left a policy for that. Pay her funeral and use the other money to fix up the three-flat. Evict the tenant in the back who isn't paying rent. I'll send you to a young lawyer for that. Rent out the other two flats and let your mother stay upstairs and live her life in dignity and peace."

The two daughters nodded, and the granddaughter smiled. She was a beautiful young woman whose energy and intelligence would save this family if they gave her something to work with, gave her a chance.

Marcus was experienced in courtroom procedure, and he knew the next step was to quickly get these ladies out of his office.

"That's it," he said, and pointed to the door.

"Thank you for your valuable time, Mister Lawyer. We appreciate it." The granddaughter shook his hand. The two daughters got up and hobbled out and the grandmother carried their coats. "Thank you, sir," she said as she passed him.

"What do you want to do with your life?" he asked the granddaughter as she said good-bye.

"I want to be a writer."

"You'll be a good writer. Have you ever read *King Lear,* the story of the mean daughters who wanted to put their father out of the castle?"

She laughed and so did the others. "You've got a good sense of humor, Mr. Marcus," the woman with the walker said and walked slowly by him, dragging her legs. "Thank you for your counsel."

That night he stayed down late and flew his dragon kite out the window and into the darkness of the city. People could get along, they could help each other. He had other ways to make $2,500. He felt good. The kite disappeared into the darkness and he could feel it straining on his fingers, but he couldn't see it. He thought of letting it go, cutting it loose. He turned off all the lights in the office and let the kite spool run out, and then he took his scissors and cut the string and sat alone in the darkness until it was time to leave and catch the 8:20. He would have to be careful, though. The streets were very dangerous at this time of night.

He took the Pedway, the tunnel under the streets of the downtown area. There was a black man standing far down along the wall in the Pedway and Marcus couldn't see what he was doing. Was the man just waiting for him? Did he have a gun or a knife? The two of them were all alone. There was no one else in the tunnel. Then Marcus heard music, and saw that the man was playing the flute, his head wrapped in a kerchief. The man was very good and had the flute hooked to two speakers. Marcus dropped a dollar in his case as he passed.

"Thanks, Doc," the man said, and Marcus headed down the long tunnel toward the train station with the notes of the flute following him.

Queen of the Voyage

I REMEMBER MRS. LEO WORMSER as a short woman, who in her late forties had already fallen into the heavy sadness of a dowager, as if her own girlhood dreams had come to a curd and the heaviness of all this sadness held so long within her had caused her body to come tumbling down upon itself. Like a candle melts, her once slim body had lost itself in layers of fat, all overlaid each upon the other, leaving as a remnant a short stub of a woman. But the eyes remained alive, shrewd and wild in the heavy lumpen face, and behind the mascara and the purple eye shadow the eyes still danced and glittered, as if a girl was alive and hiding. Mrs. Wormser's eyes would come particularly alive whenever her daughter Lois appeared, for while the girl Mrs. Wormser had been was now forever lost within her, she had in turn trapped Lois, and was molding and sculpting her into an expression of the mother's lost dreams and ambitions.

Still, Lois grew with a delicate beauty. In her adolescence, her face was pale and fragile with dark eyes and high cheekbones. She had a dark, tawny look and some ability as a dancer and an actress. On weekends, she would commute to Chicago for drama classes and during high-school summers she apprenticed in our own suburban summer theater. I often saw her, dressed in white pumps and a school blazer, shyly taking tickets at the booth or rushing on stage in the darkness between scenes to set props. Yet, she always seemed conscious of her movements, like her mother's hand lingered with her in the darkness of the theater, betrayed in the set of the daughter's shoulders and a slight, melancholy cant of her long neck.

And the mother provided a salon for her daughter's private performances, a huge, white brick house entered by a sweeping pebbled driveway. Soft beige carpets led from room to room and the walls were hung with contemporary etchings in tortoiseshell frames. The living room was furnished with low translucent plastic coffee tables, and there were stacks of lacquered tray tables alongside of two huge white divans filled with piles of designer pillows. I remember the room distinctly, for even as a youngster it struck me as unlike the living rooms in other houses. The living-room walls were paneled in pale oak, and bookcases were recessed into the walls. The bookcases glowed with hidden lights that were controlled by the same set of rheostats that directed the ceiling lights. I thought of the room as the one true salon of my childhood, but it was really a carefully contrived setting for Lois's weekend performances and all the Wormser kitsch.

The performances first became routine after high-school dances. Lois would return to the house with her friends and we would have Cokes in the living room. Then, with all of us seated in a circle on the living-room floor and a few adult friends of the family seated in chairs, the show would begin. Lois would rush upstairs, throw off her prom dress and change to a costume. She had a special closet for her costumes, kilts for Scots dances, minstrel suit, jester cap and bells, ballet skirts, a fringed Indian deerskin jacket, and different wigs. With her mother standing to one side as wardrobe mistress, she'd change and make up appropriately and soon would appear down at the foot of the stairs.

Mr. Wormser controlled the rheostats that dimmed the living-room lighting and at Lois's appearance the adults would rap on their cocktail glasses for the attention of the youngsters. Then the performance would begin. Perhaps it would be a reading in blackface, or soft shoe with tambourine. Perhaps a ballet in a pink tutu or an Irish jig in a peasant's dirndl. At the end of each performance, we would laugh and fake wild applause while Mr. and Mrs. Wormser exchanged serious little nods of approval with the adults. Then Lois would rush halfway back up the stairs, pale and intense, and then return for an encore to more exaggerated applause.

Lois's theater soon became a ritual. After her reading or a dance, Mr. Wormser would twirl the lights back up and a maid would wheel out a cart laden with sandwiches. We would rush to grab for corned beef, rye bread, thick sliced salami, chicken and mayonnaise, sweet pickles, black olives, cherry soda, Cokes, celery stalks filled with roquefort, and with paper plates heaped return to the circle on the living-room floor.

And so when I became Lois's friend, it really was as a member of her mother's salon. It must have been in the second year of high school, after a dance, that I first watched Lois from the circle on the living-room floor. It was a winter night with a fire blazing, casting her dancing shadow on the wall, while Lois was pirouetting and leaping in her stocking feet. I remember lying on the floor, head propped in my hands, and peering down through the film of her crinoline petticoats into the long smooth ivory tunnel of her legs.

During the summer following our second year in high school, the Wormsers rented a farm out in a horsey, Gentile western suburb where no Jews had yet dared venture. I drove out there one Saturday afternoon in my father's new Pontiac, a sleek gray car, with red wheels and white walls, the car polished and shining as I entered the long driveway. There was a replica of an old windmill that served as a gatehouse at the entrance to the drive, heavy shingled, with dormer windows for servants' quarters cut into the roof. The farm was named "Olde Tower Farm," but the windmill tower was long abandoned, the servants having private rooms in the house. The Wormsers had only taken the place for the summer. I did notice a big new maroon Buick station wagon in the drive. On the rear wooden panel, just below the rear window, there was written in a gold-lettered scroll in large flowing letters, "Olde Tower Farm."

The summer home was a long, one-story ranch house with a screened porch at the back that looked over a valley and a large lake where there was a smaller set of old wooden buildings, including another smaller windmill, a replica of the gatehouse. I remember being led by a servant through the living room back to the porch where Mrs. Wormser was sitting. She was dressed in riding clothes, heavy men's boots, a lavender western shirt open at the collar, a thin bandana tied cowgirl style around her neck. Lois was riding a palomino mare out in the meadow down near the millpond. Mrs. Wormser was watching her through the picture window of the porch. I remember she didn't acknowledge me, so I just stood and watched Lois through the porch window. The palomino's tail was flying in the wind and Lois rode expertly, without a saddle, dressed in jeans and barefoot, riding with abandon, far out in the distance, and then making a circle around the pond and clattering back across the little wooden bridge. She gathered the big horse in until the mare began prancing and suddenly they were off in a jump over the bushes and up into the backyard. Then she saw me watching through the window and waved. Mrs. Wormser still didn't speak to me and sat on the porch couch, hidden in the shadows. It was as if the daughter had been set free for a moment and was out of the mother's control. Lois was riding wildly, digging her heels into the mare's flanks, and when they jumped the bushes, the mother scowled. I quietly opened the porch door and left her.

Lois held her hand out to me and I pulled myself up onto the mare and, holding Lois's waist, we galloped out into the fields far beyond the house. There, we spent the rest of the afternoon talking and laughing. We'd become good friends, real confidants, we knew each other well enough to share each other's childhood secrets. She told me of her longing to become an actress. She said her mother was opposing her and while Lois was permitted to continue with drama classes, that summer she wouldn't be allowed to work in the summer theater group. Her mother had forbidden it. Instead, the family was leaving for California in a few weeks at the end of the summer. The servants would close the farm. Lois was reluctant to talk about the purpose of their California trip. Instead, she made a garland of field daisies that she gave to me. She made me promise not to ask her again about California, and she seemed distant and touched with sadness. But her mood soon passed and she began to teach me how to make the necklaces. We wove the flowers until late in the afternoon. When we rode back to the house, we were garlanded with each other's necklaces and headbands. Then Lois saw me to my car, reached out and lightly touched my face, and ran back into the house.

A few weeks later, I tried to phone her, but a maid answered and said that the family had left for California. I saw her at the high school two weeks later. Her legs were in casts, from her hips to her ankles, and she was walking with a cane. The new family station wagon was parked at a side door, and the chauffeur was rushing up the walk to assist her. I asked her what happened . . . had she fallen from her horse? She told me about the trip to California. Her mother had always felt that Lois was pigeon-toed. As a little girl she'd worn braces for the condition, but the braces hadn't helped. So, this year, Mrs. Wormser had learned of a doctor in California who would do corrective surgery. At the end of the summer, the family had flown out to the coast for an operation to straighten her feet. She hoped to be out of the casts by November. I watched her hobble to the car. The chauffeur carefully tucked a lap robe all around her and she turned toward me with an awkward twist of her body, a shadow seen through the car window, her face expressionless and grave.

I really didn't see Lois often again that year. I was busy with sports and the school paper. She was still in the Drama Club, but the private performances at the Wormser home had ended. We were in different crowds. Her friends were wealthy girls whose lives centered around social activities planned by their parents. They were still active in our high-school affairs, but they were also flying to New York with their mothers for quick little visits to eastern schools and shopping trips along Fifth Avenue and into Boston and Philadelphia. Then they'd fly back for our senior prom or other class activity.

I do remember spending an hour or so with her at our class graduation party at someone's farm just at the edge of one of the suburbs. It was an estate, much like the one the family had rented. The farm reminded Lois of the afternoon we spent together and we talked about that, and then we walked out to the barn and sat up in the hayloft and talked about college. She wanted very much to go to Northwestern, where they had an excellent drama department, or to Pasadena Playhouse. Her parents were against it. They wanted an eastern school for her. Her grades weren't good enough for Vassar so she considered Goucher, Pembroke or perhaps Sarah Lawrence. She talked mostly about her ambition to be an actress, her eyes were bright and she was more animated than I had ever seen her. I watched her face. The long black hair was now cut short in bangs across her forehead. Even at this age, her youthful softness was beginning to drain away, leaving her with a pallid, sculpted look that hardened her features. She smoked incessantly and had developed a deep, phlegmy cough that she used to accentuate her statements but that would give way to paroxysms of uncontrolled hacking when she laughed. This summer she was leaving for Europe. The family, including her little brother, was making a tour—Germany, France, Italy and England—back and forth on one of the French lines. First though, she was stopping off in New York with her mother. They were to shop for the trip and Lois was going to have a little mole snipped away from her right cheek. She laughed and bent over to show me a tiny brown mole along the top of her cheek line. Her mother had decreed that it should come off. It was really no more than a beauty spot.

Later that graduation summer, before Lois left for Europe, I saw her again one evening at a beach party. A few of us had taken some beer down to the lake and built a bonfire. She drove down on the sand in the new convertible her parents had given her as a graduation present. There were five or six girls in the car, some sitting up on the ledge of the back seat. They'd all been drinking beer and the radio was blaring as they swiveled the spotlight, searching for the party and shouting as they came running through the sand into the circle of couples sitting by the fire. The party turned out to be our last reunion. From that point on in our young lives we went separate ways. Still, I remember the laughter and the wild shrieking of the girls as they came running down the sand with Lois in the lead, barefoot and running splay-footed, dressed in jeans and a loose sweater. She jumped down in the middle of us, thudding on her knees into the sand. I remember later she disappeared, walking alone down the long strand of shoreline. When she returned she was very quiet and sat far from the fire and drank a beer by herself while we were singing.

We sang all our old high-school songs, and soon Lois joined us and sang along with the group. Then suddenly she stood and while one of her girlfriends played the guitar, Lois began to dance. It was a lonely dance, sad and graceful, in and out of the shadows of the fire. She moved slowly and languidly, kissing each of the boys as she passed, almost as if she knew she was saying good-bye. I remember the dance as her last performance and perhaps the only one that touched me in any way because of its spontaneity and simplicity. I also remember the damp press of her lips on my cheek. I had grown up with Lois's performances. They were part of my adolescence. This was the last time I was to see her as a girl, ambitious and uncertain, but dancing by the fire in a sad and graceful farewell. She was our class actress and dancer, and we were as certain that she would be famous as we were certain of our own successes.

After that night on the beach, I heard from her only one more time. That summer she sent me a postcard from the Liberté, en route. She had been voted Queen of the Voyage she wrote in her round looping handwriting, the captain had held a gala in her honor, with a menu that named the dessert after her.

On the Beach– Sur le Plage

S YLVAN KALISHER AND THE KALISHER FAMILY have come to the beach in Door County, Wisconsin; Sylvan and the family are staying in Ephraim, a tiny bay town with cottages in the hills high over the inlet. Door County is a peninsula in the northeast corner of Wisconsin, a resort area similar to Cape Cod. This afternoon the Kalisher family has decided to swim at a pristine beach they've found deep in a forest on the banks of Lake Michigan. Sylvan has brought his book on Dylan Thomas by Andrew Sinclair in his straw picnic basket, along with a denim captain's hat for the sun, a tube of Sea and Ski, four cans of Coke, a long-sleeved Yves St. Laurent silk shirt and his binoculars. Baby Kalisher, Sylvan's wife, has brought a thick book from the Winnetka library, a biography of Dorothy Thompson, her radio, some diet cola cans and towels for the family.

After they spread the towels, Baby asks Sylvan to rub some of the Sea and Ski on her back. This annoys Sylvan because his hands will get sticky, but he does it anyway. "Do it up and then around in circles," she says. "I don't want to get a bad burn." He also reaches around and rubs the tops of her thighs which feel smooth as alabaster. The excess lotion he puts on the ribs of his eye sockets and the bridge of his nose.

Sylvan lies back on his towel but before he stretches out he shields his face with his hand and searches the water for the children, Joel, six, and Katy, nine. At first the sun off the water is so bright, he can't see them, and then he picks them out of several heads bobbing. He thinks he sees them. They each have a beach ball and it looks like two heads bobbing for each child. "Do you see them?" he asks Baby. She puts the Thompson book down on her stomach and peers out over the water. Three little girls are standing on a rock and are taking turns pushing each other off into the water. "I see beach balls," Baby says. "And there, I think I see two heads."

"That must be them," Sylvan says.

"Don't worry about them, Syl . . . they're all right. They both swim like fish."

Sylvan begins to read his Dylan Thomas book. Sylvan is a psychiatrist in Chicago and a serious amateur poet. This year he's going to be published by a poetry journal in Wilmette. One of his patients is the editor, a beautiful divorced mother of three who unfortunately is suicidal and recently has been hospitalized for two months. So Sylvan's poem, "Genesis III," a haiku about the creation of man, has been on "hold" awaiting the recovery of the editor. Sylvan thinks about his poem and then he remembers asking the A&W drive-in waitress in Two Rivers on the way up yesterday where the order was. "It's on hold," she said. Everything's on hold, Sylvan thinks, even root beer. Root beer is on hold, Sylvan's poem "Genesis III" is on hold. Dylan Thomas isn't on hold. He's dead. You can't be on hold when you're no longer holding. He shields his eyes again and looks out at the water for the children. They are still bobbing. There's a gull feather in the sand beside him and he uses the feather to brush the grains of sand off Thomas's fat face, a photo of the young Thomas in Swansea.

"Cwmdonkin Park, Cwmdonkin Park," Sylvan would like to go to Swansea and walk around Cwmdonkin Park where the young Thomas played his games. He turns the page to a picture of Thomas's wife, Caitlin, and using the feather again brushes the sand grains off her face. She looks like a wild, beautiful, young Celtic bride. Sylvan would like to go to Laugharne and search for the boathouse where Dylan and Caitlin lived. Maybe Caitlin would still be there and he could introduce himself. He would like to touch the gold of the young Caitlin Macnamara's hair. He extends his fingers and notices the gray hairs on his knuckles. He begins to dream about Caitlin as the sun boils into him and her face transposes into the face of a waitress that served him last night, Swedish meatballs, limpa bread with lingonberries and fruit soup. She was blonde and bucolic with cherub cheeks puffed like a fish that swells to repel its enemies. What is the name of that fish? Sylvan's mind is slowly melting in the heat. The puffin fish? The grunt? The gub gub fish? He can't remember. She served the fruit soup and Sylvan watched her slim wrists, tanned and strong. He likes lean-wristed, thin-fingered Scandinavian women. With his eyes closed, he begins making a list of the waitresses he's seen. First the puffin fish with the fruit soup. When he left he saw her in her softball jersey outside the restaurant getting on a motorcycle with her boyfriend. Then the tall slim girl with the straight black hair at the ferry landing at Gills Rock. She looked part Indian, part Jewish, and wore a thin gold chain with a white star. "Rock Island was really neat," she said. "You should go there. It's really good." Really good, really bad, really cool. So what, Sylvan mutters to himself and snaps the Thomas book shut. He reaches over in the sand and sits up. Baby Kalisher still has her back to the sun. He drops a towel over her back and she moves her shoulders. "Don't, Syl. Why don't you take a walk?"

He gets up and heads down the beach where the children are playing. They've come in from the water and they're building something on the sand. As he walks toward them he thinks of the way the sterns of the boats flashed past him yesterday as he took the family sailing. Fantasy I, Ramona—Chicago, a huge old schooner, Pelican—Sturgeon Bay, U.S.A., Alice, Mary-Anne-Milwaukee, Love's Labor, Betty I, Elsbeth—lists of women's names on the sterns, white and black hulls tied to buoys and bobbing in the sun. Sylvan held the tiller and headed the family out to sea. From a mile out the sterns were just flashes of color, the names dissolved, just the sound of the wind in the sails. Maybe that was it, you needed distance to make the names dissolve. If Sylvan could have distance, he would stop the list making.

He reaches the children and asks Joel what he's building in the sand. "I don't know Dad. A tomb, maybe." Joel has found a discarded toy, a small plastic dinosaur, and he's burying it. Sylvan touches the little boy's head. He keeps walking. He tries to remember another waitress. In their white uniforms they all look like nurses. There was that seventeen-year-old in Ephraim with the cute incisor teeth and a pigeon-toed deferential manner. She handed Sylvan a Milky Way and he watched the sun glisten on the hairs of her arm. Sylvan sees some lettering in the sand, someone has troweled letters with a stick. He begins reading S A R A H, the first name. P E T, the last letters are smudged, E R S O N. Sarah Peterson. There's another name, R A C H E L T H O M A S. Funny names, Sarah Peterson and Rachel Thomas. He bends over and picks up a piece of light blue glass and he carries it in the palm of his hand. Then he notices another toy dinosaur abandoned in the sand. He picks it up. It's gray plastic with a high serrated fin and a single red eye. He trudges back to where Joel and Katrinka are patting the sand tomb and gives the piece of blue glass and the second dinosaur to Joel, "Here," Sylvan says, "you can make another for this and put this jewel on it."

"Dad, I've already got one buried," the little boy says with annoyance.

"Where?"

"Right here." He begins digging but Sylvan sees nothing.

Sylvan thought another dinosaur with a single red eye would be a unique find, but the kid is too fast for him. Joel digs furiously to show his father but only comes up with a rut filled with roiled water. Apparently the first dinosaur has already been sucked under into the lake. Joel shrugs and drops Sylvan's toy into the rut and fills it with sand. Then he puts the glass jewel on the mound and smiles at Sylvan. Sylvan nods and notices that another man sitting with his family along the beach has a kite. Sylvan squints up at the single kite. It looks like a Mondrian triangle. A kite is a very simple celebration, an easy way to reach up and out into the universe. Not out, he corrects himself, just up. He smiles at this little adjustment.

Sylvan rubs Joel's head and walks further down the beach. His sandals slap as he walks along the sand. There's a surfboard with a single sail emblazoned with the design of a Kool cigarette package. An old man is lying on his stomach and paddling the surfboard with his hands. He must have won it as a premium. Sylvan wonders about the names Sarah Peterson and Rachel Thomas. The name Thomas etched into the sand could be some kind of a sign. He struggles for the name of Dylan and Caitlin's daughter, some strange name, what is it? Rachel? No, Aeronwy. He remembers the daughter came to read at Northwestern a few years ago. He'd gone down to the reading but he couldn't find her. He'd wandered around and finally found the chapel where she was supposed to be reading. He opened the heavy ornate wooden door, hoping to see Aeronwy alone at the lectern and instead, he was alone. Sylvan glances at the kite weaving and surging above him in the wind. He never found Aeronwy. He just sat for a moment alone in the chapel and watched the light and shadows moving across the huge stained-glass front window. He wonders who Rachel Thomas is; he would have liked her to have been Dylan and Caitlin's daughter.

He would have taken her over to the dinosaur burial mound and introduced her to Joel and Katy and Baby would have asked her for dinner.

Later, back at their cottage, Sylvan and Baby sit outside and have a glass of wine. Two nights ago, they'd been at the Joffrey Ballet at Ravinia and Sylvan had muttered "Merde" to a woman in front of him with a big frizzed crown of hair. Sylvan found it impossible to see the stage over her hair. He politely tapped her on the shoulder, pointed to the top of her head and asked her to slump down. When she refused, he muttered "Merde" in her ear. The woman just shrugged. Baby is now chiding Sylvan for having been so rude.

"I think she might have reported you."

"So?"

"So you shouldn't be muttering 'Merde' at the ballet. Why are you so hostile lately?"

"You call that hostility?"

"Okay, why are you so morose?"

He rubs his neck. "I asked the woman politely to slump. She wouldn't."

"So you dumped on her," Baby says.

Sylvan begins making his lists again. This time lists of dinosaur names, Stegosaurus, Brontosaurus, Tyrannosaurus. Joel used to recite dinosaur names in a baby lisp before he went to bed. "Stegosaurus, Brontosaurus," Sylvan smiles. He shades his face, sips his wine and looks down the hill past the church spire. He can see far out into Green Bay and watches a regatta of small sailboats on the water. There's hardly any wind so they're flying spinnakers. He focuses the binoculars on them and the spinnakers come in like bursts of red and yellow flowers.

Sylvan puts his binoculars down. One of the orifices is wet and he rubs it with his hand. Suddenly he realizes that he's been crying. There are tears moving down his cheeks. He removes a tear with the tip of his index finger.

Baby peers at him over her sunglasses. "Are you crying?"

"No, my eyes are watering from the binoculars. I think I have an allergy."

"Maybe you're just beginning to relax a little." She's reading a paperback by Willa Cather. "You know, Capote and Cather were friends. She lived in Manhattan and he met her when he was a young writer. You're just tired, Sylvan. Why don't you get into a good book. What did you do with your Thomas book?"

"Roman women used to save their tears," Sylvan tells her. "They collected them in tear vials. Little eye-cups, only slender and fluted." He rubs his eyes.

"You know, Cather is really good," Baby says. "I can understand why Capote likes her. Do you want a Kleenex?"

"I read your book last night in the bathroom," Sylvan says. "The boy stuns a woodpecker with a stone from a slingshot and cuts out its eyes with his penknife. Then he sets the bird free in the forest."

"That was awful. But also beautiful."

"I feel like that bird."

"You're just overworked, Syl. You should stop taking night appointments."

"The Romans believed that tears were really the essence of their souls." Sylvan feels another tear on his face at the rim below his eyes. He touches it to his finger. "Sometimes they'd give their tears to a lover to drink. I have a patient that collects her tears. She brought them for me to drink. I have the vial in the office. That's how I learned about tear vials."

"She's very sick."

"She's sick. She has scars on her wrists and she picks them open when she's upset."

Sylvan raises his binoculars again and looks out at the spinnakers. There's a black kitten stalking a tiny white butterfly on the lawn in front of them. He watches the sailboats and then the kitten stalks the butterfly. The butterfly flutters away and in mid-flight another butterfly joins it and they alight on a bush and begin mating. The cottage owner's wife comes down the path from behind the cottages. She sees the kitten and picks it up. She's been cleaning and changing linen. She's a young woman, about twenty-eight, a tall pretty blonde in a white T-shirt and white shorts. Sylvan watches her bend. Suddenly she reminds Sylvan of a photograph he remembers of the young Eva Braun at Berchtesgaden holding a kitten. He watches her pick up the cat and he feels a tightening within himself. She drops the kitten over a hedge and smiles at them.

He excuses himself from Baby and gets up and begins to walk

slowly down the hill in front of the cottage. Maybe he'll do some bass fishing at the pier in Ephraim and feel better. He'll get a carton of worms at the Standard station. He feels the high grass bristling against his legs as he walks and the pebbles on the path down the hill are hot through his sandals. As he reaches the stairs, he sees the road down below him leading to the town and the harbor. There's a church at the curve of the road below the stairs with a black placard in the entrance advertising a sermon on Sunday by a minister from Minneapolis. It's a typical white frame country church with a wooden spire. He remembers that it has an apricot tree in the courtyard and last year he and the children had gathered apricots on the ground.

He walks down into the churchyard with his fishing pole before him like a long plastic wand and carefully opens the gate. There's fruit on the ground again this year. He takes an apricot. It's warm and delicious. He tastes several pieces of fruit and finds another good one. Then he sees the black kitten in front of him rolling apricots with its paws underneath a huge sunflower. Sylvan doesn't like black cats, not even kittens. Sylvan takes his fishing knife out, cuts the leader off his line and measures out a piece. He has the notion of catching the kitten by using the fishing line as a noose and then carrying the kitten back to the young woman. A monarch butterfly has come to the apricot-studded courtyard and has landed near the kitten. The kitten begins to quietly stalk the butterfly. Sylvan stalks the kitten. He makes a slipknot with his line and carefully places the noose over the kitten's neck. He gently pulls the kitten away from the butterfly. It resists. Sylvan pulls harder but the kitten insists on remaining with the butterfly. Sylvan, for his own reasons, insists that the kitten leave the butterfly and he pulls harder and then with his hands around the kitten's throat he stops the progress of the kitten. The fur is soft and silken, perhaps like Caitlin Macnamara's hair, he doesn't know. Another tear is coming. He wished he had a vial, his own personal vial. His hands tighten on the kitten's neck and then he feels a soft bone snap and the kitten stops struggling. It had tried to claw Sylvan as a last gesture and he wouldn't permit it. He then hangs the kitten from a limb of the apricot tree with the fishing-line noose. He gathers a few more pieces of fruit for his pockets and walks away down toward the dock. From the last set of stairs you can't even see the kitten hanging through the cover of the branches.

My Lights

"Nurse, where am I?"
"Where are you, sir?"
"Nurse, tell me where I am."
"You are in the hospital, sir, in the intensive-care section. You have had a heart attack."
"Am I dying, nurse?"
"No sir, but you have had a severe attack, you must be quiet and rest."
"But am I dying?"
"You are not dying, sir."
"Good."
"Now, just lie back and rest, sir."
"What are all these wires attached to me?"
"For the machine, sir. We're monitoring your reactions on a machine; you can't see it, there's a console above you with lights like a switchboard. The lights monitor your vital functions."

　　　　　o o o o o
　　　　　o o o o o
　　　　　o o o o o

"And if the lights go out?"
"Then you *will* be dead, sir."
"Okay . . . . . I get it . . . . sort of . . ."

―――――――

"Nurse?"

"Sir."

"What put me in here?"

"It's the tensions, sir, and all the women."

"Women?"

"They say you had your way with the women."

"Oh, of course, the women."

"And that created certain anxieties and tensions which . . . . ."

"Brought about my heart attack."

"Exactly, sir."

"But the lights, nurse, will they—aah—stay lit?"

"O I think they will, sir. Particularly if you can dispel from your mind . . . ."

"The tensions."

"Exactly, sir."

"The lights are lovely, nurse. They are *my* lights, you know."

"Yes, they are."

And if they go out. It will be *my* going out. And if I may say so, nurse, each light I believe is burning brightly. Aren't they? I believe so. Won't you take a peek and tell me if they're bright?"

o o o o o o
o o o o o o
o o o o o o

"Very bright."

"Good. Now shall I name the lights for you, nurse? May I call them by name? Barbara, Elsbeth, Gina, Linda, Laurie, Mary . . . . . Are you Catholic, nurse? Do you mind my calling one Mary? This is a Catholic hospital, is it not? And you must be a nun, are you not?"

"Yes, sir."

"Well then, with your permission. Then again Mary, Carol, Susan, Trina . . . . . Oh, but nurse, I could go on and on quite nimbly. Take a quick look again—are all still burning bright?"

o o o o o o
o o o o
o o o o o

"I'm sorry, sir, but some are flickering."
"Should I be afraid, nurse?"
"Don't be afraid, sir. God is with you."
"Is he really?"
"Yes."
"All right, Sister. I believe you. They must be flickering from the tension. And you're right. I do remember certain women who have brought about these tensions and cause my lights to flicker . . . . But I have my memories."
"O, I bet you do, sir."
"To sustain me."
"You will have to call upon them now, sir."
"In this rather delicate moment."
"Yes, sir. You must gather strength to face the storm."
"Take another look, nurse. Glance at the lights."

o o o o o o
o o o o
o o o

"Some have flickered to extinction, sir."
"They have gone out, you mean?"
"They have expired, in a manner of speaking."
"How many?"
"Five of them, sir."
"O, God, Sister."
"He is with you, sir."

"Sir, now you shall have to call upon your inner strength."
"O, I will try, nurse."
"To sustain you in your hour."
"I am trying."
"Find solace, sir, from your resources."
"I am trying to remember. Let's see. Now there was Barbara . . . . did I mention her? A rather fat-faced, sullen girl with silken thighs. Do

you mind, Sister, if I go on about her thighs? I think it was Barbara. Yes, I believe so . . . . heavy about the thighs. Or was that Susan?"

"Susan, sir?"

"Yes, Susan. On a picnic we were. In some forest where the trees were bent and hung with moss. It must have been in the South. Some bayou by a river . . . . . I remember now, Susan settling on the blanket. I see her sad eyes. I believe it was Susan. Or was it Carol, nurse? Anyway, she soon left me for a bright lad, full of promise. He took her with my palm print full on her thigh. Forevermore. But none the worse was she. And of course, I have the memory. Which I call upon now to sustain me. Although it is murky. Very murky. Take a peek, nurse. Are my lights strong and steady?"

"I will look, sir."

o o o o o o
o o
o

"And? . . . . ."

"More have flickered to surcease."

"Surcease, nurse?"

"Several more are in repose, sir."

"O, Sister."

"Try harder, sir. You must try harder. Surely you can."

"Will recall of hand-holding in Venice help, Sister?"

"If it helps you, sir."

"To light my lights."

"Yes, you must try to keep them lit."

"Well, there was hand-holding in Venice. Strolling along the canals. A moonlit night. The water lapping. The gondoliers hawking to each other."

"O, lovely, sir."

"I believe that was, Tina, nurse. I can't be sure. Or perhaps, Carlotta. I seem feverish. Just a touch nurse. Perhaps, some water."

"Here sir."

"O, thank you. Now then . . . . will a carriage ride in the Bois de Boulogne assist me in any way? I believe I can summon up a carriage ride or two. The horse clopping . . . . and the carriage creaking and rolling. Frolicking together we were in the back there, you know. The scent of spring in the night air. Jeannine was her name. A French girl with round fresh cheeks. I remember she tousled my hair just as she ran. 'Bon soir,' she whispered, and then she tousled me and ran. I think that was Jeannine. I am trying hard, nurse. I *am* trying. I know I must."

"O, rest a bit, sir. Sip some water."

"Thank you, nurse. A sip and perhaps a cloth, a damp one clapped upon my brow."

"Here, sir, a damp cloth."

"Will evading the house detective at the Plaza sustain me now? Silly fellow he was, dressed in a top hat and britches. We walked right past him. Like husband and wife. I remember later the way the city lights came through the window. Silver on the sheets. We rollicked in that bed—two days and nights. Ate the topiary of apples for sustenance in between frolics. That I believe was Suki. I believe it was Suki . . . . there . . . at the Plaza. Or . . . . . Janice. I can't be sure. My mouth seems so dry. Must I keep on talking like this? I mean, after all, they are *my* lights, are they not? They are bright, aren't they, Sister?"

o

o

"Rather bright, sir."

"Sister, is this how death comes?"

"Sir?"

"In little, feeble sputterings and adjustments? My lights fading one by one. My mouth grown parch. I thought death a great presence, a wild clanging. In these feeble spurts must I decline? I feel a chill, nothing more. A certain vacuity passing over me, my eyes growing hollow and my lungs rumbling."

"Death, sir, is a sacrament. It comes as a blessing from the Lord."
"My lights grow dim."
"Rather dim, sir. There is but one left."

o

"Just one, Sister?"
"Only one, sir. I shall pray for you."
"No one comes for me? Is anyone in the waiting room?"
"No one, sir."
"Then I am alone."
"Yes, sir."
"Except for the Lord?"
"He is with you, sir, if you give yourself to him."
"Shall I ask him to forgive my sins?"
"You should sir. You really should."
"Then take my hand, Sister."
"Here, sir."
"Thank you, Sister."
"Now pray with me, sir."
"You have a nice hand, Sister."
"O, sir."
"No, seriously, the hand of a young girl."
"Sir."
"Your touch, Sister . . . . it reminds me of my first love. She comes to me now through your touch, full of innocence and loveliness."
"Sir, that's very kind."
"Are you sure there's no one in the waiting room, Sister? I have such a prescience."
"No one, sir."
"And my one light . . . . it's still lit?"

o

"It is, sir, but it's flickering."
"Then I shall give myself to you, Sister, and you will take me to your Lord."
"We must pray together, sir."

"Pray, Sister, please pray. Pray for the repose of my soul. May I kiss your hand while you pray?"

"O, sir, that tickles."

"Don't let my kisses interfere with your phrasing. The prayers must be correct and properly parsed."

"O, sir, your lips feel like a butterfly dancing on my knuckles."

"I'm glad, Sister, for your feelings. But my strength is waning. I feel a great chill, an iciness coming into me, my eyelids growing heavy. I am sinking fast, Sister. Sinking. Would you kiss me on the cheek, Sister? Hold me . . . hold your face next to mine."

"Like this sir?"

"Yes, Sister. There. Now I feel the warmth of you. You do remind me of my first love. The fragrance comes to me again, a light essence of flowers, skin fresh and touched with dampness . . . . Are you crying, Sister?"

"O, sir. You say such lovely things to me. You make me seem so beautiful . . . . . and I am really quite plain."

"You are beautiful, Sister . . . . What is your name?"

"Sister, sir."

"Only, Sister?"

"Yes, sir. And your name, sir. What is your name?

"Sir.

"Sir, your name. What is your name?

"Sir?

"Sir?

"O, please sir. Tell me your name.

"Sir?

"O, dear Lord. He is dead."

"Sister."

"Yes, Doctor."

"Sister, his lights have transpired, you say?"

"Yes, Doctor, his lights are extinct."

"Then wheel him away, Sister. His family must be waiting."

"He is alone, Doctor. No family. A bachelor, I believe."

"O, a bachelor. Well then, truss him up, pull the sheet over him and wheel him over into the corner and ring for the morgue. They'll be up shortly."

"Yes, Doctor."

"And, Sister."

"Yes, Doctor?"

"What was his occupation? For the insurance card."

"O, yes."

"Sister?"

"Well, Doctor, I can't really say. I'm told that he was a professional man."

"What profession?"

"I don't know, Doctor. He only said that he had a great love for women and he was haunted by the memory of them."

"And the cause of death, Sister?"

"Anxiety, Doctor. Brought about by certain memories."

"All right, Sister. Now then, pull the sheet over him and wheel him away."

"Yes, Doctor."

"Over there in the corner."

"Yes Doctor. But first may I say my own good-bye to him? There. Let me kiss you on the lips, sir. Good-bye, sir. Please be in peace, and if you can, remember me, *Beatrice*. Beatrice, from Intensive Care. We counted down your lights together and you kissed me lightly on the knuckles and asked my name."

Henry and Gitta

I HAVE RECENTLY MET A MAN named Henry who is a Pole, a man about sixty-five. I met him in a little restaurant in Chicago at a place where people share tables occasionally over lunch. I have grown to know him better during the past few weeks and have learned that he works as a structural engineer for a large architectural firm. He's called at my law office and we've lunched together a few times. At our last meeting in a German restaurant on State Street, he began to talk about Poland in 1939, at the outbreak of the war. I remember, I was a ten-year-old in Milwaukee and I had read in the Milwaukee newspapers of how the Polish cavalry men had bravely charged the German tanks with their swords drawn.

Apparently Henry is still haunted by dreams of that German invasion. He told me he occasionally still dreams of dead horses. They were everywhere, in the roads, on their backs, upside down, feet stiffened in the air. He still dreams of these grotesque upside-down horses. He had a motorcycle. His brother-in-law rode on the rear. A very strong, well-built British motorcycle. German bombers were always overhead. He and the brother-in-law left Warsaw on the motorcycle and rode to Oswiecim in the south of Poland where Henry knew two sisters, two beautiful blonde girls who would help him. Only when Henry and the brother-in-law arrived, they found the sisters' home destroyed, the two girls dead in the rubble from the German bombing. Ultimately Henry and the brother-in-law escaped to Romania and Henry sold his motorcycle and made his way through Yugoslavia and Italy into France where he joined a Polish unit of the French army and later was wounded defending the Maginot line.

At this point during our luncheon discussion we each had to

return to work, so I left Henry in the year 1940, and I have not really had a chance to talk to him since. He did bring me a copy of J. Bronowski's *The Ascent of Man*. He left it with our receptionist with a note: "Perhaps you will be interested in this. H."

But the name of the town where the two sisters had lived, Oswiecim? "Auschwitz," he had said. "Don't you know Auschwitz?"

Then the following day he brought me the Bronowski monograph with the note. It's really a rather technical article. He brought me photostats of pages 353–75, a section of *The Ascent of Man* with the title "Knowledge or Certainty." Bronowski argues that pure science applied without human concern leads to fascism in which Auschwitz arises as the ultimate cathedral. Science applied with humanism is quite another thing and assists man to ascend spiritually as opposed to destroying himself. Apparently Bronowski's view is that war is only a technical achievement of man and can be controlled. He gives the example of the scientist Leo Szilard pleading with Roosevelt to demonstrate the atom bomb before an international audience, including the Japanese, before permitting it to be used in warfare.

Henry told me he was twenty-six and a civilian engineer in September 1939 when the Germans came across the Polish border. He had been an engineering student at a technical university in Silesia and after graduation was employed in a town in southern Poland in charge of the waterworks. He has a very precise manner when he speaks, an old-world courtliness, rather professional, and a thick accent. He looks like he might have been a very handsome young man. His hair is neatly brushed, iron gray and slicked back, and he has always worn the same black suit and vest with a gold watch chain. There is one tooth missing at the side of his mouth so he keeps his lips drawn tightly over his teeth when he smiles.

"Did you know any Jews in 1939?" I asked him at our last lunch.

"No, just a few. There were not Jews where I was working."

"What was their situation?"

"This one family I knew. They were very well prepared. They had many flags hidden. I remember, a German flag, a Russian flag, a Polish flag. Depending on what the outcome was they would drape the proper flag over their window. And of course there were very few Jews in the armed forces."

"But you were not in the army when the Germans attacked."

"No, I mean later. When I was with the Polish Army in France, very few Jews. Jews you know are not militaristic." He drank more of his tea and his voice became a bit stronger. "You know when the Jews first came to Poland? It was at the time of the Spanish Inquisition and they were welcomed by the Polish king, Casimir the Great, and were given status. They were knighted. They were treated with respect and honor as men of conscience and scholars. But they were not fighting men, horsemen, soldiers. They were merchants."

"What do you think of this Nazi march in Skokie?" I said to him. "What would you do?"

"I would fight it." He looked at me and I could see sweat on his forehead from the tea. "I would definitely fight it. You who are a writer. You should tell the Jews to make a stand. To show these people that such an intrusion will never be tolerated. You know, the Jews do not like to fight. They know that, the Nazis."

"I can't agree with you about Jews not fighting. Jews can be very tough."

"I do not deny that. I said Jews don't like to fight. They are not by nature a militaristic people. Now Begin and Dayan, they are fighters. But they were Poles. How do you think they came to Palestine? They were soldiers in the Polish Army. They came there with a Polish unit. I remember, I had already been wounded and I was in London when they bombed that hotel. What was that?"

"The King David Hotel in Jerusalem."

"Right. You think we did not know they were going to do that? Where do you think they got the explosives? They were with a Polish unit. And here we were in London and that hotel was British headquarters. Begin and Dayan, they blew it up and we kept our mouths shut." He looked around at the people sitting near us and then at me and nodded, took his handkerchief out and daubed his forehead.

"Did you ever see any Jews wearing the yellow star on their clothing?" I asked him.

"No, I never saw such a yellow star. The star the Jews wore in Poland was blue and white, the colors of Zion."

I have not seen Henry since that lunch although he did drop off the Bronowski article with my receptionist. I would like to see him again and talk more. I think he brought the article because he sensed that I wasn't responsive to his description of the Jewish situation in pre-war Poland, and being an engineer he wanted to fill out his remarks with the assistance of Bronowski. But Bronowski writes about microwaves and X-rays. I don't really understand. He suggests there is no certainty in science, only a limited certainty. At the end of the article there is a photo of Bronowski standing at the Auschwitz pond. He's squatting and sifting water through his fingers. The subcaption says that the ashes of three million Jews were dumped here.

The Spertus Museum of Judaica in Chicago has the only Holocaust exhibit that I know of in Chicago, the Bernard and Rochelle Zell Memorial. After my last meeting with Henry, I decided to visit the Spertus exhibit again. I wanted to see the artifacts there and the photographs. I remembered being there once before, several years ago, but I wanted to go again. The Zell collection is really only one room in the Spertus Museum, but a visit to it is haunting. There is a collection of children's rings behind glass panels. I looked closely at the pile of rings, perhaps a hundred tiny silver rings, mostly with a Star of David design, some with intertwined hearts. They were probably given to young women at their Bat Mitzvahs. I could make out only one inscription, "Gitta." I wondered who "Gitta" might have been. I imagined a pleasant-faced girl, a young fresh face on her Bat Mitzvah day, black ringlets under a white beret. She's smiling, a proud young Berlin Jewess. I also saw a flash of the same young girl placing her ring on the table in the anteroom that leads to the gas chamber. In my dream, there is a sign on the wall with an arrow, "Disinfectzion." Gitta is naked, standing in line, her head shaven, her small breasts pressed into the back of the woman ahead of her. Another prisoner in a blue-striped uniform shoves her into the shower room. All the other women in the shower room are also naked, many are mothers holding their children. The door is slammed and the murmuring just now begins as the sweet odor of gas trickles through the shower heads. Gitta gasps, her hands at her throat. She shrieks in German and begins to choke, screaming for God to help her. In ten minutes the Sonderkommandos will open the door and then, working with gas masks, will pile the bodies into a truck. They will then take them to the crematory and her tiny bones will burn for eternity.

The Jewish Star on display in the Holocaust room is pressed into a plastic wall plaque. It is a small yellow cloth star with the word JUDE written in black across its face in script. It's smaller than I imagined. There is also an identity card, like a passport, in one of the cases. Apparently the Germans assigned the same first name, "Israel," to all Jewish men and "Sarah" to all Jewish women. Therefore, no matter what your name, on your identity card you would be named Israel or Sarah. There is a bar of soap on display, a small oval shape. The bar of soap made from a human is placed next to a canister of Cyclon B gas. There is also a leg brace, apparently it belonged to a child, a very small child, perhaps two or three. Also a prisoner's uniform. It has faded blue stripes and a number stenciled on the left breast pocket. A red and yellow triangle precedes the stenciled number. The triangles were intended to be superimposed on each other, I suppose to resemble a Star of David, but on this pocket the triangles were two separate smudges of color.

Since I began writing this piece, I've returned to the Spertus a few more times. I wanted to be certain that my descriptions are accurate. Actually, the rings are not all Bat Mitzvah rings, and there aren't a hundred rings. There are about twenty rings in the pile, but they are all silver rings, although some of them are men's rings or perhaps they belonged to adult women. One has a Masonic emblem. There is, however, only one ring with a discernible inscription, and that is a tiny silver ring with a Star of David, and written across the star, "Gitta–1940."

The bar of soap, on each return, seemed smaller than I remembered it the previous time. It has a number incised on it, "13891." I presume, therefore, that the bar of soap was rendered from the body of a human who had been tattooed with the number 13891. The bar with the number 13891 also has a small hole at the top of the oval. Perhaps the hole was conceived as a method of hanging the soap to dry after using it to preserve it from unnecessary waste. I also noticed that the prisoner's uniform has a tag sewn into the collar for it to be hung neatly from a hook. The soap is quite chalky. Human fat apparently does not blend as easily as animal fat into a smooth emulsion. I don't know how one would go about making soap from the body of a human. I suppose you have to take a knife and slit the person's stomach open to get at the layer of fat underneath the skin. If the prisoner was particularly emaciated, this would be very difficult. Prisoners that were to be rendered as opposed to being burned to death were probably selected on arrival while they still possessed enough body fat.

Perhaps you would cut into a person's stomach with some special instrument, like a flensing knife; you would cut the fat out and collect it in a vat or a tub, or if you're rendering a child, in a cup. Of course, if you're concerned about accurate record keeping, you must number the cup with the same number you find tattooed on the person's wrist. I suppose then you add lye and boil the fat over a fire, and then when it has cooled slightly, you pour it into a small die in the shape of an oval with a hole at the top. Just before the fat has hardened, you take a stylus and carefully incise the number, 13891. This is how to make soap from a human being.

I have difficulty writing about this because as I write the stench is overpowering. My olfactory sense overcomes my visual sense and I can barely record my feelings because of the acrid odor in my nostrils. But think of the odor that must have come from those vats. And how was a person eviscerated? Did someone kneel over the body with a knife? Could this have been done while the prisoner was still alive? Most likely the bodies were hung from hooks like sides of beef in a packing house, perhaps they were pushed along a cable in order that the throat could be slit, the chest cut open and the stomach and intestines ripped out. Then the body would be pushed further along the cable where a specialist would use the flensing knife on the fat. Or perhaps the body once so eviscerated would be left to hang overnight and the fat would drip down drop by drop into a numbered vat or cup. Instead of being gassed and cremated, the young girl Gitta I suppose could have been hung from such a hook and eviscerated. Would she be left hanging on the cable, Gitta–1940 whose tiny silver ring is hidden behind the glass panels at the Spertus? Gitta, if you were cremated, again I celebrate the bright fire of your small bones. If you were eviscerated and the slime of you drawn from a hole in your body, I bless the slime which was the essence of you and that essence I call your soul. Gitta, may you have everlasting peace, sweet child.

I also have looked carefully again at the prisoner's uniform on display at the Spertus. There is indeed a tag inside the collar so the jacket may be neatly hung. The vertical stripes of the jacket and trousers are very faded, a light blue color. The inside of the jacket has darker blue stripes that show what the uniform must have looked like when it was new. There is a little metal hook or clasp at the collar. The jacket is quite stiff. I suppose it was worn winter and summer. On the right breast pocket there is a number, 17490, and preceding the number a crude red triangle and above it a daub of yellow color. I believe I was correct in saying that the Star of David was crudely reproduced on the breast pocket. The jacket has five buttonholes with three buttons in place, the top three, and they are all different sizes. The top button is a quite large black button with pink thread, the middle a smaller brownish button and the third a shiny quite small black button. In the Polish winter the jacket would be of little protection. There are also several rents in the jacket and trousers that have been crudely sewn with cross-stitching, so it must have been very important to try to close off any opening to the air.

I suppose I could have asked Henry to come with me to the Spertus to look at the soap, the uniform, the pile of rings, all the sad remains. I can see him walking from case to case, looking intently, his hands held behind his back. He is an old European gentleman and I am sure that he would have said very little, perhaps his eyes would glisten at the photograph of the young Warsaw Ghetto fighters posing as a fighting unit and he would tap the photograph and nod his head.

There are four yellow stars on exhibit at the Spertus. They are, as I said before, quite small and rather ragged. The first two bear the legend in black Germanic script, JUDE. There is another that reads JUIF, which is the French word for Jew, and another with JOOD, probably the Dutch word for Jew. I remember being a tourist in Holland many years ago and passing by a small village cemetery near the German border. I asked a man there who was placing flowers on his wife's grave if he knew anything about the three grave markers off to one side with Hebrew lettering. The graves were overgrown with weeds. Two of the stones had been broken into shards. The man slowly walked over to the three graves, picked up one of the shards and carefully inspected it. "Don't you know what is Jews?" he finally asked me.

One more speculation—suppose when Henry and his brother-in-law rode their motorcycle to Oswiecim and found the two blonde sisters dead in the rubble of their house, suppose just for a moment that instead of the two dead blonde sisters, they had found Gitta alive and standing in the rubble of that house, her face caked with ash, a yellow star sewn to her breast. Would they have helped her? Would Henry and his brother-in-law have hidden her or would they have abandoned her and rode on? What would they have done? I think Henry would have helped her. I have an instinctive feeling about him, that he was a very brave and honest man. Of course, this is speculation, and once begun leads to the next question. Who was 17490? And who was 13891? And so on.

A Woman in Prague

H E SAW HER COMING down the long path between the graves. She was a slim woman with gray hair. When he approached her, he asked her if she spoke English.

"Yes, a little."

"Do you know where the grave of Franz Kafka is?"

She gestured to him to follow. She seemed to be about his own age, in her mid-fifties, with once-darker hair streaked by gray. The graves had mostly German-Jewish names, Strauss, Friedlander, Schwarzchild, Weiss. The cemetery was wildly overgrown, and the lanes along the graves were long dirt paths winding under the archway of trees, almost like tunnels edged by foliage and the dark stones.

She pointed. "There, you see it? Dr. Franz Kafka." She nodded and folded her arms.

It was a simple brown granite gravestone with three names, Dr. Franz Kafka, Hermann Kafka and Julie Kafka, in that order. Below it was a newer, flat black marker with faded gold letters, also with three names, Gabriele, Valerie and Ottilie. There were pyres of small stones left on both graves as gifts from visitors, also some coins and a small bouquet of dried flowers. At the foot of the grave, someone had left a plant that now had a single red blossom.

"His youngest sister's name was Julie," he said to the woman.

"No, I believe Julie was the mother."

"I'm sorry, you're right. Ottilie was his youngest sister. The three sisters died in the camps. They're not buried here."

The woman pointed to a marker on the cemetery wall opposite the Kafka grave.

"Yes, I see. Max Brod. He was his good friend."

She sat down on the bench along the wall.

"How long have you been in Prague?" he asked her.

"How long?" She began to count on her fingers. "*Acht* . . . no, in English, eight days; yes, is that right, eight? I am sorry, but my English is not good."

She seemed very sad, she had a thin face etched by sadness. She was dressed in beige slacks with a gray sweater and a brown saddle-leather strap purse.

"You are English?" she asked him.

"No, American. I live in New York and teach at a university there."

"Oh, yes, New York."

"And you?"

"I live in Germany. I teach the children that do not speak." She gestured with her hand to her mouth.

He sat down beside her on the bench.

"Many stones," she said to him.

"Yes, many. Kafka is almost an industry here." He stooped over and found a small white stone and leaned over and dropped it on the row of stones. "There are some coins there too."

"Coins?"

"Yes, people have left coins."

"Oh, I didn't see."

He pointed to the names on the stone. "He is above his father here."

"I don't know if he would like being here with his family. I don't really know." She lit a cigarette.

He thought of the photograph of Kafka and his three sisters, the sisters in immaculate white dresses, all with dark piercing eyes and severe expressions. They didn't look like young people.

"Where do you live in Germany?"

"Live? It is in Heidelberg."

"I live in Manhattan."

"Yes. That is the city."

"No, it is a section of New York."

"English is quite hard for me."

"I speak some French, but you speak English very well."

"No French, please. My French is awful." She grimaced and touched the ashes off her cigarette.

It was very quiet. There was only the muted sound of traffic beyond the walls, nothing else. "We apparently are alone, the only two people here," he said to her after a few moments.

"The only two? I don't understand."

"We, you and I." He pointed to both of them. "At this moment the only two who are with Kafka."

"Oh, I see. Yes. Perhaps. The only two. I think not though." She pointed to the row of stones. "And Brod." She nodded at the marker on the wall.

There were several lines of Czech on Max Brod's memorial. He recognized the word for editor, *redaktor,* and showed it to her.

She turned and he watched her face as she turned, a long, angular face, and dark eyes. She was still a beautiful woman. "Do you speak any Czech?" he asked her.

"No, nothing. A few words."

"Have you always lived in Germany?"

"No. I am from Hungary. I am Hungarian."

"Are you Jewish?"

"Half." She made a slicing movement with her hand and ground her cigarette out. "Half Jewish and half Christian."

"I am Jewish."

SHE NODDED AND LOOKED AWAY down the path. An older man in a flat cap and blue workman's clothes was coming on a bicycle. He bobbed his head to them as he passed.

"I think most of the Jews of Prague are buried here, those that didn't die in the camps," he said.

"Probably most. But also in the Old Jewish Cemetery, there are many graves. This is the new one."

"I was in the Old Cemetery this morning. I've never seen anything like it. Graves from 1400. Rabbi Judah Lowe is buried there. The miracle rabbi who created the Golem to save the Jews of Prague. I put a stone on his grave."

She smiled for the first time and looked up at him. "I put too. I was at the Old Jewish Cemetery, and I also saw—is that right—saw?"

"Yes."

"The grave of Rabbi Lowe. But where was his Golem during the Holocaust? I have not seen one living Jew in Prague, only gravestones."

"I met some Prague Jews this morning, at the synagogue up the street from the Old Cemetery."

"I have been eight days here, and I have not met one living Jew. Only here, now, you, and you are an American."

"I would like to find a bookstore that has some Kafka material," he said. "I was told there are bookstores on Wenceslaus Square. Do you know where Wenceslaus Square is?"

"Yes, I know these stores."

"Would you care to go there? Did you come on the Metro?"

"Yes, I could go with you. Why not?" She put her purse over her shoulder and stood up. They began to walk away, and then suddenly she turned back and called to him. She pointed to several stones on top of Kafka's monument. "You see, one of them is not a stone at all, there it is—how do you call that in English?"

"A snail."

"I have been observing it all the time we have been speaking. Since we first sat down, it has moved from here to here." She traced a line of about six inches.

"Wait for just a moment."

"No," she said. "If you watch them, they won't move at all."

"Where do you think it came from?"

"I think it came down from the trees. On threads, they come down." She fluttered her fingers.

He looked up at the trees. It would serve him right to meet a woman like this, who knew about snails that descend on silken threads from trees. He would have to come to Prague to find her at Kafka's grave.

"There are raspberries here too," she said.

"And the snails eat the raspberries?"

"No. I ate them. I picked some. They were very good. And the little ones that are crazy for the nuts, what do you call them in English, they also eat raspberries."

"Squirrels."

"Yes, in Italian, *scoiattolli*."

AS THEY WALKED OUT to the cemetery gate, she pointed to several stones decorated with praying hands.

"Those are the signs of the Levites, the hands at prayer," she told him.

On the Metro, sitting silently beside her, he thought of the suicide of Primo Levi. Levi admired Kafka. He owed it to Levi to come here to Prague to Kafka's grave, and now he had met a woman, a very strange, sad woman, almost as strange and sad as himself. She hadn't told him her name, and he hadn't asked.

At Wenceslaus Square, she took him to a large bookstore and asked to see any books by Kafka in English. She asked in German.

"We have none," the young man in spectacles said.

"None?"

"No, we have no books by Kafka."

"In Deutsch?" she asked.

"No. None."

"No books at all by Kafka?"

He shook his head.

She shrugged, and they walked out, back into the sunlight and the crowds of people in the square.

"We will try another store," she told him.

At the second store, they were taken by a young woman to the manager. "Do you have anything by Kafka in English for the gentleman?" she asked again in German.

"No, madam."

"In Deutsch? In Français?"

"No, madam. None at all."

"In Czechish?"

"No, madam. Not for three years. There is nothing by Kafka in Prague."

"Nothing at all?"

"You will find nothing here."

They left the store and watched some children dancing to rock music in unison in lines under a loudspeaker in front of a record store. They were mostly little blond boys and girls, and they were laughing and doing the steps with their hands on their hips, their eyes bright with excitement.

"Are you surprised?" he said to her and touched her arm.

"I don't believe it. I know one more store. It is over there. I remember it as a literary store. More literary."

A man holding books he was putting up on shelves looked at her without expression. She asked him the same question.

"I am sorry, we have nothing here by Kafka."

"You have nothing at all?"

He shook his head and turned back to the shelf. "He is not available here. No." He bowed slightly with a trace of a smile.

"Ask him if they have anything by Primo Levi."

"No," the man said with the same expression, "we do not have Primo Levi."

"Do you have his brother, Carlo Levi? *The Christus is Coming to Eboli*?" she said.

"No."

He asked her to join him for dinner, and they went to a tavern and had some Pilsener beer and duck. The tavern was crowded with a busload of German tourists. The men were drinking shots of *slivovitz* and became quite loud. After dinner he suggested to her that they leave and have dessert elsewhere.

It had become dark, and they walked back to the main boulevard and had sherbet in a small cafe edged by bushes along the sidewalk. She told him a little about herself. She was born in Hungary but had fled the Germans and was saved by the Russians and then went to Italy as a refugee. She was in Venice in the winter. "It was winter," she said, drinking her coffee. "I was twelve, I had no money, nothing in the purse. I was what you call an orphan—yes, orphan. We lived in a shack. There was snow on the gondolas. I remember I wanted to taste Coca-Cola. I had heard of it but had never tasted it. To me it represented freedom. So I finally had a Coca-Cola, but it was awful. I hated it. It tasted like poison. Now we have eight McDonald's in Heidelberg and the place for the pizza?"

"Pizza Hut?"

"Yes, a Hut of Pizza has now also come to Heidelberg."

She was staying on the outskirts of the city in a private home. "I told *cedok* that everything they offered was too expensive. I asked them if they had a mission in the train station. They finally found me a private house. I have a room. It is quite far from here."

She asked him no questions about himself. Suddenly, as he paid the bill, she turned to him and asked quietly, "Are you a married man?"

"No, I'm not married. I'm recently divorced."

"I am a married woman," she said. She lit another cigarette.

"Where is your husband?"

"He is home in Heidelberg with our daughter."

"You are in Prague alone?"

"One can be quite alone in marriage."

"Yes, and also out of marriage. Kafka, better than anyone, I think, could write about the pain of being alone."

"He was very good with pain," she said. "Perhaps that is why they have banned him here now. Banned, is that right?"

"Yes."

They walked to the Charles Bridge and crossed the old bridge with its ancient statues of saints and the huge castle in the background. There were fishermen below with flat boats in the black water, and white swans on the river. Students were sitting in one of the niches of the bridge and were drinking beer and holding candles, singing quietly to a guitar.

"It would have been very hard for a Jew to hide here," he said to her. "Almost impossible. Everyone is blond. A Jew with dark features couldn't hide."

She stood looking down at the river. "When the Germans came to Hungary, it was late in 1944. We were living in a house. I was a child. The Germans counted ten. Everyone who was ten had to go. I survived several such counts. But why the Jews went willingly, I do not know. I still do not know. Both of my parents went. I was left alone, only with my cousin. I had in my pocket like this"—she gestured—"a small, how do you call it, nail file." She pretended to hold it in her hand. "I would not let them take me. After my parents went, I swore that if the Germans came to me as a ten, I would do like so." She thrust her hand out. "I would kill whoever came to take me." She turned to him. "You see, I think the Jews felt they had a special bondage with God." She linked her hands. "You know the symbol of Levites? They thought this bondage was special and never could be broken. So the Jews went willingly. God would take care of them." She moved her hands apart and stared at them. "But He didn't." She sighed and shook her head. "I shouldn't talk to you about such things. You are right. It was very difficult to hide. Almost impossible." She turned to him. "It's late. I should go now. You do not have to come to the Metro. We can say goodnight here."

"No, I want to come with you."

They walked together down along the bridge through the darkness, past the students holding candles, to her Metro stop, where they said goodnight. When he shook her hand, he was surprised at the strength of her hand. It was the hand of a worker, not a woman who taught children. They exchanged cards. After she left, he looked at the card she'd given him under the streetlight. She had written her name, Nathalia. Her name but not her address.

A Woman in Warsaw

He was in Warsaw for the International Book Fair. He'd never been in Warsaw before and he stayed at the Hotel Victoria and on his last night, after dinner downstairs, he went up to the casino and had a brandy at the bar. A woman immediately moved over and sat beside him. She was quite beautiful, about twenty-eight, with gray eyes, very thin, with long brown hair, and dark stockings, dressed in a suit, like a young businesswoman.

"I am tired of the Germans here at the bar," she said in perfect English. "You're not German; I heard you speaking English."

"No, I'm American."

"Good. I like Americans."

He was a divorced man of forty-eight who owned a small academic publishing company in Baltimore. He had the face of a scholar with a high forehead, and gray hair, thinning and long at the back of his neck. He felt too tired to talk to her. He'd read in the *International Herald Tribune* of the death yesterday of Isaac Bashevis Singer. If she was a prostitute, he didn't want to get involved with her. On his last night in Warsaw, he only wanted to drink his brandy and then perhaps find a cab and take it to Krochmalna Street, the street where Singer lived in Warsaw as a young boy. He'd promised himself that before he left he'd go to Singer's Krochmalna Street and to the Warsaw Ghetto monument. He had to be in London tomorrow afternoon.

Then he surprised himself by saying to her, "I'll buy you a drink, but I'm leaving."

"Americans are always in a hurry. Where are you going?"

"To visit friends."

"You have friends in Warsaw?"

He nodded.

"I'll have a vodka." She called to the bartender who brought over a bottle of Wyborowa. She drank down the shot and looked at the man defiantly and brushed her hair back as it fell across her face. "Are you a Jew?"

"Why do you ask?"

She spread her pale fingers next to his on the bar. "See how dark your fingers are beside mine. Most of the Americans who come here to the hotel are Jews. They come to walk on the ashes. Have you come to walk on the ashes?"

"What business is it of yours?"

"It is my business. We have a large industry in ashes." She looked at him again. "I will take you to see the ghetto in a Mercedes."

"I'm not interested."

"Not interested in what? I do not believe you. You do not look like a man who is not interested. Her gray eyes were very beautiful. She reached to the top of her hair and pulled her dark glasses down and lit a cigarette. As she bent her head down he noticed that her hair was really auburn colored, and as she leaned toward him, it brushed against his cheek. He wanted to reach out and touch her hair, but instead he got up and put two 50,000 zloty notes on the bar.

"You will leave me here with these foolish German tourists?"

"Perhaps I'll see you later." Then he touched the back of his fingers to her hair and then to her cheek. It was a consciously gentle gesture, but she angrily moved her face away from him and turned her back to him.

Outside the hotel he walked across the street to the plaza with the Tomb of the Unknown Soldier and stood with some people watching two young guards goose-step in cadence before the tomb. He stared at the soldiers' high-boned Slavic faces and their tri-crowned hats with chin straps, white gloves, and gleaming black boots. There was no sound other than the hollow cadence of their marching. He watched them for another minute, then turned away from them and found a cab.

He could speak a few words of Polish, enough to give simple directions. "Krochmalna Street," he told the driver. The word for street was "ulica" . . . "Ulica Krochmalna." It was an old cab and the driver was a middle-aged man with thick glasses. He drove in silence for only five or six blocks and pointed to a building on the corner. There was a sign on the side of the building, Krochmalna Street. He got out of the cab and asked the driver to wait for him.

The Warsaw Ghetto had been destroyed by the Germans in 1943. Every building was burned. Before World War I Singer's father, a rabbi, brought his young family from a small town in the provinces to Warsaw and they lived on Krochmalna Street. As he walked along Krochmalna street he saw only apartment buildings with dark courtyards, a few with strands of wash hanging over the balconies in the courtyards. A family was sitting on a front stoop of a building. There were two blonde children, with tiny, inquisitive, fragile faces, sitting with their parents who quickly glanced up at him. He nodded to them and slowly walked back to the cab as they watched him. Before he got in he touched the bricks of the corner building.

He didn't know the word for monument. "Ghetto Monument," he said. The driver seemed to understand and touched his hat. He turned on his lights and drove to the Ghetto Monument. When they arrived, after a few blocks, the driver parked the cab under some trees at the curb, dimmed his lights and lit a cigarette.

There was a large park where he got out, and he immediately saw the silhouette of the Ghetto Monument. He approached from the rear, down a long walk. The monument was in a clearing of several city blocks, surrounded by apartment buildings. Supposedly it would be the only monument in Warsaw without flowers strewn at its base. Someone at the Book Fair had told him that all the saints and cardinals and Polish military heroes would have flowers on their monuments, but the Ghetto Monument would be barren. There had been an old woman in front of the hotel selling flowers. He could have bought her last bouquet. She held it up to him as he passed her, but he shook his head.

He walked around to the front of the statue. There were some flowers lying at its base, a sheaf of dried red flowers. He picked up one, a red flower with a black throat, and put it on the arm of the figure of the man who was prostrate, lying with his head on his arm. Then he stood back with his hands clasped in front of him and bowed his head and tried to say a prayer in Hebrew. He knew only a few words of the Kaddish, the mourner's prayer. He looked up at the faces of the statue, a young man, bare chested, his coat thrown open, holding a grenade, and a young woman behind him holding a rifle. The commander of the ghetto forces in 1943 was Mordechai Anielewicz, who was only twenty-three. This was probably Anielewicz. He bowed his head and said what he knew of the Kaddish prayer. When he finished he saw someone in the distance walking at the edge of the park. A man passing on the sidewalk had noticed him and from afar lifted his hat to him in a gesture of respect.

He could then have asked the driver to take him to the Umschlagplatz, but he didn't. He didn't want to see it. The Umschlagplatz, the collection point in German, was the courtyard where the Germans forced the Jews to assemble before they led them to the trains. It wasn't necessary to see it, even though he'd been told that there was now a plaque there. Instead he told the driver to take him back to the hotel.

When they arrived the driver wanted to change money with him, and when he wouldn't change money, the driver was annoyed. Everyone in this country wanted to change zlotys for dollars. Soldiers, Boy Scouts, taxi drivers, the hotel maids. He just wanted to be left alone. He wasn't a money changer. He didn't acknowledge the doorman in the bearskin hat and gold-braided greatcoat, who solemnly held the cab door open. He ignored the doorman's assistance. He pushed into the lobby with its groups of tourists standing at the front desk and at the cashiers' cages. There were also some Polish officers and their wives, a few Russian officers in uniforms with red sideboards, and young Arab men reading and drinking coffee. He'd heard that the PLO trained guerillas in Czechoslovakia and that many of the Arab men in Warsaw were on leave from these camps. There was one fat older man in long robes who sat with them. He wore a fez, a monocle, and was reading a newspaper printed in Arabic.

He walked through the lobby and waited for the elevator to the casino bar. Up in the bar he ordered a brandy and drank it quickly. It burned as it went down and he ordered another and drank it just as quickly. Then he saw her getting up from a booth in the back of the room and walking toward him. She seemed to be covered with a green color, a soft, unusual, ancient green patina.

"Hello, American," she said. "Are you through with your communion?" She had eyes like a gray cat, and the tawny, sinister movements of a cat. "You see? I have waited for you. I knew you would be back.

They all come back in about thirty minutes. Where are you from? Philadelphia? Boston?" She snapped her fingers at the bartender.

"Baltimore."

"Baltimore? I've never heard of it. Wladyslaw, I will have another Wyborowa, but over ice. How did you like the ghetto? Did you go by Mercedes? There is nothing left to see there in the ghetto. There is no ghetto. Did you go to Mila Street?"

He signaled for another brandy. "No, I didn't know there was a Mila Street."

"Yes, of course, it was their headquarters there. Your countryman wrote a book, about it, what was his name . . . ?"

"Leon Uris."

"Yes, Uris. Are you surprised I know of him? Of course I do. Jewish writers are very popular in Poland. Woody Allen. I know of him. We all love him. Even Jerzy Kosinski. He came back here only recently. It is a pity he committed suicide. Are you surprised that I know of American literature and films? Do you know I am a student at Warsaw University? Yes, a student of English literature. I come here occasionally, and if I see a man I like who will pay my price . . . I may go with him. Otherwise I just drink and read my book and go home alone. Did you ask me my price?" She shook her hair out at him. "My price is one million zlotys. What is it for you, a hundred dollars? Nothing. A meal or two. I can live on that for two months. And never have to come here. We will order a bottle of champagne and go to your room. Are you staying at the hotel?"

"I'm not interested in making love."

"Ah, love. Is that what you call it? I am not talking about love. We can discuss literature. What is your name?"

"Mark."

"Mark? That is not a Jewish name. That is the name of one of our saints, Saint Mark. We have the name Marek."

"No, my name is Mark. What's your name?"

"My name? I never tell my name. Every time I have a different name. Tonight I shall also be a saint, Saint Magdalena. Madga. She was also a whore. Our Lord Jesus was a Jew and he forgave her. Maria Magda. He blessed her as a saint and she washed his feet and dried them with her hair." She raised her glass. "Cheers, Marek. Drink your brandy."

He took the third brandy and now he was calm. The green that had colored her face was gone and he saw that she was dressed in black, almost like a young nun in her dark suit and immaculate white silk blouse. He remembered the young nuns as a child in Baltimore in the streets near his home, passing them on the sidewalk, their slim, high-planed faces, the ivory faces of the nuns as they passed murmuring in their black robes, the rustle of the hidden legs under the long robes.

"I'll go with you," he said. "Why not?"

"Good. We will buy a bottle of champagne and we will discuss literature." She snapped her fingers again at the barman. "Wladyslaw, champagne." She smiled at him for the first time. He reached out to her and with the same consciously gentle gesture touched her hair with the back of his hand, and then her face. This time she didn't turn away. He had always wanted to touch one of the ivory faces hidden behind the coifs and so now he determined he would do this and they would go together to his room.

"Before we leave, you must pay me my fee. Do you have dollars? I would prefer to be paid in dollars."

He had five $100 bills folded inside of a pocket in his checkbook. He removed the bills and handed her one. She looked at it quickly, opened it up and turned it over, and then opened her purse, put it in her wallet, and snapped her purse shut. She got off her stool. "Okay, let's go."

"I think I'll take another brandy to the room in a paper cup."

"How many brandies have you had?"

"Three or four."

"Wladyslaw, give the gentleman another brandy. Send it to his room. They won't allow you to take a paper cup through the lobby. Not even a glass. They're very decorous here. Did I say that right? I have difficulty with certain words."

"Yes, you said it right."

Up in the room, she put the bottle of champagne in the small refrigerator, removing most of the bottles of beer and wine the hotel had provided. He sat in a chair and watched as she moved around the room touching different articles. She went into the bathroom and came out with some plastic bottles of shampoo and lotion. "May I have these?"

"Yes."

She swept them into her purse. "And this?" She was holding a bar of milled French soap. She sniffed it and held it under his nose.

"Take it."

"Good. I can sell these things, you know, or keep them. I really don't need them. I prefer to sell them. How about this?" She held up a small sewing kit.

"Keep it."

"Thank you."

There was a knock on the door. "They're here already with your brandy."

He signed the check and gave the waiter a dollar. She went back into the bathroom and opened the champagne. He heard the pop. She returned with a face towel around the bottle and poured two glasses. "There is a telephone in there!" she said. "That's really decadent. That's something new. In Poland people have nothing, and the guests here now have telephones in their bathrooms. How do you explain that?"

"That's capitalism."

"If that's capitalism, I don't want it."

"Well, you don't have to use the telephone."

She sat on the bed and raised her glass to him. "Na zdrowie, that's how we say cheers in Polish." She crossed her legs and then began swinging her leg. She leaned over to a panel at the side of the bed and turned down the lights. He reached out to her and in the half darkness traced the contours of her face with his index finger, and then her lips.

"Okay, we'll talk of literature," he said to her. "Do you know of the writer Isaac Bashevis Singer? He died yesterday in the States."

"No, I didn't know that. He was a very sweet man, Singer. He wrote the novel *Shosha.* Do you think I look like Shosha? I have her color of red hair."

He moved away from her and stood up and looked out the window. "I see Warsaw has a Coca-Cola sign. It's the only sign I see."

"Yes, it's another gift from America. Coca-Cola and a telephone in the bathroom. Just what we need." She shook up the bottle of champagne until it fizzed, and sprayed some of the champagne at the ceiling and then at him.

"You shouldn't do that."

"Why are you so quiet and sad, Marek? Is it because of Singer's death or your visit to the ghetto, or are you drunk?"

He had difficulty focusing on her after four brandies. "I may be a little drunk."

"Are you a married man, Marek?"

"No, I was married."

"Where is your wife?"

"My wife? I have no wife."

She pushed another button for the radio at the night table. "Do you like Chopin? In Poland you can't escape him."

"Leave it on."

"Do you want to stay at the window? Why don't you sit on the bed?"

"Do you think Mary Magdalene really washed Christ's feet and dried them with her hair?"

"Is that what you want me to do for you? I won't do it."

"No, I don't want that."

"What do you want?"

"Do you know how to sew?"

"Sew? Yes, of course. Do you want me to give you the sewing kit back?"

"No, I want you to sew something for me. I don't know how to sew." He finished the brandy and sat down on the bed with her. "Did you take all the pens too?"

"Yes, pens and the letter sheets and envelopes. But I will give them back, and the sewing kit." She turned on the light and sat on the bed, and poured out the contents of her purse. Two plastic pens fell out with the sewing kit, several plastic bottles, the bar of soap, her wallet, a leather folio of stationery, and a letter opener and shears.

"You can have it all back, except for my wallet."

"No, you keep everything. I just want to borrow a pen and the scissors from the stationery kit."

He began to draw a crude triangle on the yellow bedspread. He outlined a triangle, then bisected it with another triangle. He drew the design of the Star of David and then slowly lettered the word JUDE onto the center of the star. He took the scissors and cut the yellow star out of the bedspread. She watched him, sitting cross-legged, sipping champagne from the bottle. "You'll have to pay them," she finally said to him when he finished cutting out the star. "They won't allow this."

"I won't pay them. I don't care about their rules of decorum. I've already paid them."

"Now what?" She looked at him. She really was beautiful. Very inviting, very beautiful, with perfect Slavic eyes and cheekbones. She didn't look like Shosha though. He doubted if she was a student at the university. She was probably just a beautiful Polish hotel whore who liked to read. Although, maybe he was wrong, she could be a graduate student in literature. She knew too much about literature for her own good, and it disturbed him to have her as his seamstress. She was too intelligent. Now he just wanted her to leave. Maybe she was with the Polish version of the KGB, but what would they want from him? His book of photographs of the Warsaw Ghetto that he bought yesterday? "Getto Warszawskie"? Photos of Jews begging, skeletal children, hollow-eyed, dying in the streets?

He went to the closet and got his navy blue blazer and put it down in front of her on the bed. "Can you sew this star on my jacket? Right there?" He pointed to the breast pocket.

"Sew it?"

"Yes, right there. Sew this and you can go. You'll make Poland's last Jew. While you're doing that, I think I'll go into the bathroom and phone God and tell him what I'm doing. Use good strong basting stitches."

He went to the bathroom and ran water over his fingers and touched his face, and looked at himself in the mirror. She was right, he did look like a Jew. He spread his fingers in a fan in front of the mirror. He did have dark fingers.

"You're sewing?"

"Yes, be quiet. I haven't done this in a long time. You are a bit crazy, you know."

"And so are you."

"Yes, we are a good pair, a Catholic whore, Maria Magdalena, and a Jewish saint, Saint Marek from Baltimore."

"I don't know who you are, but I'm not a Jewish saint."

"Did you telephone to God?"

"Yes, I did."

"What did you ask him?"

"I asked him why three million Jews died here."

"And what did he say?"

"He said he didn't know."

"Do you accept that answer?"

"No."

"There." She held the jacket out and showed it to him with the star sewn on the breast pocket. "It's done."

"You're sure that it will hold? The stitches are strong?"

"Yes, of course. My grandmother taught me that cross-stitch. I call it Basia's stitch. It is done. It will last."

"Thank you very much. You may go now. Take the sewing kit, take the pens, all the bottles. Take everything."

She swept all the articles back into her purse. "You will be all right, Marek? Where will you go with that star on your jacket?" She looked at herself in the mirror and patted her hair. He could see that she had finished with him. She wasn't really interested in him, and in a minute would disappear forever.

"I don't know where I'll go."

She took a bottle of cologne from her purse and sprayed her wrists and throat. "I will leave you now, Marek, okay?"

"Yes, and take the bottle of champagne."

"I cannot believe you have given me a million zlotys for sewing, Marek. Only from an American. Someday, when I come to America, I will look you up." She opened the door, put her purse over her shoulder, and carried her shoes in her hand. She looked at him. "Ciao," she said, and instead of taking the elevator, she was suddenly gone, down the stairway.

He put the jacket on. She'd done a good job. He touched the star on his pocket and smoothed the hair at his temples, and caught the empty elevator downstairs. No one was in the lobby, no one paid attention to him as he passed. One man in front of the hotel stared at him and then quickly turned away.

He walked over to the plaza where the two young guards were still marching in cadence, and watched them. There were torches burning and a small crowd. No one noticed him, and he watched for a few moments and then moved to a park bench and sat down in the shadows of the trees.

If he'd had a portable phone with him, he could have called God again, but he wasn't in America so he didn't have a portable phone. If he'd had one, he could have set it on redial. He didn't have one, though, and he folded his arms around himself and sat quietly at the rim of the torchlight. He looked at his fingers. He did have dark fingers, even in the torchlight.

Suddenly she came up to him out of the shadows.

"Why are you sitting here, Marek? I saw you leaving the hotel."

He didn't answer her.

"You know, it won't do any good for you to sit here with your star, Marek."

She reached out to him and touched his cheek with almost the same gesture he'd used. "I'm going for my tram now. You really shouldn't stay here. Someone may hurt you. Do you understand that? You should go back to your hotel."

He watched her turn and slowly walk away from him toward the plaza. She turned back once more and called out to him, "You shouldn't stay there, Marek. It is dangerous for you to sit there." She stood looking at him for a moment and then shrugged and walked toward the shadows of the torchlight and she was gone.

Aliyah

He was sitting in a sidewalk cafe in Haifa wondering why he had come to Israel. It was easier to think about it drinking a banana/peach milkshake. Not really a milkshake, but a pitcher of milk blended with banana and peaches with a thin elbow straw hung with a crepe paper yellow pineapple in the shape of a bell. Very Israeli, a nice touch, the glass slender and tapered like so many of the beautiful, young Israeli women passing in tank tops with long hair, sunglasses on top of their heads, talking on cellular phones and laughing. Why had he come to Israel? To find a young woman? No, he was too old for a young woman, he was in his mid-fifties and his hair was turning gray from black, his sideburns almost white. His name was Eliott Rosen and he was from Detroit. He had a long thin face, still darkly handsome, with a high forehead and brown eyes. He was a tall, slim man and looked like an academic or a doctor on holiday. But he was a writer with a small notebook hidden in his pocket and he liked to sit in cafes and watch people and listen to them. He intended to leave the cafe soon and take a tram to the Bahai Garden and sit in the garden and just relax and read the *Jerusalem Post* he'd brought with him from the hotel.

He hadn't come to Israel at fifty-four to find another woman, although his wife had died several years ago. He'd married a younger woman, a thirty-two-year-old, a year after his wife's death and it lasted only a few months. He'd come to Israel, he thought, to find repose. It was a strange place to search for repose. In any event, after paying 4.20 shekels ($1.25) to take an air-conditioned Mercedes tram to the garden of The Bab, he found the garden closed. The security guard held him back by poking him in the chest with a cell phone. He permitted him only to use an alternative path that led to the rear of the temple, which was mostly blocked from view by clumps of cypress trees. So he returned to the hotel on the air-conditioned tram, wondering which of the passengers might be carrying a bomb in a shopping bag. They were mostly older women returning from an afternoon concert and conversing in Hebrew and German. They were dressed in silk print dresses in the fashion of Berlin of the 1930s. Some of them held straw-domed sun hats in their laps. None of them were carrying bombs.

When he returned to the hotel, he went to the lobby bar and ordered a red Cinzano over ice. Another man sat alone in the bar, about forty, in jeans, with the gray eyes of a sleek jungle cat. A man named Arnie. Arnie looked him over while asking questions about why he was in Haifa.

"To visit Israel," he told Arnie.

"You are looking for a wife?" Again the predatory stare.

"Not a wife, maybe a dinner companion."

"Don't you know the widows of Haifa are more dangerous than the Arabs?"

The bartender, who was a very short, dark, sad-eyed man, moon faced, with thin patches of black hair, poured him another Cinzano.

"What's your name?" Arnie asked him.

"Eliott. And your name?"

"In Hebrew, 'Arnat,' but that's a woman's name; my mother hung it on me. I call myself 'Arnie.'"

"Do you live in Haifa, Arnie?"

"Yes, in Haifa most of the time. I was born here in Haifa, but I also live in the States. I had two beautiful condos in Fort Lauderdale. Just gorgeous, gated, modern, immaculate, an Olympic pool, but the Haitians and Cubans ruined them. I sold them at a loss, each for $64,000; I can't believe it. I paid over $85,000."

"You're in real estate?"

"Sort of. The market here in Haifa is very hot. You're in a beautiful old section of Haifa. I'm also in American stocks. Coca-Cola. It did well for me. But I missed on Disney. Instead of buying Disney, I bought Euro-Disney. So did all my friends. Bought it at 28. It's 6."

After the Bahai and Arnie and a late dinner alone that night in a cafe, the next morning he found a bench in a small park. He'd slept fitfully and awoke with a backache and arthritis pains in his hands and legs. It was Saturday, Shabbat, the Sabbath. No one was in the park; a few cats, an older woman walking the path alone around the fountain, around and around, five circles and then she left. It wasn't really a fountain. He couldn't read the Hebrew inscription but it looked like a memorial to war dead and there were piles of withered flowers in the basin. He'd said "hello" cheerfully in English to the woman. She answered without expression, "Shalom," and then he saw it, the faded blue cross-hatching of a number tattooed on top of her left arm.

She soon returned and began circling the park again. She had a kind, sweet face and as she passed him, he stared at the faded blue numbers scarring her arm.

He thought about the cafe yesterday afternoon. There was one woman who'd spoken to him. He'd sat with his crepe paper bell and sipped the banana/peach concoction and watched two young Israeli soldiers, each about eighteen, talking to two women in their late twenties across the tables. Each soldier had an automatic rifle slung over his back. When he stood up and was thinking about whether to leave the waitress 50¢ or $1, a woman holding a miniature dachshund named "Kiwi" asked him if he was leaving and if she could take his chair. She had huge rings on several fingers, black hair, black eyes, tight white trousers and spoke a very thick accented English. She was in her fifties and had recognized him as an American.

"That's a cute dog," he said to her. "What kind is he?"

"He is a woman," she answered and smiled at him. She was the first woman in Israel who'd smiled at him and he couldn't wait to get away from her. She would be much too difficult, too tough, a pain in the neck, a real boss, a balabusta. His wife had been gentle, a very gentle, quiet woman.

He had to urinate. There was no one in the park. The older woman had disappeared again. He went into the bushes. He would never have done that in the States. When he left the park, the sun was out and there was a lovely, sea-scented wind. Haifa was built on a mountain, on the sides of Mount Carmel. Doves were cooing. Doves were always cooing in Israel. Each morning, outside the slatted windows of his hotel room, he heard the sounds of morning doves. Now, as he left the park for lunch, there was a group of boys across the street walking together on Sabbath in white shirts and white yarmulkes with strings of prayer scarves hanging from underneath their shirts. Last night at dinner at the hotel, before eating, a man and his wife stood and said a Sabbath prayer with a single glass of wine. The man held the wine glass and then drank from it standing, the woman sat. He handed her the glass and she drank. It was nice to see. He'd never seen the Sabbath celebrated, although he was a Jew born of Jewish parents, he had no Jewish background. He never went to temple and was never Bar Mitzvah. He was an assimilated American Jew. He had no children. No brothers or sisters. He was the last of his family. Last night Sabbath candles were burning on the table in the hotel corridor when he went to his room. The hostess in the dining room wouldn't even write his room number on the check. "On Shabbat, we don't write," she said. "I will remember." Still, the cafes were full, lots of wild kids dancing and shouting on Friday night, the beginning of their weekend.

As he left the park, he noticed that the building at the entrance was really a movie house. He couldn't read the Hebrew poster but it looked like a skin flick was being advertised with a poster of nudes of a man and woman, headless and without limbs—only two words in English at the bottom of the poster . . . "Live Flesh."

He had come to Israel to find repose, not a woman. He wasn't like Frank Sinatra, a fat, swollen-faced, finger-snapping Frankie who had to have every woman who crossed his path, every waitress, every little hostess. Now Frank was dead. America was in mourning and here he was in Haifa secretly watching all the young women, just like Frank, the color of their hair in sunlight, the way sunlight hits and reveals the colored strands of long hair. He watched the sway of their hips in their tight jeans and the thinness of their waists, girls in their twenties. He was always secretly watching them, chattering on their cell phones in the hoarse, throaty sound of Hebrew with the strangulated "ch" sound. The waitresses were always diffident and disengaged when he spoke to them. They screwed up their faces when he tried to speak to them in Hebrew. He'd studied Hebrew for a month from a pocket Berlitz book and brought it with him and he could say "Toda" (thank you) and "Tov Maot" (very good), "Heshbon bevakesha" (check please) and a few other phrases. With that limited vocabulary, he wasn't about to seduce any of the young waitresses. They were always laughing, heads swiveling to and from the customers, flirting with the young men at the tables. They paid no attention to him except to bring his order and then his check.

He was given the number of one twenty-nine-year-old Israeli woman in Haifa, a graduate student in comparative literature at Haifa University. Her name was Shulamit. Her father had written to her telling her that his good friend Eliott Rosen, fifty-four, from Detroit, a prominent American writer, author of four books would be in Haifa. The last book, a novel, *The Myth of Childhood,* was about two basketball players from the projects of Detroit who became NBA stars and then were charged with the rape and murder of a GM executive's wife. They were both found innocent in the novel after pages of vivid courtroom drama. He'd already made about $250,000 in royalties from *The Myth of Childhood,* not including the $75,000 option for a movie. Give the American public what it wants—lust, basketball, murder, racial hatred—mix it all up into a nice soup (marak, the word for soup) and what do you have? You wind up in Israel with a pocketful of shekels watching the sunlight play on the hair of young women. You can even argue with the falafal man, an Arab in his kiosk, whether the pita he made for you of hummus and vegetables should be 14 shekels, not 40 as he asked. A man had intervened in perfect German accented English and told him to pay only 14 and that's what he paid, 14 shekels. The man had saved him 26 shekels, more than $6.

The stock market was moving down though, the Dow down 205 points in the *Jerusalem Post* this morning. Also, the twenty-nine-year-old comparative lit student didn't want to meet with him, despite his reputation as a prominent American writer with his list of books on the Internet. Marcel Proust he was not, certainly not Amos Oz or Aharon Appelfeld, maybe a little closer to A.B. Yehoshua, *A Late Divorce.* He had Yehoshua's novel at his bedside for months but had never started it.

"I'm sorry, but I cannot meet with you, sir," Shulamit had said to him in a perfect American accent.

"Oh," he answered. "I'm sorry too. I thought your father wrote you."

"He did, but this weekend will be impossible. I am preparing job applications for interviews next week. Perhaps at the end of next week."

She sounded so bored and sure of herself. Her voice reminded him of the voice of his second wife, the same cadences. He could see her flipping her hair back with the same nervous gesture.

"I don't think I can make it next week. I'm leaving the country in a few days. I don't have that kind of time."

"Well, perhaps earlier in the week. Why don't you call me again?"

He'd called her initially two days ago and left a message on her machine that he was in town and asked her to call him at the hotel but she hadn't called.

"I doubt if I can make it," he told her. Now he would hand her the same shtick. "But your father sends his regards."

"Oh, tell him hello. I'm sorry," she said.

"Yes, I am too."

So much for Shulamit. Tonight where would he go? He'd thought they would have dinner together. He'd noticed an ad for an English language production of Arthur Schnitzler's *La Ronde* at the Haifa Museum. Maybe he'd go to the theater. Something to just get him out of the hotel. He'd rented a car but was reluctant to drive it. The city was like San Francisco, curving, twisting roads in and out of the mountainsides with great sweeping vistas of the harbor below. He went that afternoon to a park by the Japanese Art Museum. There was a beautiful view of the city and the harbor. The old white, sun-bleached apartments of Haifa were spread out for miles in the haze, the blue water of the Mediterranean, the mountains in the distance. What must it have been like to have been a survivor and to arrive in the Haifa harbor and see the city and not be permitted to land? The British would sink the ships and send the passengers to Cyprus. Thousands were sent to prison camps in Cyprus by the British or back to France or even Germany.

There was a man seated next to him in the Japanese garden. He was from Manchester, England, in his early eighties, slim, in gray trousers and an open striped shirt. He was a Jewish man and he had an ascetic, high-boned, smooth face and was here for his nephew's wedding. He was a lawyer and he said he worked only a few days a week, coming in late to help out a young lawyer. "I spend my time waiting for clients to die so I can probate their estates and taking out widows for lunch and at night I eat out of tins," he said without expression.

There was a young family of Russians seated in the garden across from them with their dog, a large shepherd with its tongue hanging out and their little girl about six pretending to use a video camera. She came over to take a pretend picture of him and the gentleman from

Manchester. Suddenly, her father pulled a tiny, slim black flute from his shirt pocket and began to play. The father played beautifully, the notes sounding in the arch of the Japanese Garden roof. The little girl began dancing. This then could be the beginning of repose. A lovely Cossack song on the flute as the little girl spun and spun holding the edges of her dress. He applauded when her father stopped and dropped the flute back into his shirt pocket.

"What was the name of that song?" he asked the British lawyer. "Was it a Cossack dance?"

"No, it was Spanish, 'La Cumparsita.'"

"Camposita?"

"No, 'Cumparsita.'"

"Not Russian."

"No. Not at all. It was a tango."

He sat a little longer in the garden. He counted the ships in the harbor, six small freighters and only two sailboats. He then walked up the path and saw a man reading a newspaper and displaying paintings on the stone wall edging the park. They were very good oils, almost like watercolors, on small canvases, the *Western Wall*, daubs of worshipers in colored robes, the Jaffa Gate, the *Bahai Temple* of Haifa.

"Kama?" he asked in Hebrew. "How much?"

"50 shekels," the artist answered and drew the number on a piece of paper.

He shook his head, no. It was about $12.

"45 shekels," the man said and drew the number.

He pointed at two paintings, the *Western Wall* and the *Bahai Tower*. "For 2—Kama?"

"80 shekels." He drew the number 80.

"Okay." He smiled at the man. That was about $20 for two original oils. A bargain. He asked the man to sign them and he did sign with his pencil, "Mikhail."

"Your name is Mikhail, a Russian name?"

The artist nodded his head.

"These are good paintings, Mikhail."

They shook hands and Mikhail gave him a plastic bag and he went up the path to look at two old cannons that pointed over the harbor.

He was such a shrewd bargainer. He'd become very good with money. But did he have to take it out on this gentle Russian artist?

Most of the Russians he saw here were big people, tough and aggressive, but not this man. Once, he too had dreamed of becoming an artist. Writing the book that would give him the stature of Bellow or Roth or maybe even Harold Brodkey. He would have settled for the reputation of Brodkey. Unfulfilled promise. Brodkey was dead now though. He'd read that Alfred Kazin died yesterday. So what had he ever done to deserve a review by Alfred Kazin? Certainly not his *Myth of Childhood*. Kazin would have never even opened it or touched it. He would have treated it like a piece of rotten herring. He'd finally learned to settle though. He'd never be in their category but he'd pulled himself out of academia and he was making money as a writer. Of course, his poor, sweet, gentle wife had never lived to see it. His second marriage had been a real disaster, with a young instructor he'd met in East Lansing when he was teaching the Bloomsbury period. The marriage had lasted six months before she'd left him for a young Chilean and his Fulbright in Chile. He'd never heard from her again except for a list of household articles that she'd wanted shipped to the young man's house in Santiago. He had done so dutifully, always a dutiful husband. After she left him, he wrote his novella, *Virginia and Leonard*, a fiction about the last days of the Woolfs before her suicide. It had been well reviewed in the *New York Times*. Then he'd written a biography of Katherine Mansfield, also well received, but more importantly it had brought him an advance of $25,000. He then did something with the money he never would have done had he still been married. He pulled down the vested portion of his pension in cash and left the university at fifty-two. He bought a condo in Franklin Hills, a suburb outside of Detroit. He put the rest of the lump-sum pension and his advance in mutual funds and sat for four months in the townhouse and wrote *The Myth of Childhood*. Then he put the money he netted from the new book into the market, this time not only mutual funds, but carefully picked stocks, such as General Electric, Gillette, Walgreens, Pfizer, Bristol Meyer, Disney, (yes, Arnie, not EuroDisney but American Disney). So, why did he have to bargain with poor Mikhail? Why was it always necessary for him to win, particularly since his young wife had abandoned him?

At the top of the path there were two bronze cannons and a plaque inscribed in fading German, English and Hebrew. Apparently, here, Kaiser Wilhelm and the Kaiserin. (Kaiserin, a strange word. He didn't want a Kaiserin in his life though. Letitia was his second wife's name and he could barely pronounce it without anger and cramping in his tongue. Letitia had certainly been his Kaiserin.) Here, the Kaiser and the Kaiserin had visited Haifa and these cannons were used to salute them. Later they met with Theodore Herzl and their meeting was described in Herzl's novel, *Alteneuland*. Also, here, the last Turkish battery was captured by the British under General Allenby in World War I. Thus, Allenby Park below, and now he was being spoken to by a young Arab man lying in the grass in the slope above him, at picnic with his family. There were two men, their wives in Arab headdress, white beaded scarves over their heads and tied at their chins and two little boys having a picnic in the grass.

He didn't understand the man. "I am American," he said.

"Ah, America," the man replied in very good English. "What are you doing in Haifa?"

"I've come to visit Israel."

"And you are American? Where do you live?"

"In Detroit."

"Detroit? They make cars there. Ford and Chrysler."

The man got up from his reclining position and came over to the black, wrought-iron fence with one of his children, a curly haired boy of about five. The Arab father seemed about thirty, handsome, clean-cut, with clear, light blue eyes.

"So what do you think of the situation here?" the man asked.

"I think that it will soon end and there will be a Palestinian state."

"You realize that we cannot live like this. We have no freedom. This is our land. The Jews have taken this land from the Arabs."

"There will be an agreement soon. They are very close now."

The Palestinian man spoke quietly. The women watched, still reclining behind him and cutting pieces of watermelon with a knife. The other Arab man, a big, heavy man with a black beard also watched and then began to call out in Arabic to his friend.

"Are you Jewish?" the man at the fence asked. "You are an American and you are a Jew?"

"Yes, I am a Jew."

"You have come here to visit. You want to be safe. To walk without being afraid. If you want that, then we must be treated as human beings." He said something to his friend and the big man stood up and cut off a large chunk of watermelon and brought it over to the fence.

"Would you like some watermelon?"

"Yes, I'd like some. I have a knife though." He reached for his Swiss Army knife.

"No, it's not necessary. We have a better knife." They had a long serrated knife with a black handle. "Take as much as you want." The man quickly cut the chunk of watermelon into six pieces. "Take all of them."

"Thank you."

The big man watched him eat and took the knife back from his friend.

"I met a young Palestinian woman on the plane coming over. We were seat mates. Her name was 'Wedad.' She told me it meant 'love' in Arabic. 'Wedad' meant 'love.'"

The younger man smiled. "Yes, 'Wedad' means 'love.'"

The big man with the knife and tiny black eyes was still watching both of them and listening.

"Jewish no good," he suddenly said in English. "You Jewish?"

"I'm an American but I'm also Jewish."

"Billy Clinton, he no good."

"My friend is a taxi driver," the first man explained. "He has lived in Haifa all his life. I cannot work here. I am not permitted. I can only work in the West Bank."

"Wedad showed me how to eat food like an Arab. To use your fingers and just pop food into your mouth with your fingers."

He demonstrated with a piece of watermelon and both men smiled, even the big man showing his brown rotting teeth. The young man asked, "Where is she now, where is Wedad, will you see her again?"

"I don't know. She was going to East Jerusalem to see her grandparents. She hadn't seen them in ten years. She'd never been to Israel."

"Jewish no good. Billy Clinton no good," the cab driver said again.

"I'm going now. It was nice meeting you and your families. Thank you for the watermelon."

The man at the fence shook hands with him and took the remains of the watermelon. The women laughed because he hadn't finished all six pieces. One of them waved from her reclining position in the grass;

propped up on her elbow she looked like a Matisse odalisque, and as she waved she smiled and called out to him in English, "Bye, bye."

That night he took his rented car and set off for the Haifa Museum to see Arthur Schnitzler's *La Ronde,* a one-hundred-year-old play about the secret sex lives of the Viennese. Schnitzler had been a doctor and Jewish and didn't think much of his play. After it caused anti-Semitic riots in Berlin in 1921, he banned it from further production until after his death.

Now, it was playing at the Haifa Museum in a production of the English Language Theatre of Haifa. But he'd driven the car in a circle, winding up miles from the museum, somewhere on Tchernikhovsky Boulevard. The museum was on Sabbtai Levi Street in Hadar, a commercial section of Haifa. He was parked under a streetlight, examining his map with his penlight. A woman approached out of the shadows. She looked at him and spoke to him in halting English.

"Are you lost? Can I help you?" She seemed to be about forty-five, probably on her way home from work. She was attractive, but tired and wary.

"Do you know where the Haifa Museum is?" he asked her.

"Yes, I know. You are very far from it." She stuck her head in the window, held her glasses up and looked at his map. "I cannot see on this map."

"How far am I from it?"

"I will take you there. It is near where I'm going. May I have a ride?"

She quickly got into the car and pointed in a direction and then became silent.

She had olive-colored skin, big cheekbones, canted eyes. She obviously wasn't afraid of him. He should just skip *La Ronde* and ask her to a cafe for coffee or a drink. Finally he'd met someone close to his own age, not carrying a dog, no sunglasses on top of her head, no cell phone.

"Now you turn there and you go straight ahead. Are you alone? Do you have family in Haifa?" she asked him.

"No, I'm alone."

"Where do you live in America?"

"In Detroit. In the middle of the country."

"I know Detroit. They have a lot of racial problems there. I came from Argentina, from Buenos Aires, because of the anti-Semitism there. I was a Zionist and I couldn't stand it, so I came here. You turn there and after some time you will drop me off by a bus stop."

Now was the time. Ask her for coffee. Ask her for a glass of wine. She was a very interesting woman. Stop being a voyeur, sitting in cafes, watching everyone. Make a simple gesture of friendship toward this Israeli woman who had come out of the night to help him.

He was at her bus stop now. She had her hand on the door. "You will find the museum over there." She pointed.

"Good night," he said. "Thank you very much."

She closed the door and stared at him. "I hope you enjoy yourself at the play. And also in Israel. I hope you will enjoy yourself." Then she walked away and didn't look back.

So she was gone. He hadn't asked her name or her address. He'd said nothing to her and by the time he found the museum, the play had almost ended. He didn't go in and instead went back to the hotel and drank a glass of red Israeli wine in the lobby bar and then went upstairs to sleep with another glass of wine he took to the room.

The next evening he decided to go back to the play and not take the car. Instead, he'd take a bus to Central Carmel and the Carmelit which was an underground subway tunneled into the side of Mount Carmel. It only ran halfway up the mountain but it stopped at Hadar, three blocks from the museum, and he could take it and walk over.

On his way to the train, he saw a display of religious articles in a small store. He had an impulse to buy one of the yarmulkes in the window. He went in and bought a green beaded yarmulke trimmed with white Stars of David and a hair clip that the clerk put into a bag. He stuffed the bag into his pocket and went to the station and dropped coins into an automatic ticket dispenser for a ticket for Hadar. This time he was prepared. He knew that the station for the Haifa Museum was Hadar, the third stop.

There were such sad faces on the street, the older people he'd seen before he entered the subway. He thought of the hundreds of faces he'd seen in Israel, so many were etched in sadness. Truly, he was a voyeur in this society. An American Jew looking to redeem himself in Israel's sadness. He had even begun to kiss the mezuzah on the door frame before entering his hotel room. What had he ever done to help these people? What did his contribution of $100 yearly to the UJA entitle him to do here? Sit in the cafes and watch the young women? He was as alien to the Israelis as the bus loads of German tourists in their silly tropical folding hats nodding courteously to everyone. He'd seen them at the Dead Sea, at Eilat, at the Golan Heights, even at breakfast at the hotel this morning. The blonde woman at an adjoining table had said quietly to the man beside her after he'd taken only two buns from the buffet, "Das es Alles?" The Germans were here atoning. There was everywhere this pervading air of sadness of the old, sitting on benches along the boulevards, like tired and sick gray sparrows, but always silent. Deep in Hadar the other night, he had walked the twisted streets and saw the men on the streets, in black hats, black caftans, black knickers and stockings. He was in an old, orthodox neighborhood. He entered some of their tiny shops. It looked like a section of pre-Holocaust Krakow in the photographs of Roman Vishniak. Children with long earlocks and angelic thin faces, with yarmulkes perched on their heads. The Germans would have taken all these people—men, women and children—and locked them in a synagogue and burned them alive.

He sat on the Carmelit and waited for the train to begin moving. He noticed a woman across from him. The train began to move down the mountainside through a dark, concrete tunnel.

He glanced at her and she looked up at him.

"Do you know the stop for the museum?" he asked her.

"Yes, of course." Israelis were always saying "of course."

"What stop is it?" He knew perfectly what stop it was.

She looked at the chart on the wall of the train.

"It's the third stop."

Who did she look like? She was in her late forties, no rings on her fingers. He was not only looking for tattoos of numbers on arms, he was always looking for wedding rings. The Germans hadn't gotten all of the rings for their smelters. The Germans and the Swiss, perfect allies, both so precise, so disciplined, so accurate. He should have never bought the Swiss Army knife he kept in his pocket, the perfect little red knife with the incised white cross. "The Jews killed Christ, you know." The wild-eyed guide in Jerusalem on the Via Dolorosa. "Here they took him and laid him on the cross and flagellate him. Do you know what is flagellate? With the thorns." He demonstrated, the black eyes darting, another crazy man. "And they bury him under his tomb and he lifted up the rock and go up to heaven. Yes, it is true. Now, sir, you give me 100 shekels and I will show you the tomb and also Dome of the Rock where Mohammed got upon his horse and rode to heaven to meet with Jesus. You give?"

"No, I will not give." Of course I will not give. Leave me alone, you madman. Here you will have to leave me alone because if you don't, one of these Israeli soldiers with his automatic weapon will send you up to heaven to meet Jesus and Mohammed with thirty-two neat, little holes in your body. He'd talked to one of the young soldiers at a post on the Egyptian border, ten kilometers outside of Eilat. The soldier's name was Eric. He'd come from Russia and lived in Beersheeba and had just completed basic training. He was eighteen. His rifle shot thirty-two bullets before reloading and he had several clips slung around his chest, each with thirty-two more bullets. He said the sight on his gun was set at two hundred meters, the next setting was five hundred meters and he demonstrated how to set the sight. There was never trouble anymore along the border. This border marker stone was No. 82, marked for the Israeli-Egyptian peace treaty. "Over there is Egypt. There is no one there. You see their watch tower has been abandoned."

Well, he would prove nothing by assassinating one more Arab guide. They would then assassinate one more Jewish tourist, with or without flagellation, and so the story goes and always has gone.

He was almost at his stop now. The woman across from him was probably one of the loveliest women he'd seen in Israel. She had no rings. She seemed to be in her mid-forties, she was thin, her eyes were warm and gracious and welcoming. He could just hand her his Swiss Army knife instead of frankincense and myrrh. Instead, he didn't say anything to her when he got off at the museum stop. She smiled slightly at him as the train doors closed.

So, the author of *The Myth of Childhood* wasn't much of a lover, apparently not, not a lover anymore. Letitia had hurt him too much for him to risk any more rejection. At least that was his excuse. He could play the stock market with assurance. But he couldn't ask out any of these women. Not even to spend an evening with him over coffee and dinner. Instead he would go alone to *La Ronde*.

He stopped in a cafe near the museum and had dinner. An omelet and red wine. He had first gone to the museum to check it out but the ticket office hadn't opened. There was a group of young Arab men sitting on a fence in front of the museum hassling the pedestrians. One of them came down to him and addressed him as "Haver" and began to follow him. He knew what "Haver" meant, "friend." Bill Clinton had a dish of sand from Israel in his office in memory of Yitzhak Rabin and on it was written "Shalom-Haver" (good-bye, friend). The man stopped following him and then he walked a few blocks, saw the restaurant below street level, and went down the stairs and took a table outside. As he ate, he asked the waitress about the young Arab men. Would it be all right to go back to the play or should he just forget about it and return to the hotel?

"No, I think it will be all right, if you are just careful."

"In the States, I don't think I would give them a second chance."

"No, it will be all right. It is okay here. This is just where they live. They are there every night. It is up to you, of course."

He ordered an ice cream sundae for dessert with chocolate sauce and vanilla ice cream.

"How many balls?" the waitress asked.

"Scoops. You mean two scoops."

"In Hebrew we say 'balls.'"

"Okay then. Two balls."

"Why are you laughing?"

"No reason."

He told her he was a writer from America and she was interested because her friend in the bar was an Israeli journalist and worked on one of the Israeli papers.

"He is brilliant. Come inside. I will introduce you."

Several young men were playing chess. The writer was behind the bar helping out as a bartender. He shook his hand and asked him the name of his paper and what he wrote about. He was about twenty-eight, clean-shaven, with a thin, dark bearded face and he had a constant, challenging, sardonic smile. It never left his face. "I write for *Ha' aretz* (*The Nation*). I write about the army and the Mossad. You know what is the Mossad?"

"Yes, the Israeli intelligence service."

Again the quick, sly smile.

"Those Arabs in front of the museum. Is it all right to go back there? Will I be able to get out of there after the play is over?"

"Who knows, it is up to you."

Hardly encouraging. A wise guy. A wise-ass writer. Still, he asked him to write his name and the name of his paper. The waitress invited him to a jazz concert at the bar tomorrow night. He said he would come but he knew he wouldn't. There were well-dressed women in the street now walking toward the play and he joined them and walked with them. They passed the group of young Arab men sitting on the fence in front of the museum but they said nothing to the women. So he was a coward, using the women for cover. He got into the theater without a problem. In most of the Schnitzler scenes, the phrase "I love you" seemed to be the key to seduction. Instead of running the gauntlet again after the play, he took a taxi back to the hotel and went for a long walk before going up to his room. It was a beautiful moonlit evening. A woman passed him outside on the sidewalk in the dark walking a tiny dog and carrying an open white paper umbrella, shielding herself from the moonlight.

He awoke to the shrieks of children playing soccer before school. He had only two days left in Israel. There was a school down the street and the voices of the children came through the windows mixed with the cooing of the doves. He'd dreamt of the open, white paper umbrella and then of two paintings of flowers he'd seen in the hotel corridors. Paintings in vivid watercolors, trailings of snapdragons, reds, purples, green, with twisting black stems, almost randomly Oriental. They were beautiful and signed in a black scroll by a woman named "Shoshanah," but her name had faded into the wash. He was certain they were valuable and he dreamt that he bought them both from the hotel for $500. He would take them to the States. The paintings would be something that he alone had recognized in Israel. It was a pleasant dream except when he awoke, he was drenched in sweat.

He spent the morning doing ordinary tasks, picking up his laundry, shopping, lunch in a cafe. He wanted to buy a tube of hair coloring cream but he couldn't find one. He had no plans, the weather was beautiful. He bought an ice cream bar from a musical ice cream truck. When he returned to the hotel, the woman clerk at the lobby front desk called him over.

"There is someone waiting for you in the bar, Mr. Rosen." She went back to answer the switchboard.

He went into the bar and there was an attractive young woman drinking a glass of wine. She had ivory skin and dark, curly hair pinned in back. Her black skirt was very short, her long legs suntanned with sandals. She had on a white tank top and she was smoking and tapping her ashes into an ashtray. Her phone was on the bar.

"I'm Shulamit," she said extending her hand. "Are you Eliott Rosen, my father's friend?"

"I'm surprised to see you here. I thought you were busy with your job interviews."

"Not so busy." She put the cigarette out. "Besides, as you know, I'm a student of comparative literature and you're a well-known American writer. I looked you up on the Internet. You have several books. Quite impressive."

"Not really."

"So, Eliott, what have you been doing in Haifa? How are my father and his new wife? May I call you Eliott? I'm Shulamit, but call me Shula."

"I've been just going around, doing the usual tourist things. Last night I saw a play, *La Ronde,* at the Haifa Museum. Your father is fine and so is Paula. They send their regards."

"Ah, Schnitzler. Very dated. An anachronism. I can't stand Schnitzler, and also Paula, I can't stand her."

"What plays do you like?" He ordered a red Cinzano with ice and lemon.

"What do I like? Not too much. I like Ionescu's *Rhinoceros.* It's playing at the Tel Aviv festival. I'll tell you Eliott, if you haven't found out already, Haifa is very boring. An old people's town. There is nothing here. Nothing at all. Everything is in Tel Aviv or Jerusalem."

"Why do you stay here then?"

"That's easy. I have no money, so I stay with my mother. As soon as I have money, I will go somewhere. Maybe India. Maybe Jerusalem. There is a nightlife there. Cabarets, cafes. So what do you think of Israel?"

"It's a beautiful, complex country."

"But you wouldn't want to live here. That's what Americans always say. You don't want to make Aliyah. My father has done it in reverse. He has made his Aliyah to America with his young wife."

"It would be very hard for me to live here. I'm too old to learn Hebrew."

She crossed her legs and looked at her watch. She tapped on her cell phone with her fingers. Her nails were painted purple and she was quite beautiful.

The little bartender who had served him when he met Arnie stood behind the bar carefully watching both of them with his dark, sad eyes.

"So you don't have to move here Eliott. Stay in the States. We can take care of ourselves. It's Israeli blood that's shed here. Not American."

"Yes, but we give you enormous amounts of aid."

"That's true, but in the end it's always everyone for themselves, isn't it? When the Syrians came over the Golan with their tanks in the Yom Kippur war, it was the Israeli Army that stopped them. Not the Americans. We stood alone. If we hadn't stopped them, they would have driven us into the sea. There would be no Haifa."

"Were you in the army, Shulamit?"

"No, the navy. I was what you call a 'frogman.' I call it 'frogwoman.' But I have to leave now. I have an appointment. Still, I could stay and we could have dinner and perhaps go down to the harbor and walk the promenade along the beach. However, there would be two conditions. First, you would pay for our dinner. Second, you would pay me a guide's fee of 400 shekels, that's about $100."

"I think not. I'm not interested in paying a guide's fee."

"Well, it's up to you Eliott." She put her hand out. She had a strong grip. "This is not Schnitzler's Vienna, you know. This is Israel. You are an older man. I am a young woman. Why should I go out with you without a fee?"

"I don't know. That's up to you. On the other hand, I know I shouldn't go with you Letitia, I mean Shulamit, even without a fee."

"Who is Letitia?"

"No one."

"You're not a very nice man, Eliott."

"And you're not a very nice woman, Shulamit."

She began to walk out and then she turned back to him and gave him a military salute and smiled. "Say hello to my father and Paula," she said.

He went back to his room and got his jacket and a cap. He even tried the yarmulke on he'd bought and put it in place in the mirror with the hair clip. He looked like an old photo he had of his grandfather. He took it off and put it back in his pocket. He'd done himself a real mitzvah by not going with her. Instead he caught the bus to the Carmelit. He'd read that Haifa's beaches were beautiful and he wanted to see them before he left. First though, he would look for the woman he'd sat across from last night on the train. This was about the same time he'd met her. He looked for her at the station in the crowds. There were hundreds of faces. Again, all the old, sad faces. Hundreds of faces. He would never find her and after awhile stopped looking for her and took the train down to the beach.

It was true, Haifa's beaches were lovely. The Mediterranean was gently crashing in a beautiful sunset, people were walking, jogging, children playing in the surf. The old, white cubes of houses were above him and on the horizon an Israeli destroyer was patrolling. He sat on an old, wooden beach chair at the water's edge. His legs ached from the walk along the beach and he took his sandals off and let the water run through his toes. He took the yarmulke from his pocket and pinned it on. No one stared at him. He was just another Jew here. The water was warm and comforting and he turned the chair toward the direction of Jerusalem and closed his eyes.

About the author

Lowell B. Komie is a Chicago attorney and writer. He received his B.A. from the University of Michigan in 1951 and his J.D. from Northwestern University in 1954. *The Judge's Chambers,* his book of short stories, was the first collection of fiction published by the American Bar Association. *The Lawyer's Chambers,* his collection of fiction published in 1994, won the Carl Sandburg Fiction Award in 1995 from the Friends of the Chicago Public Library. His stories have been published in *Harper's, Chicago Magazine, Chicago Tribune Magazine, Milwaukee Journal Magazine, Chicago Bar Record, Canadian Lawyer,* and by the Japan Federation of Bar Associations and other magazines and university and literary quarterlies. His novel, *The Last Jewish Shortstop in America,* published in 1997, won the 1998 Small Press Award for Fiction from *Independent Publisher Magazine.* He lives in Deerfield, Illinois.

SWORDFISH
CHICAGO

When my father, who died several years ago, wrestled with me or hugged me and held me in his powerful grip, the only way he would release me would be if I said our secret password, "Swordfish." He was a powerful, athletic man, a very graceful athlete and a marvelous baseball player and shortstop. He could have held me for an eternity, and I wish he had, but the secret password, "Swordfish," was always honored between us not as a sign of weakness, but as a matter of honor between father and son. So Swordfish/Chicago is named after my father. My mother would be very happy. In a way, my father was the Last Jewish Shortstop in America. He played night softball under the lights in Milwaukee in the businessmen leagues, and he had all the moves and a rifle arm as shortstop. I was the bat boy for his teams, and his fluidity and grace as a shortstop are locked in my memory.

My father was a friend of the Marx Brothers when they lived on the South Side of Chicago. His particular friend was Zeppo, who he called Buster. On Saturdays the Marx Brothers, who raised pigeons in a coop on the roof of their boarding house, would take the pigeons to Calumet City and sell them to immigrants, who baked pigeon pies. Then Buster, Chico, Harpo and Groucho would rush back to the South Side, and my father would wait with them on their roof for the birds to come flying back. If you let the pigeons out of your grasp for a second, they would be off—and would fly back to the coop because they were homing pigeons. So the Marx Brothers sold the same pigeons each Saturday, over and over again. My father swore this is a true story.

Years later, I learned that the Marx Brothers made a movie in which all through the movie the secret password was "Swordfish." So I finally learned where my father got the name, and I pass it on with these stories to you.